SO-EGH-406

Just Between You and Me
By Tamara Hanson
Prairie Girl Press

Text Copyright © 2016 by Tamara Hanson
Cover design Copyright © 2016 by Tamara Hanson
ISBN: 978-0-9949026-1-0
e-Book ISBN: 978-0-9949026-0-3
Prairie Girl Press
www.tamarahanson.ca

First printing May 2016

Thank-you!

Prologue
Every new beginning comes from some other beginning's end. - Seneca

It had to be some cosmic force, divine or not, that started things in motion. Maybe the planets aligned or maybe they misaligned. Whatever it was, it started something that ended with a conclusion that no one could have predicted. I can't really say for sure what it was or why it happened the way it did. All I know is that it set me on a course that was about to turn my world upside down.

They say every ending has a new beginning. At the time, I wouldn't have believed that. Instead, I would see it as the end of the world and blame people, like, say, my parents. But that's a cop-out. I could tell you that my parents were rarely around, off doing who knows what in some third world country. Maybe all the Christmases and birthdays they missed spun this whole thing, whatever it was, into an uncontrollable vortex.

Why don't we just get down to the bare bones? My name is Cate Chase, born the only daughter and child to Flora and Forest Chase. Yes, those are their real names. I'll never figure out how my mother and father managed to attract each other the way they did.

Actually, Cate is my middle name; my first name is something that I wish not to reveal. There are only a few people who have full disclosure of my real name: my parents, my grandmother, my best friend Susanne Hunter and the people who handle my birth certificate at the vital statistics office. I will go to the grave with that one. Or, until recently, I thought I would go to the grave with that one. More about that later.

Career: Four years ago, at the age of 33, I became the first and thus far, only female sergeant of the Riverton Police Service—and the youngest. I like to describe Riverton as a small city with a Stepford Wives' appeal. Along the river are the cookie cutter people in the cookie cutter homes, far away from the dregs of society.

The day I decided to be a police officer was the same day that I saw Charlie's Angels for the first time. I was about seven and sat fixed to the television watching three women fight crime and kick ass (insert Charlie's Angels' theme song here). I wanted to be Farrah Fawcett. Who didn't want to be Farrah? No one really wanted to be Sabrina. Maybe it was because of the turtle necks she wore.

My parents had always known I would be a police officer, much to their disappointment. My parents are of the hippy persuasion— free love and dope; living in peace and harmony. There's definitely a clash at family suppers where I'm always turning a blind eye. But, they are getting better as they get older. Turns out that Dad's sperm count was down explaining the reason why they couldn't conceive another child and name him or her Moss... Tulip... Petal.

My average build can be deceiving to bad guys. None of them expect me to chase them and throw them down to the ground in eight seconds flat.

I had a cat named Bullet. I know, original. Bullet was silvery and beautiful, and he ran away. He was really one of those high-maintenance type felines, always wanting to be scratched and petted. Probably ran away because I was always working or something. I hope someone else is taking good care of him.

No kids. Never been married.

Relationships? Well, I'll explain that as I go along. Let's just say there had been a time in my life where I sat around in my pink bunny slippers watching Dawson's Creek while eating Kit Kats and Reese's Peanut Butter Cups. In my sugar haze, I mulled over the last couple of months, sorting out what had happened and....why don't I just start at the beginning.

Chapter 1
You Put the Fun in Dysfunctional

I'm a sergeant of a dysfunctional team. It's been a progressive thing. Four years ago, I was promoted to a sergeant, got my stripes and was assigned to my own squad—a team consisting of all men. Don't get me wrong, I'm not a card-carrying man-hater.

In fact, I love men; can't get enough of them. Except when I'm their leader. You start giving them constructive criticism about a botched stolen auto pursuit and you sound like their mother.

Being a female sergeant means trying to win the respect of my troop with very little luck. I can talk till I'm blue in the face and still won't get the desired response that I want from them. Even as I stand before them pointing out how we need to work on our team skills (and some other shit that I made up but sounded good), most of them are staring idly into space.

To be fair, one guy is eating his lunch and another is picking his nose; at least these two are still alive. Another two are at the back drawing something and snickering—quite possibly a picture of me holding one (or both) of their over exaggerated large penises. No matter how much I reiterate the fact that they weren't following my orders or procedures, they still manage to come up with some lame excuse that they couldn't hear me or the siren was too loud, or some crock-of-shit that I've heard too many times before.

My efforts are futile. No matter how flamboyantly I use my hands, point out the obvious, or stand before them naked in all my glory, I'm sure I'd only get meaningful stares at my breasts, whisperings if they were real and how a Brazilian wax would tidy things up down below. Foregoing the strip tease, I escape the pasty-white boardroom without another word, only to be hounded by another sergeant.

"Lose another pursuit, Chase?" Sergeant Erickson is from the other team and somehow feels it's his duty to point out the inadequacies of mine.

"Do you have a question, Jack?" I try the tactic of sounding bored and walking past him in my pursuit of finding coffee. Coffee is my lifeline. Hook me up an IV of the black stuff and I'm good to go for the rest of the day.

"No, not at all. I was concerned about you, that's all. You know, this is the fourth pursuit this month you lost." His brush-cut looks ridiculous since he hasn't the nicest shaped head on this side of the hemisphere. I've also noticed that he is getting a spare tire around the mid-section, which makes me quite happy.

"I didn't know we were competing." I pour myself a cup of office brew, recognizing the typical sludge sitting at the very bottom—the stuff that's been there for days.

"It's always a competition between us, Chase. Isn't it ironic that your last name is Chase when that's all you do? You want to place bets that you fuck-up another pursuit?"

I open the microwave door to warm up my coffee and decide against it; the innards obviously haven't been cleaned since 1982. Yep, cold coffee is just as good. I'd have an iced coffee if someone bothered to refill the ice-cube trays.

"Don't you have some place to be, Erickson?" My shoulder brushes past him as I try to ignore his attempts to rile me up any further than I am.

"Yes, as a matter of fact. I'm just heading out to undo your last screw up." He chuckles irritatingly, finally leaving me alone.

Bastard.

Here's the thing. Jack and I had a short relationship years ago. Very short. I don't even know if you could call it a relationship since it only lasted a couple of days. He was really a cocky bastard. At first, I thought that was all part of his charm, but turned out he was like that 24/7.

Getting to my tiny office with the prison window before receiving anymore unwanted feedback proves to be a daunting task; it would take a miracle to be left alone in this place.

As I enter my so-called sanctuary, I'm greeted by the inspector, Mark Brady, who is sifting through my desk. I'm ready to take him down if he steals any of the chocolate almonds I have stashed behind the stack of sticky notes. Mark's six foot frame looks awkward in my little office, and I want him to leave so badly. It's seriously ruining the chi. I continue to watch him, and, from the angle I'm at, have a nice view of Mark's salt and pepper hair thinning on the top of his forty-two year old head. I smile.

"Looking for anything in particular?" I ask. I boot him out of the chair and take my seat while he shimmies onto the corner of my desk.

"What can I do for you?" I shuffle some papers in an attempt to look busy. This is a feat as I haven't a clue where anything is.

"We've got some more complaints about you, Chase."

"Really? And who would these poor souls be that have to complain about lil' ol' me?" I take a sip of my coffee. Gack! That's disgusting. I grimace as coffee grounds slowly make their way to the back of my throat.

"Some of your team members say you're being too hard on them. You're calling them names, getting angry over the smallest details."

I snort. "Name calling? Give me some credit. Listen, if they can't handle a little criticism, then maybe they shouldn't be in police work. I'm not going to baby them, Mark."

"I know. I know. But do you think you can ease up a bit? You already have an Internal Affairs complaint from a domestic you attended last week."

Right. The domestic. A bogus complaint if there ever was one. Some guy complained that I smashed his head into his coffee table, when what really happened was he suckered punched his wife right in front of me and I took him down. Unfortunately, he hit his head on the coffee table and had to get fourteen stitches.

"All right, all right. I'll ease up on the poor babies." I make a face and turn toward my computer.

"Please, no more complaints." Mark gets up to leave, then stops. Here it is. I was wondering if he had forgotten. "How's that boyfriend treating you?"

"Good. Never been better."

"Well, if things go sideways, let me know. I'm still available."

My eye starts to twitch as memories of Mark in our bed with the recruit he was training flashes in my mind. I'd never heard him moan that loudly with me. I'm thinking he didn't expect me to come home from work when I did. I thought I'd drop by on my lunch break to surprise him. Looks like we were both surprised. Several years have passed since I torched those bed sheets.

"Yeah, well, don't hold your breath."

"Cate." I grimace. I hate it when he says my name. It's all in the delivery. "Things are different now. I'm a changed man," Mark whispers. I open the door to my office, boot him out and slam it behind him.

Now, you're probably wondering, 'how many cops has she dated?' I think it's five. I think. Honestly, I lost track around the number five mark. Well, after three they all become a blur, morphing into the same person. Mark was the only one I lived with for a few months. Don't ask me why I did it; the guy had no idea how to pick up his dirty clothes off the floor.

It's the nature of the beast—you're in a career where men are abundant, you're stuck in the same room or police cruiser, and affairs fly left and right. Sometimes you don't even see them coming. Then, one day, you're going out for an innocent beer and end up in bed together. I swear I have a problem—an addiction. Blue fever, perhaps? Maybe it's one of those things where I have to date a cop or, what, I'll lose my mind? I'll disappear off the face of the earth? I hope I'm done with my little experiment. I guess dating Phil broke that cycle.

Before I have a chance to sit, the phone rings. It's Nan, my grandmother, the light of my life. She's the one who raised me since I was ten when my parents were off doing whatever they do. At least she's normal—except for the part about calling my father 'Forest'; I still don't know where she got that one.

"Nan, it's nice to hear your voice. How are you?"

"Great. But I'd be even better if I had my beautiful granddaughter here to talk to. Can you come over for dinner tonight? I'll get Annie to cook something amazing for us." My grandmother always has special privileges. She can ask whatever she wants and I would do it for her.

Nan has a cook, a gardener, a butler, and, well, all the help she could ever want or need for that big house of hers.

"Not tonight, Nan. I'm seeing Phil for dinner."

"Oh." I can hear the revulsion in her voice. Nan doesn't like Phil. She thinks he's too wimpy for me. Come to think of it, she says that about all my boyfriends I bring home. None of them have ever been good enough for Nan. "Then come over tomorrow."

"I have so much work to do! I really don't think I can." I glance at the sea of paperwork that has somehow migrated across my desk in a mass of jumbled documents.

"It's been so long since you came by. I need some Cate-time," she whines. Nan should have been in car sales, or maybe a lawyer.

"Fine. I'll come by tomorrow," I agree. I detect the smugness in her voice as she says her goodbyes. Yes, when Nan wants something, she gets it. There's no winning with her.

*

I'm to meet Phil at seven at the Seaside Restaurant—nowhere near the sea or a body of water, by the way. It's a little fish and seafood place that Phil loves to go to. He loves the lobster because 'they serve it up right'. I have no idea what that means because it looks like every other lobster platter I've seen at Red Lobster.

There's nothing special about this place and I honestly believe that they crack open a box of Captain Highliner, throw it in the oven at 400 degrees for twenty minutes, slap it on a plate with a sprig of parsley and charge fifteen bucks for it.

I guess I won't complain as this is a free meal and Phil did indicate that this was a special dinner. Part of me hopes that sex will be included after the fish sticks. Phil has been away for a week and I'm looking for some action.

Phil Myers is a good looking man with the bluest eyes you can ever imagine on a dark haired man. He is tall and slim, and when naked, well, he's a bit too scrawny. But I like him. We met a few months back when he did my income taxes and then did me. Phil's an accountant—well, 'nuf said.

I enter the fish place and scan the room. The restaurant is decorated in typical seaside regalia, catching the ambience of a fishing boat by tacking nets, tackle, stuffed fish, and pictures of boats and light houses to the walls. The flooring is made of wood planks, reminiscent of the pirate days.

I spot Phil already seated and enthralled by his menu. He only looks up when I'm a couple feet from the table. His blue eyes scan my slinky red dress and then he smiles. Not a 'wow, let's skip dinner' kind of smile; it's more regretful than anything. But I brush it off.

"You look beautiful, Cate." Phil misses my lips and kisses the very edge of my mouth; an awkward moment lingers in the air, but I ignore it.

"Maybe a bit overdressed for the fish house." I pour myself some wine from the bottle Phil has ordered. I peruse the menu for any new items, but already know what I'm going to order. I look up and realize Phil is watching me. "You've already decided?" I ask, surprised. Phil is the type to take his time, to savour each moment and bite—a bit frustrating, really. I'd rather just indulge, get it all down within the next ten minutes, then move on.

"We need to talk."

Oh, no. What can he possibly want to talk about? Taking this relationship to the next level, like moving in together? Or, worse, marriage? I like Phil, really, I do. We've been dating for a few months now and I get sex when I need it. Sure, he stays the night, but I don't feel obligated to make breakfast in the morning. He isn't clingy and doesn't need to cuddle all the time. See! It's the perfect relationship.

Realizing where this conversation is heading, I decide to step in and diffuse the situation before it becomes worse and someone loses an eye, or departs from the fish house humiliated—like Phil.

"Look, Phil, I know you want to take this relationship to the next level, and I don't blame you. The fact is, I don't think we're ready. It'll jeopardize everything we've worked for." My voice is sweet, my smile reassuring, maybe over the top benevolence—well, I am working with no warning here, people.

"Cate, I'm breaking up with you."

"I'm sorry." Did he say he's breaking up with me? No. He didn't say that. I'm the breaker-upper here, not Phil.

"I just don't think this relationship is heading anywhere. We are two different people with different plans. And, different personalities."

I'm still quite stunned by the words I'm breaking up with you, but manage to recover just in time to get in on the conversation.

"What do you mean different personalities?"

"Well, you're always talking about work."

"So?" I'm astounded. "What's that have to do with anything?"

"You don't hear me talking about work all the time, do you?"

Oh, god, no. I would be bored to death. Debits and credits and...yawn.

"And, you're, well, angry."

"Angry?"

"And have a chip on your shoulder."

"A chip on my shoulder?" Is there an echo in the room; my voice seems to be growing louder and ... becoming shrill.

"I'm sorry. It's just not working out," Phil apologizes. His voice is soft, his face now has the sympathetic look I was just sporting two minutes ago, and I want to slap it out of existence.

"But, please, stay for dinner. It's the least I can do," he adds reaching out for my hand. I stare down at it realizing that Phil has basically said that I don't cut it for him and, to take pity on my poor soul, he will buy me dinner. A fish and chips dinner. At least when you're breaking up with someone, make it a steak.

At this point, I fly off the handle. "Listen, you scrawny weasel," I lean across the table, my face mere inches from his. "You are lucky to have me because I can do so much better." My eyes bulge out and I know people are watching because Phil's eyes dart back and forth to the corners of the room. "Don't think you were doing me any favours by dating me, you skinny-pocket-protector-tightie-whitie-wearing accountant. I was taking pity on you." I take one last swig of my wine, then add, "Screw you and your fish sticks, Phil!" And at that, I make my grand exit out of the Captain's lair and into the fading daylight of the evening.

Angry doesn't describe it. Infuriated? Ready to snap all of my crayons? How dare that fucking bastard break up with me? Across the street I spy a little pub called 'The Black Duck'. Beer. That's what I need. I dig out my phone and punch in Susanne's number.

"Susanne, I need you to meet me at 'The Black Duck' over on the corner of Bay Ridge Drive and 23 Street." What's with the references to water? Duck, Bay, Seaside. Honestly, there isn't a lick of water in this area.

"Now?" she sounds out of breath.

"Please, I need you."

"Is there something the matter?"

"Yeah! Phil's an asshole." I flip the phone back and walk into the pub.

Once inside, I am even more aware of how overdressed I am. My red dress stands out amongst all the other people dressed in work boots, lumber jackets, and jeans. A group of men sitting at a corner table glance up and gawk as I take a seat on a stool at the bar.

"What'll you have?" the bartender asks placing a Black Duck insignia napkin before me. His hair is slicked back into an Elvis type hairstyle, including the sideburns. He almost has the body of Elvis in his later years, with his gut hanging over his brown leather belt.

"Beer. I don't care what kind." He pours me a Triple X on tap in what appears to be a dirty glass.

"You need another one, Cindy?" he nods toward the woman next to me.

"Keep 'em coming, Earl." The woman turns to me, then quickly looks away.

I know I've seen her somewhere before. I usually don't forget a face. Oh, yeah, I hauled her ass to jail one night after she started fighting with a woman in another bar. I choose to ignore her as well.

I sip my beer and stare at myself in the mirrors behind the bar. Notice how they don't show a very flattering side to a person? Faces are usually deformed, being cut off by a shelf or liquor bottle. I sit for about twenty minutes seething at the thought of Phil till Susanne walks in just shortly after I order my second beer.

"I got here as fast as I could. What's the problem?" Susanne is adorable with her dark hair separated into two braids and her trendy jeans and t-shirt. She's the only thirty-seven year old I know that can get away with wearing braids and not look like she's trying to be sixteen all over again.

"Phil broke up with me," I say, sounding disgusted rather than sad. This is the first time I've noticed my repulsion.

A smirk crosses Susanne's face, but before I can ask her what she's smiling at, she turns to the bartender. "I'll have a Strawberry Daiquiri, please." She looks down at my glass of beer, then adds, "In a clean glass."

The bartender rolls his eyes, wipes out a glass, then starts the blender. Susanne and I wait until the daiquiri is mixed and are sitting at a table away from the nervous ex-inmate Cindy, Earl the Elvis impersonator, and the prying eyes of the lumberjacks sitting in the corner.

"So, what happened?" Susanne asks. She takes a sip of her girl-drink with the garnish of cherry pierced by a yellow umbrella.

"Do you want the extended version or the Reader's Digest version?"

She doesn't hesitate. "Reader's Digest."

"He said we were different people and that I talked about work too much. He said this relationship wasn't going anywhere. Oh yeah, he also said I'm angry and have a chip on my shoulder," I laugh at the irony of it all. "There ain't a chip on this shoulder, honey."

Susanne doesn't say a word. Instead, she twists her mouth up like she's trying not to say something.

"What?"

"Nothing."

"Come on. Say it." She zips her mouth shut. "Susanne!" I whine.

"Well, you kind of are a teensy bit angry."

"Susanne!"

"You wanted to know, so I told you."

I slurp my beer.

"Come on, Cate. You're always talking about work, and always hyped up when something bothers you or doesn't go your way; or even how you should have arrested that bad guy, but didn't."

This isn't what I want to hear. I want Susanne to agree with me and to tell me that Phil is an ass. I want her to help me bash Phil all night long until we can't think of anymore accountant jokes.

"I thought you'd be on my side."

"I am. But ask yourself this: Are you mad that you broke up because you really liked Phil or because your pride is hurt?"

"I don't know," I lie. I do know.

"Okay, think about it this way, you barely introduced Phil to any of your friends. He didn't even meet Nan."

"Not true. He met Nan—once."

Susanne continues, ignoring my response. "At my birthday party, you ignored him the whole night. Phil sat in the corner while you drank your face off."

"I'm a social butterfly," I say defensively.

"The sex wasn't that great."

I stare at her. "How did you know that?"

"You told me."

"When?"

"At my birthday party as you drank your face off and ate salsa and chips all night."

"That would explain the red stain on my shirt. I loved that shirt; had to throw it out, too." It's all coming back to me now. Susanne's husband, Dave, had thrown a surprise birthday party for Susanne a month or so ago and I was wearing a brand new white shirt and Capri pants. It was a warm day and everyone was outside, drinking, eating, and I think there were a few people in the hot tub. Dave had outdone himself, and Susanne didn't suspect a thing. That's Dave for you, always treating Suzanne like a queen.

Anyway, Phil and I had gone to the party and I was drinking Long Island Iced Teas that night. I did have one too many, but Phil was driving. When I get drunk, I like to eat. Who doesn't?

"And, not only did you tell me about the bad sex, but Phil overheard you because he was sitting only two feet away."

Now all the pieces of the puzzle are fitting together. "I guess that would explain why he was trying to get kinky that night." He really did give it an honest effort. The whole legs behind the ears thing—he was a little confused.

"So, now, do you really think this relationship is a loss?"

I don't want to admit it, but Susanne is right. Phil was just someone to have mediocre sex with. If I had seen this before, I could have saved myself countless meals at the fish palace and had mediocre sex with my vibrator. Leave it to Susanne to point out the obvious when it hadn't been so obvious to me.

"Fine. The relationship was a dud anyway."

"I knew you would see it my way." She lifts her glass to clink mine. Her wedding ring glints off of the lights in the bar.

Susanne and Dave, an engineer with one of the major companies in Riverton, got married last year and they've been living in marital bliss ever since.

I've known Susanne since we were six, and she has always been the one with her shit together. She has her life all planned out. She was going to graduate from university with a doctorate degree in psychology. By the time she was 30, she was going to have her own psychology office, by 31 she'd be married to an equally successful man and at 37 she would start having kids. And, in true Susanne-fashion, she has completed every task to date, except the kids.

Then there's me. I've always wanted to be a police officer, and always wanted to be a sergeant. I've gotten there, now what? And somehow, I managed to leave out relationships in my big plan. Maybe I thought the relationships would come naturally. Shouldn't they?

"Hey, ladies." Standing next to our table are two of the lumberjacks from the group over in the corner. Their big and bulkiness tells us that they've been away from civilization, and women, for quite some time.

"Hey," Suzanne says politely. I don't say anything; I just choose to throw a menacing stare their way. This is not how I want to start another relationship.

"We noticed that you two were alone, and wanted to know if you'd like some company?" asks the one with the John Deere ball cap. It sits on top of his head as if it doesn't fit properly. Rather than fitting snugly, it's just 'there', lying on his head. And, underneath that hat is a bushel of hair so dark and thick that I'm afraid of what might be hiding in it. A squirrel? Moose? Bear? Loch Ness Monster?

"I'm sorry, but do we know you?" I narrow my eyes.

One man's grin turns serpentine. "I'm your wildest dreams!"

I scratch my chin, feeling a Godfather moment coming on.

"You lookin' for a real man?" The other one says.

I lean in real tight and tell him to come closer, which he does. "Yeah, do you know where I can find one?"

"Uh...well..." The one with the crooked nose stutters.

"Then get the fuck out of here." The two men glance at each other, turn and walk away.

"Not angry, huh?" Susanne says.

I avert my eyes from hers. "Angry works for me." I know that at my deepest level that this isn't true.

Chapter 2
When All Else Fails, Make Something Up

I've always loved driving up to Nan's house in the country. It always brings back fond childhood memories, regardless if my parents were present or not.

I lived with Nan since I was ten years old, moving out when I graduated from the police academy at the age of 21. I stayed in one of the many rooms in her house and then lived in the guest house out back after high school. After a couple years on the job, I bought my own place—a nice, older house on the south side of Riverton, near the river. See, the river is near my place, and nowhere near the Seaside Restaurant.

My house, a remodeled Victorian style, is painted a dark red with black shutters. I love the character that it has, from the squeaking floors when you walk from the front door to the kitchen, to my quaint bedroom and ensuite with the clawfoot tub. There is nothing like soaking in a bubble bath after a crappy day at work.

Crappy days seem to be the norm lately. Thankfully, today was only slightly treacherous. I shuffled the paperwork sitting on my desk from one basket to the other. I think I signed my name on a few forms—I assume I did as I blacked out for a bit during that time. I answered the phone a few times. Two times it was Nan who was making sure I was coming over and wondering what time I would be there. Another call was from Susanne, checking to see if I was okay after my break up with Phil. I think she was being sarcastic.

The inspector, my ex, whatever you want to call him, paid me a visit. He had come by with wonderful news that I had another Internal Affairs complaint. This one was from a civilian who didn't like the fact that I rammed my cruiser into his motorcycle as he was trying to get away after robbing the local liquor store. I barely touched him; but he managed to fly off his bike anyway, and into some bushes where he broke an arm. Fortunately, for him he was wearing his helmet.

But, in true criminal fashion, this guy decided that he was the victim and laid a complaint against me, crying that I almost killed him with my cruiser. Of course, Mark gave me a lecture about police procedure and how we don't run over motorcyclists. Then, he managed to hit on me again.

"I'm still free, Cate," he winks.

"And, I'm not," I wink back. Mark was on a need to know basis. In this case, he didn't need to know that I broke up with Phil last night. Yes, now I'm changing it to me doing the breaking up. Phil's a jerk and deserves lies and rumours being spread about him.

I walk into Nan's and throw my coat on the chair at the front door. "Nan, where are you?"

Syd, the butler, saunters out of the dining room with a straight-laced, almost morose look. You'd think that he wouldn't have a funny bone in his body with that short grey balding hair, the long distinguished nose and the rod-straight posture. He may act this way, but I know he's not. There have been a few times where the two of us have met in the kitchen on late nights and had a few shots of tequila. No, nothing sexual happened between us. Syd is getting up there in age, and well, that would be gross.

"She's in the living room." He nods toward the door and I head that way. Sitting on the floor in front of the fire place, looking all cozy and content, is Nan sifting through a pile of pictures. She looks up, her face glowing. "Cate, honey, come sit." She pats the floor beside her.

"Hi, Nan," I kiss her soft cheek. Her face is a venerable map of happiness; her eyes still twinkle like little stars, her skin is radiant, and her crow's feet are a testament to the world that she's done more laughing than crying. "What are you doing?"

"I've joined a scrap booking club."

"What do you mean you've joined a scrap booking club?"

"A scrap booking club. You know, you take your pictures, put them in a photo album alongside doodles and stickers and all things creative, and you're scrap booking."

"I know what scrap booking is, Nan. Why are you taking it? It's just a waste of money, you know. All those stamps and stickers and 'special' colourful markers and scissors are pricey."

"I'm doing it to meet people, Cate. I don't know if you've noticed, but most of my friends are dying off." Nan shuffles through her pictures, setting aside the ones that she either likes or dislikes.

Now I feel like a heel. "I'm sorry, Nan. You're right. I'm glad you're meeting people."

"Oh, look at this picture of your grandfather and me." Nan holds up a picture of when they were young, just shortly after they were married. My grandfather, Drew Chase, died approximately the same time I moved in with Nan. He was very young; about sixty. He always had breathing problems since he was little, and one day it caught up to him.

"I love this picture of the two of you."

"You have it, dear."

"Nan, I couldn't." I shove the picture back in her hand.

"I insist." She shoves it back at me, giving me the stare that I better take it or she'll ground me.

I relent. "Fine. I will take it. But if you ever want it back, let me know." As if I'd ever give it back. It's one of those deals that hold no weight.

"Ma'am, dinner is served," Syd the butler calls from the doorway.

"Thank you, Syd."

Annie, Nan's cook, has prepared another fine meal of Chicken Divan, roasted broccoli, baby potatoes and chocolate lava cake for dessert. This beats having cold pizza or Vietnamese food for the third day in a row. I'm not much of a cook. Actually, I know how, I just couldn't be bothered to think of something different besides Kraft Dinner and wieners.

"You know, Nan, I just had an idea. You say you want to meet more friends. Why not extend that to meeting some male friends."

"I do have a few male friends." She takes a bite of her lava cake; the chocolate oozes onto the plate. I hate when it does that—you know you'll never get all that chocolate off the plate, unless you resort to licking it up.

"What I mean is for companionship. You know, a boyfriend... sort of." I feel slightly awkward saying this. Nan with a boyfriend at her age—I don't know if she'd go for it.

"You mean for sex?"

I cringe at how simple she makes it sound.

"I'll leave that part up to you. I'm just saying that it'd be nice if you had a male to hang out with, you know, to balance your life."

"Hmm, a male companion."

"I'm sure you can meet one at the senior's hall or bingo or maybe go on one of those senior's cruises. That would be fun."

"Mmm, I'm not one for ships. Nasty scenes from the Titanic have ruined me for life. I'll consider the other options though. Speaking of boyfriends, how was your date with Phil last night?" She only asks this to be polite. It's nice that she tries.

"Phil and I broke up last night." I'm not looking up at Nan because she'll have one of those gleeful smiles plastered on her face. Those crow's feet will be more pronounced than usual, and they'll be doing the happy dance.

"Oh, that's too bad. I'm sorry to hear that." She pauses for effect, you know, to let everything sink in. "But, like I said before, you're too good for him."

"Nan, you always say that. Tell me who's worthy enough to date your only grandchild?"

"I'm not sure, but I'll find someone for you."

"Oh, you're going to find me a man, are you?"

"That's right. As soon as I find myself a man," she cackles.

"Maybe we can head down to the senior's centre together."

"I'm not sure if you'd like that type. Most of them don't even have their own teeth, or hips, in some cases."

"Well, I'm sure they're ten times better than the lot I've been dating."

We both laugh only because we know it's true.

*

I'm trying to avoid everyone at the office today. Locking myself in my own little prison doesn't do any good because no one knocks anyway. I'm not in the mood to see Erickson because he'll compare my two Internal Affairs complaints to his no complaints. He'll also compare his lack of reports sitting on his desk to my stack.

I also don't want to see Inspector Mark, mainly for the reason that he's trying to get back together with me. He thinks that we can rekindle what we had, which, when you whittle it down, is pretty much nothing. Sure, we briefly lived together before he couldn't keep his penis in his pants. That was an error and something I wish to erase completely.

So, instead of being bait for two people I didn't want to waste my time talking to, I sneak out of the office after the team briefing and into my cruiser. I haven't even made it into my office because Mark's office is only two doors down. My plan is to do some work outside of the office today, arrest people or hand out tickets. But first, I must stop at Nan's to grab my sunglasses that I left at her place.

If it isn't abundantly clear by now, I'm not as excited about my job as I have been in previous years. It's as if being promoted to sergeant has sucked the life right out of me. Plus, I'm stuck with a team that can't stand me. Each day, I hope that things will get better and that I'm just in a slump right now. Everyone goes through them. Right?

I pull my cruiser up behind a black SUV parked in Nan's driveway. I've never seen the vehicle before and think twice about running the license plate on the system to see who it belongs to; first, I'll go inside and ask about the mystery vehicle before running it on the system.

"Nan, I'm here. I forgot my sunglasses," I call out grabbing them from the table and hooking them in my front pocket.

"Nan?" I call again. Suddenly there's a giggle echoing down the hall—a high school giggle coming from the library. Then a man's voice.

Who in the world is she talking to? Maybe it's the gardener, Heinrich. That can't be Syd's voice, and they are the only two men that work here. And, besides, the cute pool boy came by already this week. He prepped the pool for the winter and I was lucky enough to witness the event.

More giggling—giggling I haven't heard since my grandfather was alive. Maybe Nan's flirting with Heinrich, that little vixen. Actually, I hope it isn't Heinrich because he's way too anal with his rose bushes. I can only imagine what he'd be like in bed. I shake the thought from my head and call out again, this time announcing I'm coming into the library in case clothes are coming off.

"Nan."

"In here," Nan sing-songs.

I walk in and realize it isn't Heinrich or Syd, or the pool guy for that matter. It's a good -looking, mysterious man, and I can't help but stare.

"H-hi," I say.

"Cate, this is Zach Kennedy. Zach, this is my granddaughter, Cate Chase."

Zach Kennedy sent to do my bidding. How wonderful. I shake his hand and feel a noticeable quiver run up my legs. I do a once over, visualizing his slim, muscular body beneath his jeans and t-shirt.

I press my hair back into place where some strays have fallen out of its bun. Now I wish I'd worn something else, something less constricting, like a pair of handcuffs dangling from my finger.

"Nice to meet you, Cate. Your grandmother was just telling me all about you."

"Oh, really?" Don't tell me Nan went out and got me a date? Well, she did damn good.

"Yes, I was just telling Zach how it was your idea that I call up an escort." My head snaps around so quick that I'm sure I gave myself whiplash.

Escort?

Chapter 3
The Train Wreck Begins

"Wait a minute. What?"

"Zach is from an escort agency."

I'm...speechless. I'm... stunned. I can't help but shift my eyes from this, this escort, to Nan. The escort continues to smile, all happy and suave, and Nan grins as if she's the cat that caught the canary.

"Well, it's my own escort agency," corrects Zach.

Like it makes a difference.

"Nan, can I see you for a moment?" I lead her out of the room and give her a sound beating when we're out of ear shot. "You called an escort agency?

"That's right. I took your advice."

"My advice?" What is the woman talking about? "Nan, did you have a stroke?"

"You said that I needed some male companionship, so I looked in the yellow pages under 'companions' and it said, 'see escorts'. So I checked for the most reputable escort ad and saw there was a website. Well, I just knew I had to check out the merchandise before calling the number."

"Of course," I say sarcastically.

"So, when I looked at the tasteful website...you should see it, Cate, it's so savvy...and once I saw Zach's picture, I knew I had to call it up."

"First of all, I don't think you can use the word 'reputable' and 'escort' in the same sentence. Second of all, I don't recall telling you to find an escort. I told you to go to the senior's centre, find some widower who has five percent of his real teeth and hair. Or get a puppy, like a terrier or poodle...or one of those hairless mole rats. I didn't tell you to get an escort." I rub my temples.

My grandmother has gotten herself an escort. What is this world coming to?

"I'm not going to have sex with him, if that's what you think. That's where I draw the line!" she says with conviction.

"Well, I'm so glad you've set your boundaries." I pace in a small circle. "Nan, he can't be here. He's an escort. It's illegal. I'm a cop. Doesn't this uniform give it away?"

"He's just here to keep me company, Cate. Like I said, no sex is involved. And since no sex is involved, it's not illegal."

"I'm here, Nan. I can keep you company. You don't need to pay for an escort. Save your money."

"If you haven't noticed, I'm not exactly broke. And you're too busy with your career to take time out for me." Oh, who turned on the violins? I choose to ignore it. "Nan, please tell him to leave."

"No."

"Nan, he can't be here."

"He's staying, I want him here." She throws me a meaningful look. "Oh, and he's moving into the guest house tomorrow." Nan strides toward the library leaving me staggered.

"He's moving in? Nan, seriously, should I call the doctor?"

Nan's hand flies in my face. "I've made up my mind. He's staying." And, with that, she walks back into the room. "So, Zach, I hope you'll stay for lunch so we can chat more."

"I'd love that, Mrs. Chase."

"Oh, call me Ursula," she giggles.

My position in the doorway allows me to send daggers from my eyes to The Escort. Maybe Nan isn't aware of his dishonourable intentions, but I sure know what he's about. I've dealt with these manipulators before, and this is one person that he will not make his victim.

"I'll stay for lunch, too, Nan." I promptly sit down in one of the leather wing back chairs.

Surprise cris-crosses her face. "Don't you have tons of paperwork to do?"

"It can wait." I glare at The Escort. He continues to smile at me as if I'm not affecting him in any way. Who does he think he's dealing with?

"Why don't you two go out to the patio for a bit while I tell Annie there will be two more for lunch? Lunch should be ready shortly." She pushes us through the French doors of the library and out onto the deck.

The air is crisp as mid-September begins to cool off in its original style. The breeze is a bit chilly and I'm not sure why Nan has sent us out here when we don't even have jackets on. But, I'll humour the old girl.

I lean over the deck edge and look out onto the estate grounds; the once green, immaculate lawn is now slowly being covered with falling leaves of red and gold; the lawn gnomes have been put away for another year, as well as the potted plants. I hate to see the summer go.

Beside me, The Escort is also looking across the grounds, finally resting his eyes on the guest house. He catches me staring at him.

"I guess I'll be staying there for a while," he says, nodding towards the small, one bedroom white guest house.

"Do you really think it's a good idea to be living at my grandmother's?"

"It's a perfect opportunity. I'm here when your grandmother needs me, day or night. Plus, I don't need to look for another place since I'm moving out of my old place."

"Did you get evicted?" I patronize.

"Nooo, I was staying with a buddy till I could find a place of my own."

"I guess at, what, 40 years old, it was time to grow up and find your own pad."

He ignores my cattiness and changes the subject. "So... Cate, is it? You're a cop."

"What gave it away? I mean, I am standing here in a police uniform." Is that not the lamest question?

"I wanted to be a cop once," The Escort continues, unfazed by my impoliteness. It's really starting to bug me that nothing I say will make him want to leave.

"Couldn't get in?"

"Actually, I got in. Was hired and everything, but then I decided that police work wasn't for me."

"Well, policing is a lot of work. You have to be a special kind of person to do it." I puff out my chest to the point where I can't breathe anymore and slowly let the air out before I turn blue.

"I declined the position because I didn't like all the politics."

"Politics? Hardly," I spit out. "There aren't any politics at Riverton Police Service." That's a bit of a lie, but whatever.

He rolls his eyes. "I also didn't want to get a fat head."

"A fat head?" I snap.

"You know. All puffed up because you wear a uniform, carry a gun and can put the boots to some guy who refuses arrest." He doesn't change his expression as he says this. Nor, does he change his tone; he says everything like he's asking for a glass of water.

I grind my teeth. This guy is going to get the boots put to him if he doesn't shut up. "You know what? I'm making an executive decision here and have decided your services are no longer required." I wave my hand in the air, erasing some fake contract between The Escort and my grandmother.

"Really?" He raises an eyebrow, staring me down. "I think I'll leave that decision up to your grandmother." He walks away, but I catch up to him and block his path.

"I don't think you heard me. I've made the decision that you should leave, or rather, you have to leave. I can't trust you and I don't think your intentions are admirable."

"What are you implying?"

"You know she has a lot of cash. You know she's in a weakened state; she's needy right now. Not thinking clearly," I whisper this last part because Nan isn't any of these things.

"I think she's a lot more cognizant than you are!" Zach spits.

"What are you trying to say?" We are in a face off; obviously this guy has no idea who he's dealing with. Doesn't he know that I can have him wrestled to the ground in two seconds with my knee strategically placed behind his ear?

"You're unstable; a loose cannon."

"I think you should leave," I growl.

"Considering this is your grandmother's house, I'll wait for her to kick me out. In the meantime, you can choose to ignore me or put up with me." Behind his eyes linger a fire that I knew wasn't about to be extinguished.

"Wait a second! I'm not done with you yet. Where are you going?"

"Far away from you!" Zach yanks the door open.

"Yeah, well, far away wouldn't be far enough," I yell.

He waves me away like a gnat and leaves me at the patio doors.

Meanwhile, I head up to Nan's room where she's brushing her hair and applying lipstick.

"Nan, he has to leave."

"Who has to leave?" she doesn't look my way, but I know she knows. Come on. How could she not?

"Zach, The Escort. He has to go. He can't be around here. It's not good for you and it's not good for my career."

"He's staying, Cate." Nan rises up from her mirrored table and walks past me and out the door.

"Come on, Nan. You don't even know who he is. He could be psycho or a mass murderer. For all you know, he could be stealing the silverware right now."

"Oh, god, he can have it. I didn't like it anyway. It was a gift from my mother-in-law."

I can't believe Nan isn't concerned. Not one little bit. "Come on, be serious."

"I am! And, Zach Kennedy is staying." Her one last look reminds me of the ones I used to see as a child when I had pushed her too far.

"Ursula, you are gorgeous." Zach Kennedy stands at the bottom of the landing, fangs gleaming, claws extended like he's a wolf in Prince Charming's clothing.

Come on. Can't you be more inventive than that? This guy is just plain cheesy and he continues to prove it all through lunch, drenching Nan with the whole charming spiel.

Oh, Ursula, you make me laugh. Oh, Ursula, you're so right. Oh, Ursula.

And to top it off, The Escort doesn't even look my way. Even when I ask him, specifically him, to pass the salt and pepper, he only pushes it towards me without acknowledging my existence.

Not one friggin' glance. Nothing. The jerk.

"Listen, Nan, I can come by after work and take you out for dinner. Just the two of us."

"What about all your paperwork?"

"Oh, that can wait. Clearly, you need some company, and I always have time for my grandmother." I kiss her.

"Why don't you come over for dinner tomorrow instead? It's always nice to sit here in front of the fire and have some drinks."

I knew I could lure Nan away from the 'dark side'; the place where only escorts roam. "That sounds even better. Just you and me..."

"Zach, we'd love to have you join us."

"No. No, we wouldn't." Did I say that out loud? I think I said that out loud. Nan and Zach both stare at me. I did say that out loud.

Nan is stunned, but Zach remains stoic as ever. "Cate!! That's not very polite."

I try my best not to turn red. Nan is punishing me in front of The Escort and I'm ten again. "But, Nan..."

"Zach, we'd love to have you join us."

She's ignoring me. She's blatantly ignoring me!

"I'd love that. I'll bring my things over during the day, and then join you for dinner."

"Oh, and I can't forget to tell you about my annual Halloween party. Big party, lots of fun, costumes, food, drink. I've done it every single year since Cate's father was young. I hope you can make it."

"What?" I squeak. "Nan! You can't invite him to the Halloween party. It's our Halloween party."

"What's wrong with you? You're being childish today." I'm suddenly struck with the notion that my grandmother is not going to be taking my side any time soon. "Do you think you can make it, Zach?"

"Of course. I wouldn't miss it." He leans in and kisses my grandmother's hand.

"I don't believe this!" I throw my napkin on the table, and stand up, or try to, but my billy club is caught on the arm of the dining room chair. I yank at it till it finally comes free, and stand straight.

"Cate!"

"Nan, you aren't going to believe any of his bullshit, are you?" Zach doesn't flinch. Why am I not getting a rise out of him?

"Cate, I will not have that language in this house. Zach is our guest."

"Please! He's not a guest, he's an intruder. He's wheedled his way in here, and believe me, he shouldn't be here," I sputter.

"No one wheedled their way into my house. I invited Zach and he's staying. You will have to accept it."

I'm ready to use the ol' I'm not coming back till he's gone routine, but I know that it's futile. It's an empty threat and she'll see right through it. She knows I'll come back the next day and the day after.

I bite my tongue and mumble something about getting back to work. I give Nan a kiss on the cheek, tell her I'll see her tomorrow for dinner and walk out without a backward glance. This guy is up to something, but what? Luckily, I have the capabilities to learn many things about Zach Kennedy.

As soon as I return to the police cruiser, I type in his license plate number and wait while it thinks.

Zach H. Kennedy
302- 2322 Harvest Valley Rd.

No license suspension. No probation. No messages. I use another search method, typing in his name, including his birth date from his license information. The computer tells me to wait.

A few seconds later, a message pops up.

This is it; I have him for warrant upon warrant. I can go back inside right now and arrest his ass. Oooo, this will be so sweet. I hit the button and bring up the message.

No files found.

That's impossible. I type in the information again, and again, nothing. Something has to be wrong with my computer. I race back to the office, suddenly realizing that I've been gone for quite a while and, well, no one has even asked me where I've been. Kind of depressing.

At my office computer, I type in the information and continue to get no hits. I walk out to the front where Joan Purvis, the secretary, is at her desk looking through a People Magazine. Joan is a middle aged woman who always seems disinterested in her work or anything else going on around her.

Actually, Joan has been great to me. Aside from the numerous silky blouses that she has an abundance of, and which always match the satiny bow in her hair, she always has her hand on the pulse of the local office gossip.

Today, she's wearing a fuchsia coloured satin top with a large matching bow that holds her hair in a bun.

"Joan, is there something wrong with the computer system?"

She glances at her computer, hits a few keys, clicks her gum and says, "Nope. Seems to be working okay." She returns her attention back to her magazine, unconcerned by my situation.

Even though Joan's flippant behaviour is slightly disconcerting, she always calls me 'sweetie'. Well, except for right now because she's more interested in the gossip on Clint Eastwood, her favourite actor ever since Bridges of Madison County.

"Chase, can I see you for a moment?" The inspector holds a bunch of papers in his meaty hands; his concerned look scares me.

"Sure, what about?"

"Let's go to your office." Great, an office talk. Maybe he needs to tell me how much he loves me or possibly wants to sweet talk me into a good romp.

I take a seat in my rickety office chair, all the while eyeing the papers in Mark's hands, catching glimpses of what it says. Mark sits on the edge of my desk as he usually does.

"By the looks of those papers, I'm guessing I'm not getting a promotion." My lightness of the situation doesn't do me any good.

Mark sighs. "You know I like you, Chase. You have always been a hard worker, always putting in 110%. But, ever since you became sergeant, you've gone downhill. What's going on?"

My brow furrows; I have no idea what he's getting at. I thought I was doing a damn good job as sergeant considering the circumstances. "Let's see, you stuck me with a team who absolutely hates me. I'm trying everything possible to please them and still getting nowhere. You tell me what the problem is."

Mark shuffles the papers in his hands and scratches his head.

"Just tell me you have another complaint on me. I can take it." I know this is what he holds in his hands. Why else would he be in my office? He hasn't hit on me yet, so obviously he has more important things to talk about.

Mark sighs again. "Yes, I have another complaint on you. Not from a call, but from a member of your team."

"There's a surprise."

"Look, someone is concerned that you aren't organizing the team well enough and that one day, someone will get hurt due to your management skills."

"Give me a break." I roll my eyes and slump down in my chair.

"I'm an excellent manager. I'm always on top of things, organizing things." Mark's eyes fall to the pile of paperwork on my desk—the paperwork that has no rhyme or reason to its filing system. Honestly, I don't know what's what anymore.

"Okay, I can't organize my paperwork, but I can organize a team. You know that, Mark."

Mark nods in... agreement? Admission? Reluctance to continue this conversation any further? "Do you want things to work out with your team?" he asks.

"What kind of question is that?"

"Just answer the question, Chase. Do you want to work things out with your team?"

"Of course."

"Then this is what you need to do. I want you to get organized. Get your paperwork out of the way. I want you to speak to your team and get on some even ground with them. This has to be taken care of, Chase. Now."

I nod, taking a few dramatic moments before I say my speech, raising my hand in the air. "As of today, I promise to get my work done, my paperwork signed and sent off to the big paperwork filing system in the sky, or archives, or wherever paperwork goes when it's no longer needed. I promise to meet with my team first thing tomorrow and I promise to get organized and back on track!"

"Get it done." Mark walks out. He obviously means business seeing as he didn't even hit on me. He must be running a fever.

Maybe he's right—I need to get organized and file my paperwork. I'm determined to make him proud. Well, not really. But even as I make my plan of action, a big part of me feels absolutely doomed.

Chapter 4
Death by Ceiling Tile

I had stayed late last night finishing up most of my work that had been lingering on my desk for many days. Actually, it was more like me staring into space for a couple of hours and only doing some paperwork. My mind had been a jumbled mess, wondering what the hell I would say to my team the next day.

The second thing that preoccupied me was Zach Kennedy. As much as I hate to admit it, my mind strayed to The Escort more often than not. For one, how was he planning on manipulating my grandmother? And, two, why did he make my body hum?

Even as I sit here, early morning, waiting to start the staff meeting, I'm still thinking about him. Thankfully, Susanne phones to snap me out of my fantasy. "I can't talk long, Susanne. I'm about to give a riveting speech to my team."

"I'm calling to see what you're doing later this evening."

"Going to my grandmother's for dinner."

"How about tomorrow night?"

"Paper work. Why do you ask?"

"I want you to put aside your paperwork and meet Dave and me Carlos' at seven tomorrow night."

"What's there? Is it Tequila night again? You know I can't handle tequila night."

"No. Margaritas."

I sniff the air. "Wait, I smell a blind date brewing."

"How do you always do that?"

"I'm a trained professional. So, who's the engineer?"

"How do you know he's an engineer? He could be the guy that works at the 7-11."

"The pimply-faced kid that spits when he talks? Not really my type."

"Okay, he's a co-worker of Dave's. I think you guys would get along really well."

"Susanne, I just got out of a relationship."

"A relationship you should have ended months ago."

"We only dated for three months."

"Three months too long! Look, come meet this guy. He's nice, he's an engineer and he's good looking."

"Can I call you back with my answer? I'd like to think about it first."

"No, you can't. You are meeting us there at seven tomorrow night."

"Fine." I cave too quickly. I hang up and look at the clock. Grudgingly, I stand. Time to motivate my team.

When I arrive at the boardroom, my entire team is waiting patiently. They know what's coming seeing as I sent them all an email the day before indicating my need to speak to them about the situation. I'm surprised they all showed up.

I stand before them, my hands flat on the boardroom table, leaning forward. I want to demonstrate my ability to be a team player; I want to show them that I can mesh with them.

"I don't want to waste your time, guys, so I'll cut right to the chase." The last word hangs like a smelly shirt as I realize how ridiculous it sounds considering it's my last name. This is not a way to start a heart-to-heart. I recover myself and continue.

"For the last two months, our team has sucked. Now, I know some of you don't like me or appreciate me being your sergeant, but this is something we all need to accept. I mean, we've had some really shitty things happen lately. Calls have been mishandled; an abundance of miscommunication and mistrust.

I'm just as much to blame as the next person. So, starting today, I would like to start new. I want us to forge a new relationship built on trust, teamwork, and respect. I know we can be an excellent team if we just work at it." I look around.

Blank stares.

I'm having a hard time gauging what's going through their minds. There's a few looking at their phones. Some are writing things in their notebooks. Overall, no one is paying attention.

"Guys?"

"Guys?" I say, this time more firmly.

Then, I notice something. Something that's been hidden for a long time. It's subtle at first, but slowly, I recognize the anger that starts to bubble in my chest, ready to split wide open. It takes everything in me not to flip a table; unfortunately, it's not enough to bite my tongue.

"What do I have to do to get you guys to work with me?" I yell.

"Please. Someone. Tell me!" The words spill out before I can catch them. "You all are bunch of jackasses!" I turn my back, throwing my pen across the room.

"You suck!" The words reverberate around the room. They didn't come from my mouth, but from the back of the room. I turn around and see Rob Spears, senior constable, smirking.

"Pardon me?"

Rob stands. "You suck. You wanted to know why we can't stand you...you are a shitty sergeant."

I scan the other faces in the room. Most of them refuse to look up.

I'm speechless. I don't think I could say anything if I tried.

The anger that had been present moments ago is slowly turning into tears.

"Everyone, back to work." I growl leaving the room. I slam my office door and slide into my chair. What the hell happened in there? That entire meeting exploded into a mushroom cloud of toxic doom. I hold back the tears and vow that this is not going to make me cry. I know I'm an excellent cop. I know it. What has happened to make me suck in their eyes?

The paperwork is still glaring at me, ready to mull me if I don't show it who's boss. God, I'm really starting to hate my job. I used to be kick-ass at this work. It's like I had a sixth sense about criminals. Now, I question everything I do.

I recline back in my chair and stare at the water-stained ceiling. I will most likely die drowning from this water leak before I finish my paperwork. Actually, death by ceiling tile sounds much more fun than paperwork.

There's a knock at the door but I don't answer. It doesn't matter anyway because Joan pokes her head in, sees me staring at the ceiling and closes the door behind her.

"See anything interesting?" she asks, clicking her gum in that 'Flo-like' way that she does.

"Yes. Alert the presses. The Virgin Mary has moved from the taco she was last seen in to the water stains on my ceiling tiles."

Joan gives me a quirky smile like she's ready to tell me to 'kiss my grits'. "How are you doing, honey?"

"Oh, fine," I lie. "Why do you ask?"

"You look as if things have been troubling you for some time. Bad meeting today, hey?" She moves in closer, now leaning up against a filing cabinet.

"Yeah, you could say it was shitty. I really don't know what to do next. They hate me." The heaviness in my chest lingers, like someone sitting on me.

"Humans will attack like a wild cat when they become threatened."

"Hmmmm...I don't think I'm that threatening."

"It's funny what we do when we aren't thinking clearly." She pauses for a second, then changes the subject. "How is that boyfriend of yours?"

"Mmm, we split."

"Sorry to hear that."

"Don't be. We weren't a good match to begin with."

"You know what you need?"

"A shot of bourbon?"

"A man who treats you right. Someone who can handle your strong constitution." Joan sits at the edge of my desk, her face serious. There's an excited flicker in her eyes.

"I suppose that would be nice." I agree with her. At this point, I'm thinking the conversation will end right here. You know, it's like saying, 'yeah, you're right. Maybe one day.' Or even, 'yeah, maybe one day, but I won't hold my breath.' Then we'd laugh and she'd leave, never really resolving anything.

"And I have just the man for you." Before I can protest, Joan utters two words I don't expect, "My son."

"Oh, Joan, I don't know. I've just recovered from dating my co-workers, I don't know if my next pursuit should be dating my co-worker's children." That sounds absolutely horrible once said out loud.

"Sweetie, my boy is a perfect match for you. He's going to be a doctor soon, so he understands overtime, stress and shift work. At the very least, meet him. His name is Ian, and I'm not being biased when I say that he's gorgeous. You'd be doing me a favour.

"All of the other women he's dated have been so clingy. He needs someone independent. And if it doesn't work out, at least you gave it a shot. No harm done." She says it all so fast that I'm almost convinced that he's the man for me. And, before I can ponder the situation further, sleep on it, or tell her I have a blind date for tomorrow night with some engineer, Joan is dialing.

"Joan, I don't think I'm in the mood to plan a date. This day has been the worst day ever, and it just started."

She shushes me and talks into the phone. "Hi, hon. How was your day?" Joan winks at me and I groan. "Hey, I won't keep you, but I think you should meet a friend of mine. She's wonderful." Joan pauses as Ian says something to her. Maybe he doesn't want to meet me and is telling Joan to stop setting him up with her friends.

"You don't need her number, hon. She's sitting beside me right now." What? He wants my number after a thirty second phone call with his mother?

"Okay, her name is Cate." Joan cuffs the phone with her hand. "He wants to talk to you about going out."

I hesitate for a second and then take the phone.

"Hi, Ian."

"Cate." His voice is comforting and sweet. "When can we get together?"

This guy doesn't waste any time. "Um, I'm on four days off starting tomorrow. Anytime then works. Oh, except tomorrow."

Right. I have another date tomorrow.

"Hmmm...let's see," there was a pause. "How about the next night? Dinner?"

"Yeah, dinner, sure." Do you think I'm capable of say anything half-intelligent?

"Great. Give me your address and I'll pick you up around seven."

"Okay." I give out my address and phone number, the whole time Joan clicks her gum and beams like she's ready to accept me as her daughter-in-law. I tell him I'm looking forward to meeting him then hang up the phone, my head reeling at how quickly this all has happened. Three minutes ago, I was having a pity party. Now, I have two dates; I'd shoot for a third if my social calendar could handle it.

Sensing my uneasiness, Joan places a hand on my shoulder. "This is how you get things done, honey. You do it whole-heartedly or you don't do it at all. But never, ever regret your decision."

"Listen to you being all philosophical." I smile.

"You'll love my son. I know it!" She winks at me then sidles out of my office.

I leave work a little early so I can get home and change into something a bit nicer for dinner at Nan's. I sift through my wardrobe and pull out a pair of grey pants and a blue top. I shake my hair out of its bun and let my hair fall around my shoulders.

I check myself over in the mirror, and tell myself I'm not dressing up for The Escort, and that this is how I always dress for dinner at Nan's. Truth be told, I have shown up for past dinners wearing frayed jeans and a brown short sleeved shirt that said, 'Al's Hardware- We'll find the right screw for you.'

*

Syd greets me at the door and takes my jacket; he smiles appreciatively at how I look. "Your grandmother and Mr. Kennedy are in the living room," Syd winks.

Mr. Kennedy? When did we resort to using a title when addressing the hired help? And when did we ever use a title to address any of the escorts we've ever hired? Not like we've hired escorts before. And why was Syd winking at me?

In the living room, Nan and The Escort are chatting on the sofa, intent on their conversation. Their voices are hushed and the minute they see me standing at the door, they stop talking.

"Cate, you look nice. You didn't dress up for us, did you?" Nan looks especially glowing in her crème coloured pant suit.

"This is how I always dress for dinner, Nan."

The Escort sits casually on the sofa, a drink in one hand and the other draped across the back of the couch. Tonight, he's wearing all black—a black button down shirt and dark fitted jeans. Not that I'm paying attention to these fine details. There's a familiar ache inside my belly, which I promptly turn off; I'm not here to make friends, no matter how delicious he smells tonight.

"I see you're still here, Zach," I say. Nan brings me a drink and gives me a dirty look in the process.

"It would appear that way considering I'm sitting here," The Escort replies. He remains cavalier, his gaze not moving away from mine.

"Zach only has a few more things to pick up and then he's all moved in."

"I'll get the rest tonight after dinner, Ursula. I'm really feeling at home in the guest house. Thank you for letting me stay there."

"You're welcome. It wasn't being used anyway. Cate moved out ages ago."

My grandmother turns to me. "How was your day, dear?"

Shitty. It sucked. My team hates me. "Fine. I have a lot on my plate right now. You know, there's a ton of responsibilities as a sergeant," I say, haughtily.

"You mean lots of paperwork," The Escort flies back.

I raise an eyebrow. "And what would you know about my job?"

"Enough to know that you're mainly overloaded with administrative duties than doing actual calls."

"I put in a lot of time on the street. Actually, last week we busted a ring of car thieves." Of course, this isn't true, but it sounds good anyway.

"Oh, dear. That sounds dangerous." Nan puts a hand to her chest.

"It's just another way of saying a group of teens were stealing cars for joy rides." The Escort flashes me a contentious look.

How does he know? Before I can throw a comment back, Syd is at the door calling us to dinner.

Nan and The Escort walk ahead of me, arm and arm, while I fall behind them, trying to hear their conversation; I have somehow been deleted from the picture.

All during dinner, Nan and Zach talk amongst themselves. Zach is blatantly over- friendly and sweet to the point that it's sickening, and Nan sucks it all up like a woman in the desert finding an oasis after three weeks with no water. By the end of dinner, I'm so overloaded with his saccharine dialogue that I just want him to leave.

"Don't you have some place to be, Zach? Like another escort job."

"Nope. Your grandmother is my only client. I'm here as long as she needs me." The Escort smiles.

"Great," I mutter. "I'm going to go now, Nan. I'll call you tomorrow." I stand up and lean over to give Nan a kiss on the cheek.

"All right. Drive safe." I turn on one heel, give Zach a nod and leave. Why do I even give him that much? Why did I acknowledge him when he wouldn't even pass me the salt at lunch yesterday?

I drive out onto the country road, my head full of Escort. The dark clouds from earlier produced a rain of monsoon proportions, and my windshield wipers are barely able to keep up. On the other side of the road, a few cars drive by; other than that, the dark road is all mine. The drive home, if anything, will give me the time to think of how to wean Nan of The Escort and how to rectify my team situation. Even as I formulate my plan, the only thing that creeps into my mind is the way he smiles and how those smoky grey eyes seem to look right into me.

As I turn the bend, my mind continues to flip to The Escort. Any effort into making him into some sort of monster is futile. What is this man doing to me?

Pop! Crack! Ping!

The car suddenly wrenches forward and banging noises echo from under the hood. The car spasms and lunges forward, choking to its death as I pull to the side of road. Steam billows out from under the hood and the engine light flashes on, almost like it's telling me I'm doomed.

"This is not fucking happening!" I slam my hand on the steering wheel, as if that will get the car going again. "This is not fucking happening!" I look out into the dark night realizing that I haven't passed anyone in a long time.

I pop the hood and more white smoke pours out from underneath; I wave it away and peer inside. The rain pelts the hot silvery engine and it sizzles like a cat hissing, telling me to leave it alone. I know how to service my revolver, but, for the life of me, cannot figure out the innards of a car.

The rain continues to run down my face, down the length of the coat, and into my shoes. There's really no use standing out here if I can't see a single thing. I'll just grab my phone and get some help.

I slide back into the car and reach for my purse, only to discover the phone is not in there but sitting on the kitchen counter at home, charging.

Could this day spin any further into a deep dark pit? Okay, I'm about a twenty minute walk back to Nan's place. I could wait it out till the rain tapers off or I can head off now and be a drowned rat when I arrive.

"Why, why, why, why?" I bang my head on the steering wheel, only because the steering wheel had it coming and all. Just as I think of other ways to take it out on the car, there is a loud tapping on my window that scars the shit out of me.

I squint into the dark night but can't make out the face of the hooded figure wearing a raincoat, so I reach for my mace and open the window an inch.

"Cate, it's Zach."

Zach! As much as I hate to admit it, I am relieved. "Zach, what are you doing here?"

"I was heading out to pick up the rest of my things. Are you all right?" He calls from the still partially opened window.

"Yes, I'm fine."

"Come on, I'll take you back to your grandmother's, or have you called a tow truck?"

"No. I forgot my phone at home." My stubbornness wells up before I can even think clearly. "And, besides, I don't need your help." See? What am I saying? Wasn't I the one that just said I needed help?

"Fine. Have it your way." Zach walks back to his vehicle, leaving me, and I realize that if I'm going to get home in this century, I have to be nice.

I fly the door open and yell, "Wait. I do need help."

Zach stops and waits for me to walk to him, the water now steadily dripping from my curls and down my face. He jerks his head toward his vehicle. "Get in the car."

I slide into the seat and am grateful for the warmth and for the fact that he didn't leave me stranded. Okay, be nice, be nice.

The guy is giving you a lift home. He didn't have to stop. I glance at Zach, his eyes fixed on the road, his face damp from the rain.

"Your grandmother's?" he asks.

"My house. 822 Brookside Lane."

He nods and continues to drive, silence awkwardly fills the air; the only noise is the rain pounding down on the car while the windshield wipers whoosh back and forth at lightning speed.

"Some rain." I uneasily make conversation.

Zach murmurs in agreement. More silence.

"I don't know what's with my car. It's brand new. You'd think the brand new ones would be better than the old ones." That sounded absolutely pathetic.

"I'm sure they'll fix it for you at the dealership."

I stare out the window. More silence. Can't we turn the radio on or something? This is just too uncomfortable. Okay, think of something to talk about. Anything remotely interesting. Maybe I can impress him with one of my cop stories.

"So, how long are you staying with my grandmother?"

Zach looks out of the corner of his eye for a split second then sighs. "As long as she needs me."

"Hmm."

"Hmm, what?" he says.

"Oh, nothing."

"Obviously there is something or you wouldn't be muttering to yourself."

"I'm not muttering to myself. I just said hmm."

"Hmm is a sound that means there's something else hanging there, something else the person wants to say—so, say it."

"I just don't see what service you are to my grandmother. I'm here for her. She doesn't need you to take her places. Honestly, it's a waste of her money. Plus, what you do is illegal."

"Oh, yes, the old it's illegal bit. Well, if you stopped yakking to ask me about my business, you'd understand it better." Zach pulls onto my street.

Finally.

"What's there to understand? You provide a sexual service for money. I don't like it. I think you should leave my grandmother alone and I'll see to it that you do."

Now stopped outside my place, I turn to him, ready to say something else, but he beats me to it. "You can get out now."

"I'm watching you, Zach." I point a finger at him and leave the car.

"Fine, fine, watch me all you want." Zach puts the pedal down and takes off just as I barely have time to slam the door.

I'm left standing on the street watching his taillights disappear into the distance. A feeling of disappointment washes over me. I'm not sure exactly what I was expecting to happen. All I know is that I have to start pulling it together.

Chapter 5
After the fifth blind date, I get a free toaster.

"What are you and The Escort doing tonight?" I am sitting outside Carlos' in the rental vehicle the dealership gave me till my car was fixed. I didn't see Susanne's car anywhere, and I wasn't about to go in and make small talk with my blind date.

"Nothing. Zach is out this evening. I'm here doing my scrapbooking."

I sit up in my seat. "Where'd he go?"

"Heavens, I don't know, Cate. It's his life. He doesn't need to report to me."

"Aren't you paying him good money?"

"I'm not a slave driver. I do let him have time off. Or should I keep him under lock and key?"

How about handcuffs? I shake that thought from my head. "If he does anything to you, you let me know immediately. I haven't found anything on the guy yet, but I'm willing to bet—"

"Cate! Shame on you. I can't believe you checked him out."

"I had to! Did you expect anything less?" The other line beeps. "I better go. I'll talk to you later." I click over to the second call, which is Susanne.

"Are you there yet?" She's almost yelling into the phone.

"Yes, I'm sitting outside waiting for you. Where are you? It sounds like you are standing on the side of the road."

"Ya, well, we won't be able to make it."

"What? Why?"

"Our car broke down and we're waiting for the tow truck."

I do a fist pump in the air. "No problem. We'll do this some other night."

"No, you have to go. Go in and meet Ethan. We couldn't get him on his cell phone. He'll be waiting for us."

"Ethan? I don't want to meet Ethan!"

"Listen, please go meet him. Tell him we're really sorry."

"Do I have to?" I whine.

"Yes, you do."

"Okay, but I'm leaving right after I tell him."

"Fine, do whatever you have to. He has light blonde hair and black rimmed glasses. Oh, I gotta go; the phone is dying. Talk to you tomorrow." And she's gone.

"Perfect." I whine, pulling the keys out of the ignition and debate if it's really rude of me to not show up. I think I'm more scared of Susanne kicking my ass.

I walk into the pub and scan the tables for a man I've never met before. It doesn't take too long as I spot the only man in the place that's sitting by himself. He nervously taps his pint of beer with his finger, leans back, wipes his hands on his pants, and shifts in his seat. I walk toward him; his blank stare hasn't clicked in that I might be the one he's meeting tonight.

"Ethan?"

"Yes?" It took him a second till he realized who I was. "You must be Cate." He stands, and I realize that I am quite a bit taller than him. He shakes my hand and gestures for me to sit down.

"Actually, I can't stay. I just came to tell you that Dave and Susanne had car troubles. We will have to reschedule."

His face falls. "Oh, that's too bad. I was looking forward to this."

Really? That's what I want to say but instead choose, "Yeah, me too." My eyes catch a glimpse of the door and I recognize a tall, dark haired figure standing with two women on either side of him.

The Escort. What's he doing here?

"Um, on second thought, I can stay for a little bit." I sit down beside Ethan while maintaining a view of The Escort.

"Good. I just ordered some nachos; we can share. What do you want to drink? I'll get the waitress over here." Ethan does the waitress sign language and she makes her way over.

"Um, Corona, I guess."

"One Corona, please," Ethan repeats my order to the waitress and she leaves.

"So, you're an engineer." I smile, still keeping an eye on Zach. I watch him walk to a table nearby; he doesn't realize I'm in his line of sight. "That must be exciting." I turn my attention back to Ethan.

The waitress puts a beer in front of me.

Ethan takes a sip of his pint. "Big stuff happening. We have a major project that we're working on right now." He takes off his glasses, and swipes his hair back. He's nervous, that much I know. He's also kinda cute; almost the boy next door cute, which I do find attractive.

"Oh, ya? What's it about?" The waitress places the nachos in front of us and Ethan digs in. I turn my gaze toward Zach. The two blonde women, flanking either side of The Escort, are laughing at something he said. I can't help but wonder if they are prostitutes, or strippers. Who else could Zach be friends with?

Ethan continues to talk about his engineering stuff, and I have not paid attention to a single word of it. If there's a test later, I'm sure to fail.

He leans forward and whispers, "That's all top secret stuff, if you know what I mean?"

"Right, right. Your secret's safe with me." I pat his arm. I turn my attention back to Zach.

"Dave says you're a cop," Ethan whispers in my ear; his words are almost on top of me. I don't notice how close he's gotten until I feel his thigh pressing up against mine, and I try to move away.

"What?" I shift in my seat. I can't focus on what Ethan is saying, when I can hear Zach laugh from where he's sitting. I feel a twinge of envy in my belly. Meanwhile, Ethan continues to shimmy his leg closer to mine no matter how much I shift away.

"A cop. Dave says you're a cop." Ethan's tone is edgier and sharper. It catches my attention.

"I'm sorry. What?"

He glances at Zach, then glares at me. "You are a cop." Every word is terse and accentuated.

"Ya. Sergeant." My gaze quickly shifts to Zach, and then back to Ethan. But, it's too late; he's figured out what's distracting me.

"Am I interrupting something?"

"What do you mean?"

He nods toward Zach. "You've been watching that man since you sat down."

The air stops in my throat. How awkward. "Um. Looks like someone I know."

He nods, satisfied with my answer. "Soooo," he leans in. "You cops must have some top secret stuff too."

My eyes meet Ethan's, which is really the first time that I've looked at him since I sat down. "Oh, totally. There's so much on the go that I can't even keep track of it," I smile willfully. I pick up my beer and steal a glance at Zach again.

Ethan leans in and whispers, "What kind of top secret info? A raid on a donut shop?" He chuckles, leaning back and slapping his knee.

I snap my head around because my date now has my complete and undivided attention.

Ethan sees that I'm not laughing. "Come on! Donut shop. It's funny."

"Are you a fucking moron?"

"Whoa!" He leans back, his hands raised.

"You are a fucking moron, aren't you?"

"Oh, come on. We all know why you guys go blazing through the stoplights with lights and sirens. It's to get the fresh donuts." He laughs again, but this time I sense hesitation.

"Excuse me, but do you have a problem with police officers?" I ask. This guy is going to get his ass kicked.

"Well, no. Yes. Maybe in my youth. I mean, I did do some drugs...." He shifts uncomfortably. You'd think he'd stop talking at this point, but he keeps going. "I'm sure you're fine. Actually, I'm surprised you're in such good shape, you know, considering you sit on your ass all day."

His words penetrate through to my bones; the anger beginning in my stomach and moving its way out. "Sit on my ass all day? Sit on my ass all day!" My hands slam down on the table as I stand. "You are a moron! Is this how you impress a woman? Insulting her?" I throw my coat on.

"Listen, lady! You're the one staring at some dude and gettin' your panties all wet."

The embarrassment rages through my face as I can feel all eyes on us, including Zach's. I have no response to this. Instead, I grab the bowl of salsa and pour it on his lap.

"You're an ass!"

I don't look back; I just keep on moving towards the doors, hoping to escape this place without having to endure more embarrassment. But, before I can make it to the exit, The Escort has his hand on my elbow, pulling me back.

Fuck!

"Do you need help?" He nods toward my blind date, a smile playing on his lips. I glance over and watch Ethan clean salsa from his lap, mumbling under his breath.

"Nope, I think I got it covered." I can't face Zach right now. Zach's dates are watching from the corner. "You better get back to your dates."

"Oh, they're just friends."

"Right. People from the business, hey?" I zip up my jacket, pretending not to be interested in his answer.

"No, actually, they're friends from high school. They're both financial advisors."

I glance at the twins, and roll my eyes.

"You wanna meet them?" He's serious.

I let out a throaty laugh. "No, not really." I pause, and decide to be nicer. "I mean, thanks, but, no." I leave the pub thinking what a waste of time this whole thing was. How did that go south so quickly? Clearly, I shouldn't go on blind dates ever again. And then I remember: Tomorrow is blind date number two.

Chapter 6
Save a boyfriend for a rainy day—and another in case it doesn't rain.—Mae West

The next day, I force Susanne to agree to never set me up again with one of Dave's friends. I tell her Ethan was rude and that he'll have a nasty salsa stain on his khakis.

I don't have time to shake last night's bad date from my head as my next blind date is on his way. It's almost seven and I take one last look in the mirror, telling myself not to expect too much from this Ian guy because his mom set us up.

Headlights flash through the room, and a car pulls into my driveway just as I'm adjusting my dress.

From the corner of the window, I watch Ian get out of his car and walk to the front door. He's nicely dressed; handsome, actually. Maybe tonight won't be so bad. After last night, I certainly deserve to have a good date.

The doorbell rings and I open it to a tall, dirty blonde haired man wearing a dark jacket.

"Cate, I'm Ian. It's nice to meet you." He instantly takes my hand and meets my eyes.

"Nice to meet you too, Ian. I'm ready." I hate standing in the doorway, chit-chatting and looking awkward.

By the time Ian pulls up in front of one of the nicest restaurants in the city, I have a feeling that this one is a keeper. The wine, the candlelight, the music, and the intelligent conversation—these are all things that make me want to see him again. Not that I'm making long term plans here, but at least he has stirred something inside me. I guess it all depends on how the evening ends. At this point, it has great potential to end very well.

*

"What are you grinning about?" Susanne asks, she pours herself a cup of tea. We are sitting at our regular lunch place that we meet at every couple of weeks. She looks rather sophisticated in her business attire: black pant suit with her hair done in a twisty bun. Actually, she could pass for a naughty librarian if only she had worn glasses. I don't answer her question, I peruse the menu instead.

Susanne gasps. "You had sex last night."

I drop my menu. "How could you have known that? You didn't even know I had a date last night."

"I know that look. You're glowing." She points a finger at my face.

I hold the menu up and hide my huge smile.

"So, are you going to tell me the details or what?" Susanne probes. "Who's the guy?"

I grin stupidly, and start to tell Susanne all about Ian, how easily we got along, how nice he was, and how he woke me up the next morning with that special thing he did with his tongue.

"I'm glad to see you're finally over Phil," Susanne teases. "It's been what, two days?"

"Four days." I giggle.

"What?"

"Nothing really. I was just thinking about how funny life is. I mean, I met Ian after being set up by his mother. I actually like him. I end up having sex on the first date. And, here I thought my life was going downhill after Nan hired an escort..."

"Whoa, whoa, wait," she interrupts. "Nan hired an escort?"

"Shit, I forgot to tell you. Ya! My grandmother hired an escort."

"Why did she do that?"

"She got this idea in her head that she needed a companion," I sip my water.

"Where would she get that from?"

"Me. I told her to find a boyfriend. I didn't think she'd get an escort."

"An escort? So, what does he look like?" Susanne stirs sugar into her tea.

"Oh, you know, hairy chest, shirt unbuttoned all the way down to his bellybutton, gold chains....a real Chachi." I roll my eyes.

She eyes me suspiciously. "You have a crush on him."

I snort. "I do not."

"Yes, you do."

"Susanne, he's an escort, I'm a cop...see how this doesn't mesh?"

"So? You still have a crush on him." She wiggles her finger.

"I don't have a crush on him. He's macho and reeks of Hi-Karate. Definitely nothing to talk about." I take another sip of my water and almost choke when I realize Zach is walking up to our table.

"Cate! Nice seeing you again." How does he manage to find me? He looks amazing and reeks of sexiness, not Hi-Karate. Damn him.

"Zach." I mumble feebly. "Um, what are you doing here?"

"Same as you." Zach extends a hand out to Susanne who eyes him with much interest. "Hi, I'm Zach Kennedy."

"Susanne Hunter." She shakes Zach's hand. "How do you know Cate?"

Zach eyes me up. "I work for her grandmother, helping with a few things."

Susanne's mind races; I can see the wheels spinning like a hamster on his running wheel. "Ohhhhh," she says excitedly.

"You must be the escort."

Oh god, please, strike me down now!

"Oh, I guess Cate has been talking about me." He raises his eyebrows.

"Let's just say I'm glad that you're not wearing gold chains." Susanne throws me a dirty look.

"Ya, me too." Zach is perplexed but plays along anyway. He turns to me. "So, I see you bounced back from your date the other night."

"Date? The date with Ian?" Susanne questions. "Or the date with Ethan?"

I bite my lip. "Ethan. Zach happened to be there as I was pouring salsa on his lap."

Susanne nods in understanding.

"Turns out Cate isn't as intense as I previously thought her to be. I really expected beer to be her weapon of choice," Zach jokes.

I cringe. "Um, don't you have some place to be?"

"Yes, I'm meeting up with a buddy." He turns to Susanne. "It was nice meeting you." Then me. "See you later, Chase." He winks. He's never used my last name like that before. What the hell?

I give a careless wave, although, knocking him down to the ground and ripping his clothes off is a good option too.

Susanne's smile turns to skepticism. "I don't know what you're talking about. There's no machismo there. What's really going on?"

"Nothing is going on," I protest. : The only thing going on in my life is Ian. And good sex."

"Riiiggghhhtt. You're crushing."

"I'm not!" Susanne is not convinced.

"Okay, let's talk about Ian then."

"See. That wasn't so hard." I pick up a piece of bread and butter it. "Besides, Zach is more interesting to talk about anyway."

"A-ha!" she spits. People around us start to stare.

"What?" I say with a mouthful of bread.

"There is a crush there."

I cross my arms. "What are you talking about?"

"You said Zach, not Ian."

I think for a second. "No, I didn't."

"Yes, you did. You are so crushing on him." Her gaze moves to where Zach is sitting. "He's watching you."

"What? He is not." I turn around and see that Zach is indeed looking over. He smiles and waves.

"I think there are mutual crushes happening here." She has a grin like a Cheshire cat.

"Susanne, there's no mutual anything. We're constantly at each other's throats. Honestly."

"You know what they say about these types of relationships?"

"What? What do they say?" I wanted to sound irritated but it came out sounding eager.

"All that anger and resentment is just a mask for pent-up sexual attraction."

I glance back at Zach again. Pent-up sexual attraction? Okay, maybe I do engage in a few miniature fantasies about him, and maybe I do wonder what's under those clothes, but that has nothing to do with Susanne's so-called pent-up sexual attraction. They're just harmless daydreams. Every woman has them. Like a two-minute commercial break to help you get on with your day. Like a piece of chocolate cake for dessert or a cigarette or a cup of coffee; the only difference is that I'm having fantasies about The Escort. Harmless.

"Impossible," I disagree.

"I'm just calling it as I see it." Susanne returns her attention back to her menu.

I've known Susanne for a long time, and she always manages to peg me. But this time, she has it all wrong. I'm not interested in The Escort. Okay, so he's attractive, and I am attracted to him. But that's where the line is drawn. There can never be a hook up with that man.

Chapter 7
How do you solve a problem like Zach Kennedy?

After several minutes of denying any attraction to The Escort, Susanne and I manage to get onto other conversation topics, the hot one being Ian. I don't want to talk about Zach anymore; it's causing lots of confusion in my brain and I don't want that right now.

I'm seeing Ian this evening and, well, I haven't a thing to wear. Of course, Susanne and I have to go shopping for the perfect outfit with matching bra and panties. The matching undies are in case there's a repeat of the night before. Last night, I wasn't prepared. I didn't think we would hit the bedroom that quickly, so I hadn't bothered to match anything. I believe the underwear I was wearing may have been my bloated day underwear or my laundry day underwear. You know, the grey ones with the hole in the ass or the elastic waistband falling apart.

Tonight, I'm dressed for success.

When Ian comes to pick me up, he grabs me, kisses my neck and whispers, "I missed you."

"You just left this morning," I laugh.

"I know, and I couldn't wait to get back to you."

Is this guy for real? I mean, it's nice to have the attention, but when are things going to crash and burn? Yes. I think about these things because, as history dictates, things will crash and burn eventually.

He eyes my low cut army green top with the black pants and boots. "There's a surprise under here when we get back from wherever it is that we're going." My voice is raspy in a sexy kinda way. Ian grins evilly.

"By the way, where are we going?" I ask.

It turns out we're going to a movie—Tom Cruise's new flick. One I hadn't intended on seeing, but Ian is convinced it'll be amazing since the trailer looked amazing. I think 'amazing' means lots of boobs and action sequences.

We get our tickets and wait in line at the concession where I discover that Ian enjoys talking about his work about as much as I do. I love this about him. His stories are interesting and relatable to my line of work. I'm beginning to think that being set up with Joan's son is the best thing for me.

The downside of this is that I can only listen once to the same story of a guy puking on his shoes or how the blood squirted out of some artery and how it left a slippery mess all over the emergency room floor. Nice stuff. I don't really need to eat those chocolate covered raisins anyway.

"We meet again. Either you're following me or I'm following you." A familiar voice comes from behind as I stand at the condiments counter removing the wrapper from my straw. I pause. No. It can't be. I turn around and find myself face to face with The Escort who happens to be on a date. However, I'm not really looking at her; I'm too busy staring at him. He looks the same from earlier today, but better. I'm not sure how that's possible. I blink a couple of times and put on my stone cold, ruthless cop face.

"Do you have a homing signal on me or do you have nothing better to do with your time?"

"I think I should be the one asking this question since you are dead set on digging up any kind of dirt on me." He's serious. He holds my gaze for a few seconds longer than what I would normally allow, then turns his attention to Ian. "I'm Zach Kennedy." He sticks out his hand and Ian takes it.

"I'm Ian, Cate's boyfriend." Ian places an arm around my shoulders; it is a move that has me uneasy, like he's protecting his property and doesn't want the other kids to play with his things.

Zach raises a brow. "I didn't know you were seeing someone?"

"This just happened last night," Ian announces for me, which is quite annoying.

"I see. Congratulations." Zach's date elbows him. He introduces her as Mindy, a 'friend'. Mindy isn't dressed like she's just a 'friend'. I think Mindy wants to get laid.

"I'd love to stay and chitchat, Zach, but the movie is starting soon." I nod at Mindy, tell Zach that maybe I'll see him at Nan's place and leave with Ian.

The whole time during the movie, I wonder what's going on with Zach and Mindy. What will they be doing after the movie? Will she be going to the guest house and having sex in front of the fireplace? Should my grandmother be alerted that Zach might be having consistent sex with women at the guest house? The guest house isn't a place to be used for carnal pleasures. Look at me; I've been reduced to sounding like a nun.

Oh, what am I saying? If I'm getting laid tonight, the chances are good that he's getting laid tonight. And what do I care if Zach is getting laid? That's his business, right? Right?

What it all boils down to is, I don't want Zach to get laid by Mindy; I want to get laid by Zach, in the guest house on the floor in front of the fireplace. Is that too much to ask? Can't I just have one night with him just to see how it is? All my questions will be answered and I'll possibly find the meaning of life while I'm at it.

Unfortunately, my constant questioning to myself doesn't give me answers, they only occupy my thoughts throughout the night, even with Ian in my bed.

The next morning, the irritation is prevalent. I need Ian to leave. I've never had someone stay this long in my house, not even Phil. He was always great about leaving the next morning.

I hint to Ian that maybe he should go home in case he has any messages from the hospital, or any emergencies they need him for, like to perform a tracheotomy or something. But, he doesn't budge. So, not till after we have morning sex, and not till after I make breakfast (frozen waffles) and lunch (frozen waffles), and not till after we have sex again, does he decide to go home.

However, as luck would have it, he informs me we'll hook up a bit later. And, just when I think the rest of the day is mine, the phone rings.

"Hello, dear."

It's Nan. "How are you?"

"Fine, Nan. And yourself?" Her tone tells me something is up, which doesn't surprise me considering I saw this one coming.

"Fine. Anything you want to talk about?" See? What did I tell you?

"Like what?" I play.

"How's your love life?"

"Fine." I stuff an olive into my mouth seeing it's really the only thing snacky that's in my fridge, aside from waffles. I wait for the next question to hit. I wonder how long we'll play this game before one of us actually says what the other wants to hear.

"You seeing anyone new?"

I guess it didn't take as long as I thought it would. Nan's going right for the throat. "Yes. I guess you've spoken to Zach."

"Uh-huh."

"Okay, I'm dating a guy named Ian. He's the son of one of my co-workers. He's nice and he's going to be a doctor." Maybe the word 'doctor' will soften Nan up a bit.

"When can we meet him?"

"We? Who's we?"

"Zach and I. When can we meet him?" It rolls off of Nan's tongue like it's the most natural thing in the world.

"Zach and you? What? You're a couple now?"

"I know Zach met him last night, but I'd like us to sit down with him and get to know him a bit better."

"Nan, where have you been? Zach and I don't get along. We're arch-enemies. Foes. If we were comic book characters, he would be The Joker and I'd be Wonder Woman." The image of using my magic lasso on Zach pops into my head, easily turning into a fantasy.

It's just a harmless fantasy, nothing more. I have Ian, right? And that whole thing last night about me and Zach and the fireplace, all just fun fantasy games. "By the way, did you see anyone sneak out of the guest house this morning?"

"No, I don't think so. Zach was having breakfast with me this morning. Unless someone escaped during that time," Nan teases me.

But it gives me some hope that Mindy didn't make it home with Zach last night. Or, maybe Zach was at Mindy's and arrived back to Nan's just in time for breakfast. Before I can ask what Zach had been wearing at breakfast, she continues with what she's called for. "Okay, so dinner tomorrow night will work for you two?"

Have I been talking to myself this entire time? Nan has totally missed my whole caped crusader analogy. The thing is, I know I'm not getting out of this one. Nan wants to meet Ian and there's no way I'm getting off this phone in the next year if I don't agree.

"Fine. We will see you at dinner tomorrow night. Oh, and tell your escort to mind his own business." Where did The Escort get off telling Nan about my date? I would have told her myself—when I had time. In the next year.

Running into Zach at all of these places cannot be a coincidence. Maybe Nan has sent him out to follow me. Well, he did show up at the pub, and he did appear at the same lunch place I was at with Susanne. He was at the theatre last night. There has to be a connection. I'm being stalked by The Escort. That's gotta be it!

I knew there was something wrong with him!

*

Later, I warn Ian about his upcoming appearance at my grandmother's house, which he takes rather well. He was really cute when he told me he couldn't wait to meet my grandmother. It's so endearing when a man says something like that.

Then Ian mentions he's coming over to spend the night, which I don't find endearing. This is getting annoying. I want to spend the night by myself in a nice hot bath.

"Look, Ian, I really would like to see you tonight, but..." I pause. If I tell him I want to be alone tonight then he'll incessantly beg me till I give in. Do I really want to be stuck on the phone for a couple of hours having him plead to me? I can spend that time watching Dawson's Creek re-runs. Plus, there's a bigger chance that he'll stop by 'unexpectedly'. You know, he was in 'the area' and thought he'd pop in to make sure I'm okay because I hadn't answered the phone, or some other ridiculous excuse like that.

It's happened before. You tell them you want time to yourself and they don't believe you, and all of a sudden they're on your doorstep with beer or Chinese food or something. There's no way around this—I'll have to lie.

"...I've already made plans with Susanne tonight. Oh, darn." Maybe the 'darn' was a bit over the top.

He sighs. "That's too bad. I really wanted to see you."

How many times do we need to see each other in a week? I feel like asking this question but decide I would let this 'honeymoon phase' run its course. He's bound to get bored of me, right?

"But we'll see each other tomorrow night," my voice lightens. I then continue with a few more encouraging words, more than I want to, and hang up. The next call I make is to Susanne since we're pretending to be out tonight.

"Where do you want to pretend to go tonight?" I ask as soon as she says hello.

"A small outdoor café in France?"

"Not believable enough. It has to be somewhere in the city."

"Lied to another one, did ya?"

"Tell me, how many days in a row do you need to see someone in the first stages of dating?" I ask, while I stare into my fridge looking for sustenance.

"Dave and I saw each other every day for the first three months. Then it tapered off to every second day till we moved in together. Now we see each other all the time." She sounds too happy about this.

"You're too in love. I think you need a pill for that or something. It's not natural."

"You only say that because you haven't found the perfect one for you."

"The perfect one what? The perfect pair of shoes, the perfect hair-do, the perfect steak? Everyone keeps talking about this perfect thing, and I haven't a clue what they're talking about."

"You'll know when it happens," she says sagely.

She may sound like she's giving wise advice, but I think she's talking nonsense. "That's a load of crap and you know it." My defenses rise.

"So, what happened with Ian?" She changes the subject—sort of.

"He wanted to see me, even though we spent the last two nights and two mornings together. And tomorrow, I'm taking him to meet Nan."

"Really? This must be serious."

"No, not really. If The Escort didn't see us at the theatre together, my secret love life would still be ….secret."

"You saw Zach again?"

"Either Nan has him following me or he's stalking me. I'm going with the latter. He looks like the stalker type." Actually, he doesn't look like a stalker, but it makes me feel so much better when I add reasoning to his good looks and clean record.

"Let me get this straight, you're already telling lies to your new boyfriend, your grandmother's escort is a snitch…"

"And stalking me," I interrupt.

"And stalking you, and you and I are not on the phone right now but stuffing some fivers in a strippers G-string."

"Yeah, that sounds about right."

"Cate," she whines. "Why didn't you tell him the truth… that you wanted to be alone tonight?"

"You know how it is, Susanne. You tell them you want alone time and suddenly they're at your door because they can't comprehend that you really do want to be alone. And besides, he's getting a bit clingy. I needed a break."

"Oh, yes, here we go. The clingy part. It must be about time to break up."

"Susanne. Come on. I don't do that."

She fakes a cough, hiding the words, 'ya, right' as she does so. "I don't know why you don't go for Zach anyway. He's more your style."

"Susanne! I will never, ever go for Zach. Never. Don't even go there."

"Denial," she mutters.

"Listen, I have a great relationship with a future doctor. He's just a little clingy right now because we're in the first stages of dating. It happens to everybody."

"Not to me."

"Well, you're weird. I like him, the sex is good, and the company is good.... we just need to set a few boundaries, that's all." Even though this all sounds pleasant, I'm cringing inside knowing Ian will be with me tomorrow and being overly clingy. I definitely have to set those boundaries very soon. Tomorrow night, after Nan's, we will have a little chat.

Chapter 8
Change never happens gracefully—it always sucker punches you in the face.

"I'm sorry this is so strange. My grandmother is relentless. I swear, she won't stop asking about you till she meets you." Ian had arrived right at six to pick me up to have dinner with my grandmother.

I look over at Ian sitting in the driver's seat and realize how amazing he looks tonight; almost boyish-looking. His pressed green shirt suits him, bringing out his blonde hair even more.

"It's no problem. I'm looking forward to meeting your grandmother. I want to get to know every part of you, Cate." Ian places a hand on my knee, running it up my blue skirt. He winks then removes his hand as we pull into the driveway of Nan's place.

"Wow. This an amazing place. You grew up here?" Ian peers out the window.

"Yep."

"Very cool," he murmurs.

The moment we walk in the door, Syd takes our coats and sends us to the living room. I catch Nan sneaking away from her perch where she was spying on us. This is not a surprise to me; of course she would be standing at the door, waiting.

She sticks out her hand at Ian. "I'm Ursula Chase."

"It's nice to finally meet you, Ursula. Ian Purvis. Cate talks about you all the time." Ian clasps her hand, cupping it with the other.

"Come in. Have a seat." Nan points the way, and we take a seat on the sofa. Ian takes my hand and pulls me closer to him.

"I hope Cate is telling you wonderful things about her dear old grandmother," she smiles sweetly. Right there. That look right there tells me what I need to know. She doesn't like Ian even though she only met him sixty seconds ago.

"Oh, Zach. You're here." Nan's hands are outstretched. I roll my eyes.

"Zach, you remember Cate's boyfriend, Ian."

"Nice to meet you again." Zach shakes Ian's hand. Ian looks surprised.

"I didn't know you were going to be here." There's an understandable hint of surprise in Ian's voice.

"Oh, didn't I tell you? I'm sorry. Zach is my grandmother's ....helper." I say. I only steal a glimpse of The Escort before turning my attention to Ian.

"How are you, Cate?" Zach asks.

I finally take in a full look of The Escort, peering into those silvery eyes and feel my cheeks reddening. "Fine. Doing fine." I turn my attention to something safe—my grandmother. "Um, so, when's supper?"

Nan stares at me, perplexed. "In about a half hour. Do you have some place to be tonight?"

"Um, no. I have to work tomorrow. Early." Obviously, this isn't the truth. I should be struck down by lighting right about now.

"I thought you were working afternoons this week?" Ian asks.

"Oh, I am. I just wanted to get in early to do some work."

"I thought we were having breakfast together tomorrow morning," Ian whispers through clenched teeth. I'm not sure why he's whispering seeing as everyone can hear him. Nan has this amused expression twitching on her face, and Zach has raised an eyebrow. He's glaring at Ian as if he were the antichrist or something. And I really just want to eat and get the hell out of here.

I slug back my rum and coke Syd brought me two minutes ago, and decide that this rum and coke needs a chaser, like, say, another rum and coke.

At the bar, I schlep some ice into my glass, pouring out a bit too much rum, when Zach joins me.

"He seems nice," Zach comments.

"Yeah, thanks." I slop some coke in the glass and pick it up, not sipping, not slurping, but gulping. Why am I so nervous? What the hell is wrong with me?

"A bit of a colt though, hey?"

I blink. "What are you talking about?"

"You know, young."

"What do you mean?" I look back at Ian who is still chatting with Nan; he seems nervous as he glances back at Zach and me, like Zach is going to throw me over his shoulder, carry me off to the guest house and make love to me in front of the fireplace. I really need to stop these fantasies!

"Actually, any younger, and he'd be Doogie Howser." Zach leans against the bar and takes a sip of his drink.

"How do you know how old he is?"

"Let's see, the way he's acting is a big tip off."

"How's he acting? What are you talking about?"

"He's acting as though he's afraid someone might steal his girlfriend."

I have to agree with Zach on that. He did act quite possessive at the theatre. I blow it off. People are nervous on dates. Right?

"Well, ya. He's meeting my grandmother for the first time"

"Nervous or not, the guy is young. Have you checked his ID?"

"No. I work with his mother. I don't need to check him out, unlike you."

"You were checking me out?" Zach says quietly, a small grin lingering on his lips.

"I don't mean it that way. Look, just keep your theories to yourself. Okay?" I walk back to Ian and sit beside him; he throws an arm around me and I cuddle in closer.

Zach returns and sits across from us. This time he's fully engaged in the conversation. "So, Ian, Cate says you're in medicine. How's that going?"

Ian sits forward, now completely interested in the conversation. "Great! I'm working the ER right now and it's been totally awesome."

Totally awesome?

"I can't wait to start my own practice."

"Oh? That's going to be soon, isn't it?" Zach presses on.

"Soon? Nah. I've got a while to go."

"How long till you're done?" Nan asks.

"Oh, about seven years."

"I didn't know it was that long." I turn to Ian, realizing that there are some things we haven't talked about.

"You must have started university a few years after high school," Zach presses. As Zach interrogates, I'm trying to figure out where this is headed and exactly where it will end.

"Nope, nope. I started right out of high school. Wanted to get a head start on this whole doctor thing." By this time, I'm confused.

"Right out of high school? How old are you?" Zach asks, clearly leading the conversation intentionally.

I can see it on his face. He's planned this! He wants to prove me wrong. I hate him! I officially hate him.

"Oh, I'm only 23."

The buzzing sound in my ears won't go away and the rest of the conversation is non-existent. I picture the floor opening up and swallowing me whole.

Unfortunately, that's not what happened. But, what did happen is Ian swiftly transformed into a completely different person. Suddenly, he looks young to me. Where are the wrinkles and the five o'clock shadow that I've seen Zach have so many times? He has none of that. His complexion has none of the mature etchings of stress and too much sun. And where did that little cluster of acne on his cheek come from?

Avoiding any and all stares from Nan and Zach, I ask Ian to step out into the foyer to have a little chat.

"It's going well isn't it? But I'm not sure about that Zach guy. Did you check him out?"

"You're 23?"

"Yes." He says this with confidence, not seeing what the problem is.

"No one told me you were 23."

"I didn't think it was an issue. Anyway, that Zach guy...."

"Ian, hang on a second. Your mother didn't tell me you were 23."

"So?"

"Don't you think it's something I should know? I mean, I'm more than a decade older than you."

"And? There are lots of women who date younger men. I've dated older women before. They have never had a problem with it."

My stomach churns. This isn't sitting well with me. He's 23. I can't date someone younger than me. Much younger. It's weird; it's strange. We're at different stages in life. I need someone mature; someone who really gets me. Someone not right out of high school. I could deal with this later, have dinner and keep going on with the evening. But, how do I walk back into the living room appearing as if I'm unrattled by this turn of events? Why hadn't I been asking these questions on the first date?

"Ian, I don't know what to say."

"What?"

The more I stare, the more I see the boyish looks peeking through. "I might regret this later, Ian, but I don't think I can go out with a 23 year old."

It takes him a few seconds till he realizes what is going on. "Are you breaking up with me?"

"I hate to do it because I've had so much fun with you, but I can't see how this will work. We're both in different stages of life."

"Come on, what does it matter? If we like each other and we get along, then who cares how old we are, right?" His hands slide around my waist as he attempts to kiss me.

Now those lips belong to someone that I'd meet bagging my groceries at the local store. Those lips now belong to a younger brother, if I had one. Or maybe the pimply-faced kid at the 7-11. I push him away. "If you were seven years younger, you would be jail bait."

"But I'm not." He leans in again, but I push him away. "Listen, I'm just as good as that Zach guy."

"What does Zach have to do with anything?"

"Come on. Clearly he's my competition. The way he's always staring at you."

"He doesn't stare at me." I protest. However, part of me wonders if it would be totally inappropriate to ask further details on the whole staring thing.

"Ya, he does. And, you want to know what else? I'm 23 and just as mature as he is. My mom even says so."

My mom even says so? What the hell? Now this is getting weird. The clinginess, the need to see me constantly—it all making sense. "Ian, I like you. We've had some good times in the last...three days, but we are two different people. I mean, I'm 37. I could have babysat you. Changed your diapers. Doesn't that make you feel....icky."

"No. I really don't know why you are freaking out about this." Ian puts his arms around me again. "I love you, Cate."

He loves me? How can he love me? We barely know one another. "We've known each other for three days. You can't love me."

"I love you." He grins. "I've been wanting to tell you."

There's a horrified look on my face. He loves me—after three days! This isn't where I want it to go. Not this soon. Not now. Help! Someone help me! I'm trapped in the commitment abyss, and I can't get out!

"I'm sorry, Ian, but this isn't going to work out." I pull away and then say something that I promised I'd never, ever say, only because Susanne thought it was too cliché. "We can still be friends."

Apparently, Ian doesn't like that word and by the sounds of it, has heard it a few times too many because he flips out.

"Friends? Friends. Are you fucking kidding me?" Ian raises his voice. I just want to be his friend. It could have been worse; I could have asked him to never call again. "Go fuck yourself, you bitch." Ian yells, slamming the door as he leaves.

"And there it is," I murmur. In the distance, his car squeals out of the drive and I wonder how his mother will take it when she finds out I'm not going to be her daughter-in-law.

I don't feel like eating, and don't feel like chatting with Nan or Zach. Especially Zach. I don't feel like telling them that my boyfriend is now my ex after three days. But I can't leave without saying goodbye. I'll bite the bullet. I'll have to tell them what happened.

I stand at the doorway, refusing to enter the room. "Nan, I'm leaving now." They both look up from their deep conversation with each other, which irritates me.

"Where's Ian?" Nan asks, walking toward me.

"Oh, he left. It's not going to work out with him being 23 and all." I glance at Zach who is gazing at me or something. I can't say for sure if it's gazing or daydreaming, because my mind has been playing tricks on me lately. I mean, look at the way I thought Ian was my age. We do choose to see what we want to see.

"He wasn't your type anyway," says Nan.

"You always say that."

She pulls me toward a seat. "Only because it's true. Now sit down and finish your drink."

I stare at my half-full glass of rum and coke still sitting on the table; the ice cubes now melting in the glass. I'm already feeling the effects of the last one I slugged back, on an empty stomach, no less.

"Okay, I'll finish my drink. I'll have to call a cab, seeing as my date left. I shouldn't be driving anyway."

"Oh, I'm sure Zach can take you home. Right, Zach?"

"Of course, Ursula." Zach nods.

I swallow hard, and take a seat. As it turns out, my half-a-drink converts into four others, without dinner; I am now completely sloshed. Because I don't feel like eating, Nan has Annie bring out some snacks so at least I won't be absolutely sick, only just a little sick.

Zach and Nan listen intently to my ramblings about how it's impossible for a 23 year old to get involved with me and why hadn't his mother mentioned his age. And did his mother really condone him dating an older woman? Also, was it just me or was it creepy when he said his mom thinks he's mature? By the time I stop talking, it's midnight and I feel woozy.

"I need to go home." I don't want to close my eyes knowing that the spinning will start and never stop till the hangover takes place the next morning, or the puking; both have a good chance of happening.

I say goodnight to Nan, blubbering something about how she has never seen me drunk before and hoping she won't judge her granddaughter, being a cop and all. If my memory serves me correctly, I think she said she loves me no matter what. But I could have made that up.

I don't remember much about the ride home with Zach. There is a slight possibility of me rambling and Zach not saying anything. I don't remember Zach saying anything, just listening or maybe tuning me out. One thing I do remember is him helping me into the house and ordering me to go to my bedroom while he fills a large glass of full of water.

By the time Zach brings the water up, I'm sitting on the edge of the bed and staring at the floor with my shirt half-off. The floor doesn't spin as much as the rest of the room; it's better to keep my focus on the dark brown area rug that pokes out from under my bed.

"Oh...um...here you go." Zach sets the water down as I lie on the bed, my shirt still around my neck, trying desperately not to close my eyes. But since blinking feels really good, completely closing my eyes will feel like heaven.

Zach pulls the blanket from the foot of the bed and covers me up, then pulls the shirt over my head. Good thing too; I probably would have strangled myself in the middle of the night.

"Cate, I have to go, okay?" Zach's hand offers much warmth to my lonely shoulder, his face close to mine.

I blink, literally staring intoxicatingly into Zach's eyes, and do something extremely stupid—I kiss him—hard, on the lips.

Zach draws away, his gaze unflinching. He grasps my hands. "Get some rest."

As far as I can remember, he left at that moment, and I have a terrible feeling that, by tomorrow, I will be regretting bigger things than drinking those rum and cokes.

Chapter 9
It Seemed Like a Good Idea at the Time

8:23 a.m. That's what my clock says when I open my bleary eyes the next day.

I look at the water and crackers on my nightstand and realize what happened. I'm feeling like complete shit and to top it off, I made an ass of myself. Shit and ass. It's funny that I'm comparing myself to both seeing as they are related.

Slowly, slowly, slowly, I sit up, the blanket falling to the side and revealing my bra and skirt, which somehow has become twisted and bunched around my hips. Not the bra, just the skirt. A true vision of loveliness. Who says drinking isn't glamorous?

Memories of kissing Zach flood my senses and I decide right then and there that I will never be able to go to Nan's place again, at least not while The Escort's around. I kissed him. Nothing like adding more problems to my life. The most heroic thing to do in this situation would be to pretend that nothing happened. That's right, feigning stupidity is the best course of action.

After a shower, after much water and dry toast, after scraping the fur coat from my tongue, and after watching one and half episodes of Dawson's Creek, it's now 11:00 am and I need to get my ass going so I can get to work for two. It all sounds like a really good idea, but it doesn't happen that way. Instead, I continue lying on the couch, now dressed in my robe and slippers, my wet hair semi-dried and pasted to my forehead and a cup of tea sitting on my stomach, hoping these skull cramps will subside. That's when the doorbell rings. Shit. Maybe if I don't answer they'll go away.

No luck. The doorbell rings again. I slowly shuffle to the window, trying not to rustle the curtains in case it's someone selling religion.

Shit! Zach. And he saw me too. What does he want?

He knocks a couple more times, each time louder than the first time. My brain aches with every rap on the wooden door.

I unlock the door, much to my distress and embarrassment, just so the knocking would stop. "What are you doing here?"

"I brought you some chicken soup." Zach holds up a thermos and pushes his way inside. I like how he assumes I'm letting him in.

"You didn't need to bring me soup." I close the door and glance at my reflection. My hair is worse than I thought and my face is a sickly, elfin-green. Almost like Shrek.

"I didn't. Your grandmother sent me over with it. She's worried about you." In the kitchen, Zach is pulling out a bowl and spoon, then pours out hot soup. He places everything on the table with crackers alongside.

"What if I don't like crackers?" I say, defiantly. I notice that he looks fresh, and smells fresh too. And I feel like an overused cigarette butt.

"Then why would you have them in the cupboard?" Zach points to the seat at the table and I reluctantly sit. Zach takes a seat beside me.

"Are you just going to sit there and watch me eat?"

"You're grandmother asked that I stay to make sure you ate properly before work."

"So, you're here only because it's your duty."

Zach doesn't think about his answer. "Ya, pretty much."

"I see." I'd be lying if I said I wasn't disappointed. And, yes, I kinda am. Although I don't want him to bring up the kissing scenario, part of me wants him to agree to replay that moment now that I'm thinking straight.

The pregnant pause made me realize that Dawson's Creek was still playing in the next room. Zach gave me a crooked smile.

"Dawson's Creek?"

"Maybe."

"You watch it often?"

"I watch it ....now and then. So what?" I watch it more than now and then, but he doesn't need to know that.

"It was a simple question. I wanted to know if you watched Dawson's Creek because I heard it playing."

"I guess the real question is do you always ask idiotic questions?" I fire back.

"Why do you have to be so angry?" he counters.

"I'm not angry."

"Yes, you are. You've got this huge chip on your shoulder." He runs a hand through his hair, which is really quite sexy in a tormented hero sort of way. "Look, let's lay it out on the table. You dislike me, you think I'm out to get your grandmother, and you wish I hadn't ever showed up in your life. I get it! But you don't need to keep hammering it into me. I just wanted to bring some soup to you."

"You wanted to bring me soup?" I need clarification, but I'm not about to get it. He looks frustrated, not knowing what to do or say next. Then suddenly he stands up, his chair almost tipping over in the process. I'm a little shocked by this outburst. And when did I ever say I disliked him?

"I don't know why I came over in the first place," he mumbles striding to the door.

"Don't you remember? It was your duty," I yell after him.

"I'll promise not to impose on your time with your grandmother anymore." The door slams and he's gone.

I stare at the closed door and wonder what just happened. The way he made it sound was he wanted to come over. As much as I would love to call Susanne and analyze this for the next three hours, I have to get ready for work.

*

It's five minutes to two when I arrive at work. That's not like me. I'm usually early, like by an hour or two. My team has already gone out on to the street before I can speak to them, which is very unprofessional of me. I have tons of announcements and updates to talk to them about... and...who am I kidding? They won't listen to me anyway.

In the front office, Joan is sitting at her desk typing or filing or doing her nails or something. I know it's inevitable; she's going to have to see me eventually. She'll have to talk to me and she'll certainly know about my breaking up with Ian. She'll know the whole story—she'll see me as a gold-digger or heartbreaker or home wrecker or something. She probably has some sort of speech planned about me breaking her poor son's heart. There's no way I can avoid her unless I crawl on the floor, past her desk and down the hall, which is beginning to sound like a really good idea.

Before I have a chance to duck down, she glances up, her smile regretful.

"Hi, Joan. I bet you heard about Ian and me." I dive right in, ready to hear it all—how I betrayed her beloved son after he had treated me like a queen. I'm getting this over with, like pulling a bandage from a hairy arm. I sit down near her desk.

"Yes, I did. I'm sure you have your reasons, sweetie. I don't hold it against you." She smiles.

"Holding what against me? That I broke up with Ian because of his age."

"Well, yes, and that you broke his heart. He was devastated, Cate, just devastated. He told me all about it when he came home last night." She shakes her head as if to say 'what a tragedy'.

"You saw him last night?"

"Yes, of course. Well, he does live with me."

Of course he still lives with his mother. How ridiculous that I would actually think he lived on his own.

"I'm sorry it had to be that way. But the age difference is a big deal for me." She nods not saying anything. "But, I do thank you for introducing us. He is a very wonderful young man. He'll definitely go far." Yes, I am blowing sunshine up her ass.

After giving her a reassuring hug, I hide in my office where I proceed to phone Susanne, telling her my sob story of my break up with Ian. That I was completely drunk last night, and that Zach had taken me home and I had kissed him—and how he had returned this morning with chicken soup. And, while I explain to her that my head is ready to explode because rum and cokes seemed like a good idea at the time, Inspector Mark is standing in the doorway grasping a pile of paperwork in his little, sausage fingered hand. Didn't I close the door?

"Susanne, I'll call you later."

Mark doesn't crack a smile.

"Hmm, by the looks of those papers, something tells me that my promotion didn't come through yet." Mark shuts the door, still gloomy, not getting my joke. "Okay, what is it this time? One of the guys is saying I hit on him?" I lean back in my chair. I think I'm being funny but he doesn't smile. I've nailed it this time. Two points for me.

"What? Someone said I hit on them?" I sit up, the chair spring forward with force, almost launching me out of my seat.

"Cate," he says. I can't tell if he's remorseful or angry. "There's been a complaint of sexual harassment. Another police officer claims you sexually harassed him in the after a night shift."

I suddenly feel as if I'm sucked into a vortex, clinging on to the edge of the desk. One slip of my hand will mean I'll be eaten up by the black hole. Wind whooshes through my ears as Mark speaks but I can't hear what he's saying.

"He has filed a sexual harassment complaint saying you cornered him in the men's locker room, demanding sex."

The vortex stops and I'm suctioned to my chair. "What? Mark, that's not true."

"According to the complainant, he said," Mark glances at the folder and reads,

"You asked him if he wanted to touch your..." Mark clears his throat. "Wanted to touch you."

I snort. Maybe that wasn't the most appropriate thing to do since Mark is staring at me in surprise. "And you believed him?"

"I have to. Until it's proven otherwise, I have to believe him."

"Mark, you know as well as I do that I would never do or say those things."

Mark doesn't say anything. He's not on my side, now? Mark hits on me all the time and I don't say one god damn word, and now a false complaint is issued against me and I'm suddenly the villain here.

The tears well up, but I bite them back. "I don't fucking believe this!" I put my head in my hands.

"Listen, the victim won't press charges if you agree to transfer out of this district."

"Victim? Victim. Are you fucking kidding me? I'm not going to let them chase me out of here. That's what they've been planning all along, Mark, don't you see that?"

"If you don't, Cate, you will have a hearing."

I swipe at all the papers from my desk, which float unenthusiastically to the floor. Not the effect I was hoping for. I'm looking for drama, for stuff to make noise; all I got was a whooshing sound.

Transferring out of this district is equal to admitting that I did do it. And I didn't do it! Regardless if I transfer or not, this will get out to everyone on the force and my name will be shit. If I don't prove them wrong, I'll get no respect. If I stand my ground, it will prove that I didn't do it. I'm not taking the easy way out; they will have to drive me out of here with pitchforks, burn me at the stake, use thumb screws... I don't care. I'm not going anywhere.

I grit my teeth, "I'm not letting them chase me out of here."

"Then I will have to suspend you till this is resolved." Mark is stoic.

Suspension. I never thought I'd live to see the day. I never thought it was possible. Me. Suspended. I suddenly feel sick. Not rum and coke sick; more like my world is crashing sick. Thoughts and words and my life flash by in a millisecond. Then there's my grandmother. "Mark, I need a favor. Please don't take this to the media right away. Please. I can't have my grandmother finding out before I actually tell her."

For a second, I see a flicker of compassion in his eyes, like he's on my side. "I'll do what I can." And he leaves.

*

Have you ever had a dream that seemed so real, you actually thought it was? That's me this morning as I crawl out of bed about to get ready for my job. I then remember that you can't go to a job that has suspended you.

Yes. This morning's realization hits me like a Mack Truck. Suspension!

I'm not the person that gets suspended. I'm a model employee. I'm the person they bring in when the others can't do the job. I'm the poster child for top-cop. I am! I'm completely embarrassed about the whole damn thing. I can't tell a single soul. I can't tell Nan, I can't tell Susanne, or my parents. Okay, my parents don't count because by the time they get my letter in whatever the hell third world country they're in, things will have changed.

All right, I'll just go about my business like nothing happened. I have some time till they announce it on the news. I don't know how much, but some. I may have to remove all of Nan's televisions and radios and she won't be able to get the newspaper anymore. I'll have to go over to Susanne's and do the same thing. No one will notice. I can probably carry this on for few months, and, by that time, this whole thing will have blown over. Hopefully.

As I contemplate my next move, I decide to don my uniform and head on over to Nan's as if on duty. I can't even pack heat at this point because they confiscated my service revolver. This all seems so insane, but at the same time, I think I know what I'm doing. Yes, I could get fired, and well, that would be worse than suspension, but I have to maintain the illusion that I'm still on the job. Right?

I arrive at Nan's shortly after ten; Nan isn't expecting me. I pull up in my rental vehicle, and in my uniform as planned. If she asks where my police cruiser is, I'll tell her I'm just heading into work and haven't picked it up yet. If she asks where my gun is, I will have to tell her it's being cleaned. This is so ridiculous but I'm desperate.

"Nan, are you awake?" I call out from the hall.

"Cate? I wasn't expecting you." Nan is at the top of the stairs, her hair brushed back in an attractive sweep; today it appears more thick and glossy than ever.

"I thought I'd just come by and say 'hi'...hi." I wave. I'm slightly edgy right now as I didn't watch the news or listen to the radio on the way over, especially since the car doesn't have a radio. But, before that can worry me any further, Zach materializes from behind Nan.

"What's he doing up there?" I head for the stairs, ready to kick some escort-ass if I need to.

"Cate, you're being rude. Zach was helping me with a leak," she explains. Why is she protecting Zach from my wrath?

"I bet he was." I glare. His expression doesn't change. How does he do that? Look all calm and collected while I'm seething and ready to take someone down.

"I stopped by to make sure you were okay, Nan."

"I'm fine. Zach and I were about to go on a picnic to the botanical gardens before they close for the season." She walks past me and so does The Escort, not saying a word. After yesterday's debacle, I suppose he's trying to maintain some composure.

"Oh....I can come with."

Nan glares at me as if I'd said a dirty word. "Aren't you working today, dear?"

Right, my uniform.

"Yes, but I have some time. I don't need to be in till this afternoon. Actually, I was on my way to work when I thought I'd pop in," I explain. Okay, I've covered my bases. That'll explain why I didn't bring the police cruiser and why I'm in uniform and that, yes, I'm still 'on the job' rather than on suspension. She hasn't mentioned the gun, so it's good. The illusion is complete.

"Well, okay, then." I give Zach a haughty look. He only raises an eyebrow.

"Here, Ursula, let me help you with your coat. There's a slight chill out there." Zach breaks his apparent vow of silence.

"Thank you, Zach." Nan turns to me. "Zach has been an absolute god-send, Cate. You should see all that this man does. He helps Annie with the cooking, me with any maintenance problems. He helped Heinrich cut down a tree the other day. I'm definitely getting my money's worth."

I roll my eyes. Zach's arrogant grin is worth ignoring.

"I've got the picnic basket, Ursula." Zach grabs the dark brown basket and opens the door for Nan. He nods his head toward the open door, indicating that I should step through, which I do reluctantly.

I drive myself to the botanical gardens, following close behind Nan and The Escort. The whole way there, I have a few things on my mind, like, how did The Escort manage to move so gracefully into my grandmother's life? And how long do I have till someone finds out that I'm not really working? And will I see someone I know that knows I'm on suspension while I'm in uniform? And why does The Escort make my loins ache every single time I see him? At this point, though, Zach should be the least of my problems. My career is hovering in the balance.

*

The botanical gardens are a gorgeous place to spend the day. It's a huge canvas of different flowers and plants from around the world and Nan loves coming here. I do too. The reds, greens, yellows, blues, and purples are an oasis from the intensities of police work. Yes, I admit it. Police work is intense sometimes. It's also nice bringing Nan to the gardens because she enjoys it so much. The day is great for a picnic; too bad The Escort is joining us.

"Oh, can we sit near the ferns?" Nan asks in her girlish voice.

"You can sit wherever your heart desires, Ursula." Zach uses his smooth operator voice and I want to gag.

"I just love ferns," she coos sitting on the blanket.

"Why's that?" Zach sits next to her; I bend down, sitting as best as I can without my duty belt digging into my legs or any other major organ.

"It shows that even rough things have a softer side."

"Even Cate?" Zach asks in his menacing way.

"Even Cate," she laughs.

I glare at The Escort; maybe he'll get the picture that he doesn't mess with me.

"Go ahead and laugh on my account."

"Oh, Cate, we're only teasing," Nan swipes my leg, which I can't feel because the blood has ceased to pump into my extremities. Maybe the uniform wasn't such a hot idea.

"I'm not," The Escort chuckles

"Really, Zach, in Cate's defense, she does have a softer side. She's only putting on a show for you. I know deep down that she's fond of you." I almost fall off my ass, if that's possible.

"What? Nan!" I can't even look at The Escort now that my face is glowing red.

"Really? You think your granddaughter is fond of me?" Zach's eyes are on me. I don't even need to look up, I can feel them. If only there was a dark gopher hole I can escape through. Maybe a large meteor will suddenly fall from the sky and kill me instantly. Oh, Nan, you've become a traitor!

"Oh yes. I know her better than she knows herself. I see the way she looks at you."

Please, someone, something, kill me now and put me out of my misery.

"Really?" The Escort continues with his stares. I have to save this moment, my sanity, my decency. I take a breath. Yep, his eyes are on me, and there's something in them, something deep and promising.

And then, "No, I wouldn't say she's fond of me." The Escort doesn't remove his gaze. "I think she likes the chase. The fact that I'm unobtainable to her." Zach winks.

"Are you kidding me?" I blurt. "You're really full of yourself, aren't you?"

"Cate," Nan sputters.

"And I thought you weren't going to impose on my time with my grandmother."

"Yeah, when it's your time. You're the one imposing." Zach looks past me. "Hey, Cate, aren't those your buddies over there?"

I turn around. Shit. Two cops are making their way across the grounds, oblivious to me sitting in the grass in my uniform. I slide onto my belly and use my elbows to slither on the ground till I can peek around the ferns, trying to do the covert thing.

"Why are you lying on the ground?" Zach asks.

"Oh, no reason." I realize they're from Erickson's team. Not good. I can't be seen. This could be termination rather than suspension.

"Uh, Nan, I need to get to work. I'll talk to you later." I slither over her, kiss her awkwardly on the cheek and crawl back to my spot, waiting for the perfect moment to leave.

Zach clears his throat. "Do you need help? Should I call them over here for you?"

"No," I squeak, and then say quietly, "No. Don't do that."

"Aren't you going to say hi?" Nan adds.

"No, I try not to interfere with their work. Besides I'm not quite on duty yet," I mutter, bending and standing at the same time, waiting for the perfect opportunity to run across the grounds.

"Cate, are you okay?" Nan asks.

"Fine, fine. Just trying to get a good look at who they are, that's all. Making sure they're doing their jobs properly." Lame, lame, lame. Once they're heading in the opposite direction, about fifty feet from me, I take my chance and dash across the grounds, quickly saying my farewells to Nan

I cross the green space, half bent over, moving in towards the trees. From there, I weave my way to the building and out to the parking lot to my car. I get in just as I spot another police cruiser entering the parking lot. Sliding down, I wait for them to pass.

Oh god, can you say Internal Affairs? Can you say 'inquiry'? Can you say 'canned'?

Chapter 10
The past called...I should have let it go to voicemail.

I avoid Nan and everyone else for a week. I watch TV, listen to the radio and read the newspaper to determine if they've released anything on me and my so-called 'deviant' behavior. As far as I know, Mark has kept his promise and doesn't leak it.

Thank goodness. It gives me some hope that he's really trying his best to work this out. But this isn't much of a reassurance.

There's a strong possibility that someone, anyone, can reveal this indiscretion to the public somehow, some way and at any moment. The media will be all over it like flies to a dead body. It goes without saying that I'm antsy whenever the phone rings, or whenever it doesn't ring, for that matter. If it rings, I cringe, and my brain goes into overdrive, telling me to hang on for a bumpy ride.

Clearly, I know that the day will come when I'll have to tell Nan and Susanne, and whoever else gives a shit. But, till then, it will be my little secret. Really, how long can this sort of thing go on for? It should be over by next week, maybe the week after by the latest. Until then, I'll make sure to avoid everyone.

Oh, sure, people call me, leave messages, tell me they've tried my work number and keep getting someone else's voicemail.

Hi, sweetie, it's Nan. Did you change your work number? Every time I try to call, I get someone else. Call me. We need to talk about the Halloween party!

Someone else's voicemail? They've replaced me already. I can make a few good guesses of the person that took over.

Oh, yes, the Halloween party; the party that I help Nan with every year. How am I supposed to plan a party when my life is in shambles?

Unfortunately, it has quickly come to my attention that there's only so much avoidance you can manage before someone takes evasive action. Like Nan, for instance, who has sent out the reinforcements in the form of Zach.

When he arrives, I refuse to let him in; instead, I make him stand at the door. Of course he looks good; I don't recall ever seeing him looking bad, even when he's had the 'I-just-woke-up' look, which I only caught a glimpse of a few times while being at Nan's early in the morning.

"You're not at work today." I can sense the skepticism in his voice. It's a statement, not a question.

"You're really quick, aren't you? And to think, the police service let you get away."

He flashes a slightly dimpled cheek, which I hadn't noticed before or maybe paid attention to. Whatever it is, it's sexy and I feel a little fluttering in my chest. "Your grandmother said you were working today, but she couldn't get you at work, so she sent me over."

"I'm fine. I took the day off and besides, I thought you weren't going to interfere anymore?"

"You have a short memory. I said I wouldn't interfere with your time with your grandmother. I'm just over here 'cause your grandmother asked me to."

"Right, the sense of duty thing."

"Right." He doesn't make a move to leave. Instead, he digs his fists into his pockets as if he's going to stand there all day and have a chat with me.

"Is that all?" I ask.

"I thought you never took time off."

"Well, I did. Is this inquiry done?"

"I guess." He shrugs.

"Bye, then." I close the door refusing to let myself watch him walk away from the house, but I do anyway—surreptitiously, of course. I shake my head. I don't have time to be fantasizing about The Escort. My life is spiraling out of control. How much longer can I continue this lie?

I give Joan a call at work, hoping that she's heard something. But, she hasn't heard a single thing. She doesn't even know if there is a press release slated for this week. "Listen, honey, if it'll help, I know you didn't do it."

"Thanks, Joan. By the way, who's taken over my spot?"

"Walters," she says this with some disdain.

"What? That cretin." This really shouldn't be a surprise. They passed him up for the promotion giving me the position he wanted. He has more seniority but everyone knows he's an idiot.

"Cate, you hang in there, okay?"

"Thanks, Joan."

I get off the phone with her and decide that I can't just sit around waiting; I'll have to take matters into my own hands. I'm calling a lawyer; something I should have done in the beginning.

I locate an attorney by process of elimination: the one that is closest to my house, one that has the nicest ad and someone I haven't heard of before. How does a criminal, or a falsely accused criminal, go about this sort of thing? Since waiting is no longer an option, I can't just sit around and hope for something to turn around; I need an opinion.

Being on the police force for as long as I have has introduced me to a few lawyers and judges, people I can certainly call on in times like these. However, I don't want any of them knowing my business. I'll stick with someone I don't know, and someone that looks inexpensive. Since this one looks like a small firm in a mediocre end of town, I deduce that it'll be cheap.

I arrive at the law office of Danforth Sherman, Lawyer, which is what it says on the door in new black lettering. The ancient office is in the district known as Cobbler's Lane. The office has a distinct smell of rusty pipes and new paint with a hint of freshly brewed coffee.

The six chairs in the office are a retro orangey-red vinyl that may have been bought at a second-hand office furniture store, and I'm guessing they were.

The secretary greets me with a wide smile and what I guess as an Australian accent. Her dark hair is perfectly coifed, curled, and sprayed to perfection. "May I help you?"

"I'm here to see Danforth Sherman. My name is Cate Chase."

"I'll let him know you're here, Ms. Chase. Have a seat." She leaves only to return a few seconds later, telling me that he'll be with me in a moment.

I flip through a magazine, not really interested in the contents and more concerned with what Danforth Sherman will have to say. My mind works over time as I wonder if this is a lost cause. How in the world will he be able to prove my innocence? Just before I consider any other factors, the door opens and out walks Danforth Sherman.

I'm stunned. "Dan Sherman?"

"Cate! I was hoping it was you. How have you been?"

Chapter 11
The First One Naked is a Rotten Egg

Did you ever have one of those relationships where sex didn't happen, but had lots of amazing foreplay? And, did the relationship end before you could explore sex with that person, making you wonder 'what if'? What if you stayed a little longer in the relationship and consummated it? What would sex be like with the person that was the ultimate at foreplay?

Well, for me, that was Danforth Sherman, or Dan Sherman, the guy I dated way back in high school and the man who is now standing before me in a black Armani suit. His dark brown hair is slicked back and his black rimmed glasses accentuate his strong, square jaw.

"Dan." I shake my head, trying to rid my mind of the numerous flashbacks that are flooding in. "I didn't know you were Danforth Sherman."

"Ah, yes, my real name. Never used it in high school. Thought I'd get beat up." Dan leads me into his office and shuts the door, finally hugging me. "It's so good to see you."

"It's great to see you!" He releases me and I take a seat in his chair. His office is much nicer than the reception area. It's complete with leather chairs, mahogany desk, and a fridge for drinks.

"So, you're a lawyer now." I really am stunned.

"Yep. I'm sure this is hard to believe."

"I mean, last time we were together, you had a tragic hero complex." He did. He was extremely deep and brooding and, for some reason, I loved it. I loved the drama.

"You remember that?" He asks, grabbing water from the fridge and handing it to me.

"Ya. The whole world was against you and you were against the world." I notice his eyes are the same, he's gained a bit of weight but it suits him. He also doesn't look lost or sad anymore. Whatever changes he has made, they're all good.

He blushes. "A lot of changes happened since then. After high school, I took some time to reflect, went to some monasteries, did the whole celibacy thing, the vow of silence. While I was at a temple in Tibet, I realized something—I wanted to be a lawyer."

"How are those things even remotely related to being a lawyer?"

"Enlightenment happens when you least expect." He sits up straight in the chair behind his desk. His smile is calm, and I immediately relax.

I am amazed at how much he has changed. This guy was knee deep in negativity, Nietzsche and Leonard Cohen. I can still hear him recite an entry from 'Thus Spoke Zarathustra' as Leonard Cohen sang 'Lover Lover Lover' in the background. His bedroom was always dark with only a candle burning in the corner. We had just finished making out.

Orgasm score:
Me: 4
Dan: 0

For some reason, the guy couldn't have an orgasm, (or refused to) no matter how hard I worked down there. If I remember correctly, he didn't want to because he felt he was losing control or some other excuse like that. The bonus was he was always obliging on my part, making sure my needs were met—each and every time. Yep, he was good at foreplay, no doubt about that. He's the only guy I'd dated who knew where that 'spot' was; the mysterious spot that every man searches for, but cannot find. He somehow knew exactly where it was. And now, as my mind races back in time, I find myself blushing before him. I shake the thoughts from my head and get to the point of why I am sitting in his office.

"So, Dan, as you know, I always wanted to be a cop."
"I remember. And? Did you?"
"I'm now sergeant of the local police force."
"Congratulations. Not surprised though. You were so focused on the police career. Always making plans."
I pause for a moment, unsure of what to say. Dan will be the only person outside of work that will know about the suspension. But, no matter how I formulate my first sentence, the words aren't coming easy.
"Cate, are you all right?" Dan walks around his desk, sitting on the edge.
I shake my head. I muster up the courage to tell him, stamping down the emotion. "I've run into some problems at work and I don't know what you can do for me. I really need solid advice." I start to tell Dan my story, all the details of what I know, hoping that he won't think I'm a sexual harasser. Maybe he will, you know, after how badly I wanted to have sex with him and he would never give in. Now that I think of it, I must have looked desperate.
After I finish talking, Dan only nods his head, remaining quiet for a minute. He jots some notes down while I wonder if I should tell him more.

"Any other incidences happen where your words could have been misunderstood?"

I shake my head. "I rarely interact with anyone on my team, except for the pre-shift meetings. I especially don't make a point of going into the men's locker room. Dan, they won't even tell me who the complainant is."

"What's internal affairs doing about this?"

"They are gathering information, so they say."

"Have they asked for your side of the story?" He puts down his pen and sits back. "No. That's just it. They suspend me but no one has asked me what happened. Even though I have no story to tell, no one has asked me."

"Unfortunately, we will have to wait on this to see what they find. If we see no movement, we will have to press for details." He walks around his desk and sits on the edge facing me. "Cate, I know you would never do this. Please, let me take care of this."

My body visibly relaxes. Having Dan in my corner, having someone I know and trust behind me gives me the boost I need.

"Thank you, Dan. This means a lot to me."

"Oh, but this doesn't come without a price."

I sit up, shifting in my seat, ready to hear how much. "Oh, I know. I'm prepared to pay you. What am I looking at?"

"Dinner with me tonight?"

I smile. Dinner with Dan Sherman? Definitely.

*

I slip into something a bit more suitable for our dinner date and meet Dan at an Italian restaurant just around the corner from his place, or so that's what he tells me. I think it's foreshadowing on Dan's part. He's trying to give me a taste of what will happen later on. Maybe I shouldn't jump to conclusions, but I'd bet there's a good chance that he planned it this way.

Dan is still in his Armani when he sits down at the table, looking dapper and fresh from earlier today. Age has really enhanced his features; he's more attractive, more mature. In the past, he looked so lost, his eyes empty and unsure. Now, they're a warm, rich brown, vibrant and lively. I like the new Danforth Sherman.

We talk about the past, about when we dated, about how much we liked each other. It's a bit surreal but exciting all at the same time. I really did like Dan.

"You know, I was crazy about you," Dan announces.

I raise a brow. "Really? Well, why did you break up with me then?"

"I didn't break up with you. You broke up with me."

"I did not. You were the one that told me on our prom night that this couldn't work out anymore." I take a sip of wine.

Dan shakes his head. "No, that's not how it happened. You told me on prom night that we were going different directions in life and that you didn't want to be committed when you entered the police academy. You broke my heart, Cate." He doesn't look up.

I'm stunned. I didn't know I had done the heart breaking? I realize right then that I can be a bit treacherous when I do the breaking up. I was hasty. Then again, I was only, what, 18 or something. Still, it's obvious I haven't learned anything new.

"Well, I was young and stupid." I finally say. That's my excuse for everything.

Dan continues to smile as if he's remembering something. He plays with his wine glass, swishing the liquid around carefully.

"Welllll, you're out of the academy now. Maybe we could see what happens. I think fate has brought us back together. Don't you?"

I blink. Does this mean what I think it means? Do I want to get back together? I've heard of high school sweethearts rekindling or finding each other after years apart; I never thought I'd be one of those people.

"Hmmm, we'll see," I say in a sexy but non-committal voice. I don't want to turn him off from a possible interlude tonight; an interlude I've been wondering about for the longest time. And, as far as a potential rekindling of a romance—we really would have to see. That's the best I can do. Considering I had broken his heart once already, it's probably a good idea to wait before breaking it again.

Two plates of Linguine Carbanara, four glasses of red wine, and one invite to his condo later, I find myself naked before him.

Somehow, we got on the topic of police work, and really, I'm a sucker for it. The conversation didn't end there; he invited me up for a night cap, or that's what he said.

To me, it sounded like an innocent drink that would carry on our conversation; however, I knew what was going to happen. This part of him hasn't change—luring me in, making interesting conversation, then getting me naked—I was always the first one naked. I'm curious to see how it'll all play out. I can honestly say that there's still something there that has me intrigued by him, and I want to find out what it is. I guess that's one of the reasons why I went up to his place; the other reason could be the wine—it makes me do unrestrained things.

The whole nakedness thing started when we walked hand-in-hand back to his place and got on the elevator. I was yammering as usual (too much wine), about the damn thirteenth floor. That thirteenth floor phenomena of how the twelfth floor magically goes to the fourteenth floor, giving the illusion that there isn't a thirteenth floor, when really the fourteenth floor is the thirteenth floor.

That's when Dan turned to me, his arms around my waist and said, "You always knew how to make me laugh. Let's rid ourselves of the bad voodoo of the fourteenth/thirteenth floor and create our own good luck." With one quick flick of his fingers, he had undone my bra right there in the elevator as we passed the eleventh floor.

Once Dan had me inside his place, he immediately dimmed the lights, lit some candles, and put on Leonard Cohen (like I said, some things never change). I kicked off my shoes and pulled my bra from my shirt, throwing it off to the side somewhere. I didn't take much notice of his place, aside from the fact that it's the typical bachelor style of black leather couches, a large TV, and a left over pizza box sitting on the counter. Otherwise, the place was a blur because Dan brought over more wine and a bunch of moves—some old, some new.

I took a sip and set the glass down on the table before Dan moved in, kissing my neck and pushing me down to the couch.

Things were slowly unbuttoned, unbelted and thrown to the floor. He was still in his pants; his shirt and jacket already strewn about the condo just minutes before, which brings us to me being completely naked—like I said, I was always the first one.

I'm not bothered by this because Dan and I are going to have sex. This is what I've been dreaming about since dating him; the thing that has kept me wondering for almost two decades.

This is new territory, new things explored. All my questions will be answered and more. Will Dan be just as good at sex as he is at foreplay? And will he have learned any new moves since the last time I saw him?

He makes his way down my belly and my legs, and finding the spot he had found so many times before, and I confirm that, indeed, he has learned new tricks.

At that point, the orgasm score is,
Me: 1, Dan: 0

The stickiness of the leather glues to my back as our bodies begin to burn, and I can't wait any longer. Hasn't it been long enough? I yank at his pants and shimmy them down to his ankles. He continues to move up my body kissing, licking and tickling. He's hard on my leg and grazes it up and down a few times. He won't let me touch it. Instead he prefers to tease me, rubbing up against me a few more times.

And then he moans.

My eyes fly open, my mouth in a halfway 'O', my spidey-senses tingling. Why in the world did he moan like that? This isn't an 'I'm-so-turned-on-get-ready-for-a-crazy-ride' moan; this is one of satisfaction. Complete satisfaction. He slightly rolls off of me, wedging himself between me and the back of the couch, saying, 'Wow.´ I know this night is done.

'Wow? What's wow? You came on my leg', I want to yell out. He came on my leg. One more time—Dan came on my leg! I don't fucking believe this.

I grab his underwear that is still hanging from his ankle and wipe my leg. Dan has a post-coital glow that really can't be classified as post-coital, because you'd have to have some coitus to get to the coital. He rubs my back, gives me a satisfied smile and says, "Let's go to bed."

I blink and nod like an idiot, getting up and crawling into his bed in the next room. He kisses me good night and in a few minutes, he's asleep.

And I was robbed.

You'd think that any normal woman would have gotten dressed, picked up her dignity that had been abandoned there on the sticky couch, and left after that performance. Nope, not me. Instead, I stick around. Maybe because I'm slightly drunk and slightly tired, and maybe a bit hopeful for the morning. At least I'm getting good foreplay. But, sometimes, a woman wants more than foreplay. She wants some good, blow-your-mind sex.

That's not too much to ask, is it?

*

I'm dreaming about this gigantic bee buzzing around my head. Whenever I try swatting it, it buzzes louder and longer, driving me absolutely nuts. I'm afraid it might sting me with all the swatting I'm doing. But here's the thing, it doesn't have a stinger.

"Hello?"

I wake to the sounds of Dan answering the intercom.

"Hey, man, it's Zach."

I sit up. Zach? No! It can't be. My Zach? What are the chances? Do Dan and Zach know each other?

"Come on up." Dan presses the buzzer and I grab my clothes.

"Zach? Zach who?" I attempt to slip on my skirt, forgetting about my underwear. I will have to leave it behind seeing as I can't find it. I have to save myself.

Dan watches me run around as I pull my shirt on. I now can't find my bra; I think I tossed it by my shoes. Being slightly intoxicated when clothes are flying off can have its drawbacks, namely trying to find missing underwear. In my frenzy, I notice Dan doesn't seem to care that Zach's coming up the elevator.

He's still naked and erect. Isn't he going to get dressed?

"Zach Kennedy. A buddy of mine." It looks like the chances are really good that this Zach is the Zach. "We're going for lunch today. You wanna come with?" Dan grabs me, kissing my neck, hard against my leg.

I push him away. I grab my shoes and coat, not bothering to put them on. I'll carry them and deal with it downstairs. "I have to go." I rush to the door, putting an ear to the wood, checking for elevator sounds. Nothing.

"Bye, Dan. Uh, it was nice seeing you again." What else am I supposed to say? Thanks for the memories?

"Wait, Cate, stay. I want you to meet Zach."

Does he think we're in a relationship now? The sex part isn't working and I'm not interested in sticking around to find out if it ever does. I ignore his request and check the hall. "I'm in a hurry," I whisper.

"I'll call you later to give you an update on the case."

The case? Shit! I hired him as my lawyer. And I paid him with sex. Oh, god, I'm worse than Zach! "Yep. Okay." It occurs to me that I will have to find another lawyer. Hopefully, I won't sleep with the next one.

The elevator pings and I do the 100 yard dash down the hallway, dodging around the corner and peeking with one eye to catch a glimpse of Zach striding off the elevator in his confidant, good looking way.

Jerk.

*

Is it me, or does everyone on Dawson's Creek have their shit together? Even if someone is suffering a meltdown during that episode, one of their buddies is sure to give some sort of philosophical viewpoint—the viewpoint that is going to change their lives forever. You know, the a-ha moment we all look for. Well, look no further, because you can find it all on Dawson's Creek. Even Jen, the one that's a little messed up, did make sense on occasion.

But, if I were to have anyone figure out my life, I'd leave the job to Pacey. Although his family members are slightly dysfunctional—he's the only one that has it solved by the end of the day. If I could, I'd have him come over to my place and he'd have my life worked out in a few hours. He'd probably give me some sort of speech using a pencil and eraser as an analogy, and ta-da! Everything would be explained. Ah, Pacey, I love it when you wax philosophical.

As I consider this, somewhere in the back of my mind is wondering if Dan told Zach he had sex with me last night. Sex—ha! Far from it. What am I thinking? Of course he told Zach. What guy isn't going to tell his buddy they came all over an old girlfriend's leg?

They'd give each other high-fives, maybe slap asses then go for lunch to celebrate. Now the question is, did Dan mention my name, and if he did, would Zach put two and two together? What are the odds that Dan and Zach know one another and that I would be there, naked, after having non-sex with Dan when Zach came to the door? Dan couldn't have told him my name. He would just mention that an ex-girlfriend came over. That's all. Men don't really share the names, do they? They just describe the act with some nameless, faceless woman. That's me—the incredible nameless, faceless woman.

So, just as I put that all behind me, wash Dan-smell off of me, and sit down with a nice cup of tea and Pacey, I actually think no one is the wiser. Really.

That's when the doorbell rings. Part of me wants to believe that it might be Pacey at the door or even Dawson; but when I open it, it's Zach.

"What are you doing here?"

Zach doesn't flinch at my impoliteness. Instead, he continues on as if he hasn't heard me, entering my place uninvited.

"So, I had lunch with a buddy today."

"So?" I reluctantly close the door.

"He said he ran into an old girlfriend last night. I guess she stayed the night."

"And?" My throat closes up and I feel a headache coming on top of my slight hang-over headache. "Why should I care about your buddy and his ex?" I cross my arms in front of my chest. I'm hoping my face isn't matching my gut feelings, which are of sheer dread.

"She left her purse at his place." Zach pulls his hands from behind his back. Hanging from his index finger is a purse. My purse. "I believe this is yours."

"That's not mine," I say automatically. I've heard this phrase too many times from the people I've arrested when I'd find drugs on them; it sounds funny coming from my own mouth. Can I get away with I was just holding it for a friend?

"He said that her name was Cate," Zach counters.

"Newsflash, there's more than one Cate in this world."

Zach smiles knowingly, as if we're playing chess and he's about to call out checkmate. "I recognized the purse from the other night at your grandmother's place, and..." he pauses on purpose, "I checked the driver's license."

I snatch the purse from his hands, pissed that he has me. I want to ask if he found my underwear too, but decide against it.

"So...I met an old boyfriend last night. What? I can't have fun, is that what you're saying?" I walk out to the kitchen and grab the Double Fudge Chocolate Ice Cream from the freezer, eating it straight from the carton. Zach follows me. Why is he following me? Why isn't he leaving?

"No, not at all. What I am saying is if you're going to sleep with someone, find someone better to do it with. Not Dan Sherman. The guy has some sort of penile irregularity." Zach leans up against the counter, arms crossed over his chest, a Cheshire Cat grin.

God, I'd love to jump him right now. Is that too slutty? First Ian, then Dan and now Zach. Well, Dan doesn't really count, I mean, he just came on my leg. So, no, maybe not too slutty. And besides, Dan is just a rebound thing after Ian. Zach is—God! What's wrong with me?

"First off, how do you know he has a penile irregularity?"

"Trust me. I lived with the guy and heard his girlfriends complain about him too many times. Walls are thin."

"Secondly, who is worthy enough to sleep with me?" I question.

At that moment, I'm standing about two inches from Zach in my ripped sweats and bunny slippers, holding my container of ice cream. He doesn't do or say anything for a few seconds then suddenly reaches out to touch one of my brownish-red ringlets, gently pulling it till it springs back.

He then shrugs and says, "No idea." Then winks, leaving me breathless.

A few days have passed since that incident. I haven't gone by Nan's place and Zach hasn't come over, bringing me soup or anything else for that matter. I spend most of my days phoning Joan, asking her if she's heard anything.

Then I talk to Mark who assures me he's working on it and to be patient. Although, he can't guarantee that a press release won't be sent out in the next week. I beg and plead with him to hold off as long as possible.

He reprimands me, saying I should have told my grandmother by now and it's my own fault. He always liked Nan, even though Nan didn't like him. She saw through him the moment she met him. Why is she always right about these things? Maybe I should start listening to her; it may save a lot of headaches.

So, after not seeing Nan for a few days, I decide to go over there. I'll tell her I took some time off and will be around her place more often, which happens to work. She's pleased that I'm taking a break. Yes, it's a lie, but I just can't face her with my suspension story. I can't tell her that her granddaughter, the one she's so proud of for making sergeant, is now suspended for something so ludicrous. It'll crush her.

Nan and I sit in the kitchen, coffee for me and tea for her. I look out the window at the guest house wondering if Zach is in there. Wondering what he's doing. Why isn't he servicing my grandmother? Isn't she paying him good money for him to do things, whatever those things are?

Nan catches me staring at the house and pipes up, "It's Zach's day off today." I stare at her. She sips her tea, looking above the rim of her cup directly at me.

"I don't care what Zach does with his time, as long as he's not a jerk to you."

"He's absolutely wonderful, Cate."

"Hmm, I guess that remains to be seen." I stir the cream in my coffee.

"Oh, shoot." Nan sets her cup down.

"What?"

"I forgot to make a call to one of the ladies in my scrapbooking club. I'll be right back."

Nan leaves me in the kitchen staring out the window at the guest house. I can't just go over there to say hi. I mean, what will that look like? Or can I? Considering we are nemeses, it might look like a surrender, and I'm not about to surrender to Zach Kennedy. I suppose I could thank him again for bringing back my purse, but then we'd have to bring up the whole Dan Sherman thing again, and I really don't want to relive that.

I guess asking if he managed to locate my underwear isn't an option either. Although, we would get on the topic of underwear and maybe that will lead to something else. All I know is that I really need to control my adolescent hormones around Zach.

I eye-up the sugar bowl and lift the lid. I grimace. It's full. I walk to the garbage and dump out the sugar then walk out of the kitchen to the front door of the guest house, knocking a few times. A few seconds later, the door opens and Zach's brows crease at the sight of me standing on his doorstep. He's wearing jeans and an untucked button down blue shirt.

"Hi?"

"Hi. Um, sugar." I hold up the sugar container. I clear my throat. "I mean, we ran out of sugar at the house."

"You ran out of sugar? Are you sure? Because I'm certain that this bowl was full when I made your grandmother tea yesterday."

Fuck. I bite my lip. "Well, it's empty now. And I can't find any in the pantry. Do you have any?"

Zach grins lopsidedly. "Uh, yeah. Come in."

I walk in, looking around. Everything seems clean and in place. No stolen artifacts lying about. Not like Nan had artifacts to begin with.

"Bring the bowl to the kitchen." Zach breaks my concentration noticing I'm surveying his place—a football game on TV, beer and chips sitting on the table, no grow-ops or the smell of weed. Lucky for him or I'd have to handcuff him or something else nasty like that.

"So, what were you doing?" I hand him the sugar container and he starts spooning sugar into it.

He looks up. "I was watching a football game."

"Oh, right." I'm starting to think this is lame.

"Heard from Dan lately?" Zach asks, putting the lid back on the container and turning toward the sink, his back facing me.

"Um, no. Not lately. He said he'd call though." Here I am trying to make it sound like I want Dan to call, when really I couldn't care less if he called ever again. Except for the fact that he's my lawyer and I used semi-sex for payment.

"Here's your sugar. Tell your grandmother I have more if she needs it."

"Right. Thanks." I don't reach for the sugar; rather, I just hang around, waiting for something to happen. Maybe I'll use the bathroom or just go straight to the fridge and rifle around for a beer, saying, hey, I love this team. Who's winning? Can you believe they put him in as starting quarterback? Do you wanna order pizza? Then we'd sit and watch and eat chips and whoop when our team (whichever one it is) makes a touch-down.

"So. You're just going to watch the game."

"Yep." He leans against the counter and crosses his feet. I'm finding him to be irresistible standing there. There has to be something else wrong with him. Bad in bed? Small penis? Psychological issues from years of abuse at the hands of his parents? Those are all good options.

"I better get the sugar back to my grandmother. Thanks, Zach." I take the container and head for the door. Now, really, this man needs to show more hospitality. I mean, isn't he going to ask me to stay for a beer? Eat some chips? Make out?

"Cate, wait."

I stop and turn. "Yes?" And before I have a chance to ready myself, Zach leans in and kisses me hard, his strong hands cupping my face, his lips meshing with mine. I drop the sugar bowl ignoring the fact that it crashes into a million and one pieces on the hardwood floor. As my heart drums wildly against my chest, I rip open his shirt as he kisses my neck and undoes my bra in one seamless act.

"Cate?"

I snap out of my fantasy. Zach is still standing a few feet away, his face is screwed up in a question mark, and I'm still standing at the door holding the stupid sugar bowl.

"Sorry, what?"

"Tell your grandmother I'll see her at ten tomorrow morning."

I attempt a nod. "Ten, right. Again, thanks." I indicate the sugar container and walk out the door, not looking back, and desperately needing a cold shower.

Chapter 12
If you tell the truth, you don't have to remember anything. --Mark Twain

When Susanne had invited me to her psychic party, I thought she had lost her mind. I'm not one for signs, symbols, and the flying tables crap. I would have sooner gone to a Tupperware party than this.

Frankly, I think it was a conspiracy. It had been a while since we had seen each other. I had been avoiding her because I knew that she would have picked up on the fact that something was wrong. If I would have told her I was working, she would have seen through that lie. Susanne knows me better than anyone else, that's why I had to go.

When I sat down amongst the other women who were eagerly waiting for a reading from Madam Kitty (yes, that was her name), I was not too kind, whispering under my breath to Susanne about how I was waiting for the psychic to apparate before my eyes, only to discover the psychic was sitting right next to me, hearing every word I was saying. The dirty looks from Madam Kitty had me thinking that she didn't see that coming.

Madam Kitty had gone around the room, giving tidbits of information to all the guests, a bit of a teaser to quench their thirst for more info and cough up the $100 for a reading.

She started with Tabitha, a slender woman who was in need of a Big Mac or two, who was told she's pregnant. Tabitha managed to share with us that her period was definitely late and she was running home to take a pregnancy test.

Christine, a short, stocky woman with short curly hair, was told her grandfather was watching over her. According to Christine, she has had a feeling all along. Right, Christine.

The psychic continued to the other women in the room, and then she stopped at me, leaving me shocked. She had said, point blank, that I wasn't working at the time. If you Google 'deer caught in the headlights', you would get a picture of me. When Susanne heard those words, I knew I was done for. I tried to side step and tell her that I was on holidays, but Madam Kitty insisted that I was off of work. She said something along the lines of, "I'm sensing something about being pushed...no...wait. Forced. Yes, forced to leave. For two...no, four weeks. You haven't been working for four weeks." Then, at that moment, she closed her eyes and whispered, "Your guides have a message for you."

My guides? I didn't even know what she meant by that. What guides?

"YES. About losing...loss of self. You need to find yourself, or you will lose."

I'm so wrapped up in Madam Kitty that I blurted out, "Lose out on what?"

"On love."

At that point, Madam Kitty moved onto the next person, and I was left wanting more. And, that's where we are at this point in the story. Me, standing in the Susanne's kitchen, shoving cheese and olives into my mouth while the other women talk amongst themselves, waiting for a full reading from Madam Kitty.

"Is it true?" Susanne presses.

"What? About love? I have no idea what she's talking about." I stuff a couple of olives in my mouth so I can't speak. Maybe I'll stick some more cheese in there too and Susanne will get bored thinking I'm just going to stuff my face all night and leave me alone.

"No, about you not working. Why haven't you been at work?"

My cheeks flush. I know I'm giving myself away. "I've been working," I say through my mouthful of shrimp.

"Cate." She puts a hand on her hip.

I take a gulp of wine, finish it off and place the empty glass on the counter. "They've suspended me, okay?" I can't look at Susanne. Why? Because the tough cop now looks like she can't handle her job.

Susanne places her hand on my arm. "Cate, why didn't you say something?"

"I didn't think it mattered."

"What? Of course it does. You should be able to talk to someone—and you didn't. It must be eating you up inside." She hugs me and I try not to cry. After so many weeks of hiding this secret, this is the first time I feel like crying.

"Does anyone else know?"

I shake my head.

"Not even Nan?"

"Nope. No one."

"She's going to find out sooner or later. She'll be hurt to discover you didn't tell her."

I nod. But that still doesn't change the fact that I'm unable to tell Nan. She has been incredibly proud of me ever since I entered the force. I can't let her down. She'd be crushed.

"What are you going to do?"

"Funny you should mention that. Remember Dan Sherman?" I proceed to tell her about Dan and our strange one night stand. Then I tell her how Zach knows Dan and the whole sordid tale surrounding that odd night.

She stifles a laugh and pulls me into a hug. "Oh, sweetie. We will figure this out, okay?" She rubs my back, makes me feel better and hands me another glass of wine. "So, now, what about the true love thing?"

"I have no idea. Madam Kitty is not very accurate." I laugh maybe a little too nervously for my liking.

"Maybe you should get a full reading from Madam Kitty."

I shake my head. "No, I don't think so."

"Cate, she's not a fraud. She's clearly proven that."

"I can't," I say, my tone matter of fact.

"What are you afraid of?" She questions.

"Nothing. I just don't think it'll be beneficial."

"You're difficult." She pours herself some wine.

"But you still love me!" I clink her glass. Deep inside, there's this place where I know I need the answers soon, but I knew that Madam Kitty couldn't give them to me.

*

It's been a long road so far; four weeks of not doing the job that I love. Four weeks of not hearing a single thing and of not knowing what the plan is. How long do I have to put my life on hold? Dan had called saying he received information from the case, and would review it. And, maybe we could meet for dinner at his house. It was a cringe-worthy moment. I'm not feeling it from him, and maybe it was safer that we stay strictly in a lawyer-client capacity.

At work, Joan overheard some guys talking in the lunch room about my suspension and how it's about time someone put me in my place.

When Joan transfers me to Mark, he announces his plan for a press release as soon as all the information has come to him from internal affairs. He doesn't give me a time frame, and I argue how unfair this is and how can he release it to the media when there is no evidence but hearsay? I feel the stress throbbing in my head.

And, then there's my other stress, Zach. I make a point of being with Nan more now. I'm able to keep an eye on her and monitor what Zach is doing on a more consistent basis.

Even if he's not in my grandmother's house, I manage to concoct some story to check in on him, like, say, borrowing a hammer from him as I pretend to hang a picture for Nan. Nan wasn't even around at the time, so I just walked over to the guest house and asked him for a hammer.

"Why do you need a hammer from me when there's one in the shed?" He asks. He looks good today. Well, he looks good every day. I wish he would look like crap at least once so I can stop thinking about him.

"Heinrich is using it and won't give it up. Not even for a few minutes." It's a dumb line.

"For his gardening?" Zach asks.

"Yeah, you know. He needs it for when he plants his tulip bulbs next year."

Zach shakes his head. "Okay, come on in." He walks to a closet and pulls out his red toolbox, lifting the lid; the hammer is sitting right on top. "Do you want me to give you a hand?"

"You don't think I can handle a hammer?"

"I was just wondering if you needed a hand. I wasn't questioning your hammer-handling capabilities."

"I can handle any type of hammer, thank you." For a minute there, I wonder if we're still talking about tools or something else; especially when Zach smirks. "I'll bring it back in a few minutes."

"If I'm not around, just leave it on the step."

"Oh? Where are you going?" I say it before I even think about it.

Zach looks surprised. "I have some things to do today, if you really need to know about my whereabouts. Don't worry, I won't be doing anything unscrupulous." He shows me the door, obviously wanting me to leave at that very moment.

"I don't care what you're doing, Zach. Do whatever you want."

"Thanks for the permission. Now, if you don't mind, I have things to do." I leave with him slamming the door behind me. Hammer in hand, I feel completely unsatisfied.

That day, I decide to stay late into the evening. Zach had been out for most of the day and returned just shortly after Nan and I had dinner together. I didn't see any packages with him and he looked the same as when he left. Before he enters into the guest house, he picks up the hammer I had left on the front step, and casually looks around, then disappears inside. Nan catches me watching from the window. "Anything interesting?" She flicks on the light to the kitchen where I'm standing.

"Oh, no. Just deciding if I should have a nice dip in the hot tub before I head home, that's all."

"Hmm, you should. And you should also see if Zach wants to join you."

I freeze. "Why would I do that?"

"Because it's the polite thing to do. Zach doesn't have a lot of friends here."

"Trust me, Nan, he knows lots of people." I turn my attention back to the guest house and realize Zach is coming this way with his swim suit on and towel in hand. I jump back from the door and lean against the counter flipping through a flyer.

Zach enters and I try not to look up, but can't help it. He has no shirt on and I feel the drool edging to the corner of my mouth. Thank goodness he isn't wearing Speedos.

"Cate," he nods.

"Zach," I say to the top of his head because I can't look him in the eyes.

"Hey, Ursula. I was just going to head out to the hot tub before calling it a night. Did you need anything before I do?" I shift my eyes around from the ceiling to the floor and back to the ceiling again.

"No, no. I'm fine."

"See you in the morning then," he turns ready to leave.

"Oh, there is one thing," Nan blurts.

"Sure."

"Take Cate with you out to the hot tub. She's so tense."

Zach grins, his dimple showing.

"Nan, it's okay. I don't need to go."

"Yes. Yes, you do. Go get your swim suit on and meet Zach out in the hot tub. It'll be good for you." She pushes me to get changed and I do, still stunned by Nan's behaviour. A few minutes later, I walk out to the hot tub where Zach is reclined, eyes closed. He looks like he's sleeping and I slowly turn around, glad I dodged this bullet.

"Leaving so soon," his voice is soft. I turn to see dozy bedroom eyes, and I imagine that they look about the same after waking up in the morning.

"I didn't want to wake you." I pull the towel from my shoulders and climb into the hot tub. My eyes meet Zach's as he watches me get in. His hair is wet and glistening.

I lean back, hoping to get some relaxation in. Hoping that I don't need to keep up a conversation with The Escort just to please Nan. Suddenly a pair of feet kick me in the knees and I abruptly sit up. "Do you mind?"

"Sorry, do my feet bother you?" He sits up giving me the same look he's been giving me since we met, like he knows something. Like he has a plan.

"Hell, yeah, especially when they're kicking me."

"Sorry, didn't see your legs there."

"How can you not see where my legs are?"

"I said sorry. What more do you want?"

"How about some consideration and make yourself invisible while you're here."

Zach sits up straighter, slapping his arm on the side of the tub. "I'm not sure what your problem is, Cate. I've tried to be nice, tried to be friendly. Let you borrow my hammer for whatever pretend picture you were hanging—"

"It wasn't a pretend picture. I don't know where you get your ideas from."

"I know you're only coming over to spy on me. Is that why you refuse to be nice to me?"

"I can't be nice to you because you're my grandmother's escort. You have chosen an illegal career. What part of this conversation do you not get?"

"Hey, there are lots of things you don't know about me, so I wouldn't make assumptions if I were you."

"Are you an escort?" I ask

"Yes."

"Then we have nothing in common. The only thing we will have in common is when I arrest your ass for the crime you'll be committing."

"Tell me something, are you constantly PMSing?"

My head is ready to explode. "Aaarrrghhh! You are so infuriating. You know I have the right mind to..."

"Cate. Zach." Nan stands a few feet from the hot tub, looking completely pissed; more pissed than I've ever seen her. "Pack your bags. We're going to my cabin tomorrow." That's all she says and she walks away.

Her cabin? What's all this about? "But, Nan. I have to work." I protest. I'm so wrapped up in my lie that I don't know what's real anymore.

"No you don't." My heart stops. Does she know something?

"You told me you took time off, remember?" Right. "If you two can't get along, then I'm forcing you two to become friends." She leaves, yelling out, "Pack your bags."

Zach grins. "You heard the woman. Pack your bags." He hops out of the tub, and, when he reaches the guest house, slams the door behind him.

*

Nan's cabin with Zach. That's where I'm going to be stuck, for my holidays, which really aren't holidays. How can Nan be so cruel? I'm not ten, Nan! What is with her anyway? On top of everything else, she has decided that part of our punishment is to sit upfront together in the car. I think I'm getting the butt-end of the deal since Zach is driving.

"Do you even know how to drive this car?" I demand. My arms have been crossed over my chest since we left about forty-five minutes ago.

"Much better than you can drive it," he snorts.

"Hey, buddy, this is what I do for a living. What do you do?" I glare at him.

"I give women what they want," he grins slyly. I'm ready to say something, but Nan cuts me off before I do.

"Okay, enough. I'm trying to read back here."

"But, Nan, he's driving like an idiot."

"I'm driving as your grandmother asked me to. Now drop it," Zach says.

"You both drop it, or I'll leave you out on the side of the road."

"Nan—"

"Cate." That's her warning voice. I know that voice all too well. I don't know what she can do to me now that I'm older, but dropping us off at the side of the road isn't beyond her. I clamp my mouth shut and notice The Escort grinning smugly. I mouth the word, ass. He raises his eyes in mock surprise.

"Cate..." Nan does her warning voice again. How did she know I was mouthing words? I square my shoulders to the front and watch out the window till we arrive at the cabin shortly after 4; a whole hour and twelve minutes of sitting in the vehicle with The Escort. A whole twenty minutes of not saying a word to anyone. A whole twenty minutes of complete and amazing quiet. I hated it.

Nan's cabin, if you can call it that, is a two-story cedar home with loft, three bedrooms, two bathrooms, a living area, dining area and kitchen. No, it's not really a cabin but more like a home away from home. It's perched on the most beautiful lake that I've ever seen, and, when we pull up, I'm actually glad that I came.

I sigh at the sight of the trees changing colour; the lake glistening in the late afternoon sun and memories of my childhood flood back to me of when Mom and Dad were still around and they would watch me dive off the dock. I stand at the top of the small incline overlooking the water, breathing in and deciding that I won't let The Escort get to me. I'm going to enjoy myself. Maybe I'll read, or do yoga or something like that. Or maybe meditate. I haven't done that in ages.

"Nan, do I get to sleep in the loft?" I lug my bag into the cabin, perching it on the stairs that lead to the loft. She'd always let me sleep up there when I was younger. It was a given every time we came out here.

"Nope." She's been quite abrupt over the last 24 hours. She's obviously still pissed.

"What?"

"No." She eyes me seriously. "You two are in the bedrooms down here."

"But Nan..." I whine.

"No." She turns abruptly, obviously ending this conversation.

"Boy, is she in a rotten mood," I mutter.

"I'd say," Zach agrees. We both stare in utter shock that we actually agree on something. I shake it off and haul my bags to my room, unpacking my toiletries and putting them in the bathroom adjoining the bedrooms.

Zach walks in the other door. "The bathroom joins our rooms?"

"Yes. Is there a problem?"

He slides his toiletry bag onto the counter. "No, do you?"

"No."

"Fine, then. There's another thing we agree on." He walks out and I follow, standing at the door.

"I'm not going to let you get to me this weekend," I say triumphantly.

"Ooookay."

"I just thought I'd make that clear."

"Fine. It's crystal clear." He moves toward me, reaching around me. He's so close, pings of electricity bounce off of him. He looks deeply into my eyes and I swallow hard. What is he doing?

"In or out?" he whispers.

"Sorry?" My palms sweat.

"I want to close the door to the bathroom so I can change. Are you coming in or are you leaving?"

I realize he's grasping the doorknob behind me. "Oh. Um, I'm leaving." I quickly shut the door behind me. Oh, god. What was that about?

*

That night, Nan's mood has simmered down, maybe because Zach and I aren't at each other's throats. Nan makes dinner for us and we all have a nice time around the fire pit roasting marshmallows and making s'mores. Amazingly, not a nasty word is uttered, or not while Nan is around. When she heads off to bed, it's fair play, everything is on the table, and the worst insults can be spewed.

Zach says something about how Nan's really enjoying herself since he came to stay and that sets me off on a tangent of how he wouldn't be here if I had any say in the matter. Then he rebuts that I'm so angry and bitter that I need to seek help. Then I tell him to go screw himself and leave for my room. He's just some big, good looking jerk, anyway.

A big, good looking jerk that I spy on the moment I return to my room. He doesn't do much of anything. Just poke at the fire a bit, looks up at the night sky, stares dreamily into the flames. All right, dreamily is my word, I'm not sure if that was what he was doing or not.

Ten minutes later he's dousing the fire and walks into the house. Once I know he's outside my door, I open it.

"Zach." I realize that I have no idea what I'm doing. Am I going to ask him to have sex with me? That's a dumb move. I mean, it looks good on paper, but a really dumb, dumb move.

"Yeah?"

"Um, so, did you..." my eyes shoot around. Think of something. Anything.

"Did I....what?"

"Did you put the fire out?" I cross my arms, my head held high.

"Ya. Remember, you saw me do it from your window," he says.

Shit. "Right. Well, good night then." I slam the door, feeling like a dumbass.

*

The next morning, I awake to the sun streaming through my bedroom. This was definitely a good idea—coming out here, the fall smells, the lake. I missed this place. I climb out of bed, stretch and decide that avoiding The Escort and relaxing all day is exactly what I need. This place is big enough for us to avoid one another.

I'll have a shower, eat some waffles, read a book and nothing will get in my way of enjoying myself. I do deserve some much needed rest. After all, look what I've been going through.

I open the door to the bathroom to find Zach just coming out of the shower and wrapping a towel around his waist. I freeze, unable to move.

"Hey, don't you knock?"

I stare at him for a split-second, my mouth agape. It takes me a few seconds to snap out of it. "Well, you should have locked the door," I say indignantly, still standing there, not looking at his face. Instead, I look at his chest or somewhere in that vicinity. I'm not sure where I'm staring, but all I know is I'm not making a move to leave.

"Are you going to continue to stare or are you going to close the door?" Zach is still holding the towel around his waist. I continue to stand there, stuck to the floor. Why can't I leave?

"Well?" Zach snaps me out of it.

I pull my eyes away, mutter a bye and slam the door. That's embarrassing and a bit, oh, I don't know, arousing.

By the time I get out of the shower and head to the kitchen to eat, Zach has already finished and is outside, according to Nan, which she gave to me on her own. There was absolutely no provoking on my part.

"Good, now I can eat in peace."

"He's a nice guy, Cate. Why won't you give him a chance?"

"Because he's a criminal, Nan. He has sex for a living."

"He hasn't had sex with me, so that's not true."

"Regardless if he hasn't had sex with you, and I want to say thank you for that, he still has done it with other women in the past."

"How do you know? You haven't even bothered to talk to him."

"I know, Nan. It's my business to know." I finish up my waffles, do the dishes and head outdoors to read my book. It's a beautiful day to just relax. The sun is warm with no breeze, and the sound of the lake lapping at the water's edge is completely soothing. Except there's another sound intermingling with the water—a guitar and singing.

Where the heck is that coming from? I scan the area till I finally see a person on the dock playing guitar. It's Zach. I stand at the edge of the deck making sure it really is Zach. Zach can play guitar and sing?

"Isn't he wonderful?" Nan startles me. He's more than wonderful, I want to say, but decide on a different opinion.

"He's all right." I plant my nose in my book.

"He's better than all right."

I shrug showing disinterest. "If you say so." But I know she's right. I can't even concentrate on my book as he continues to play his guitar and sing his little tune. His voice carries across the water and I find myself becoming entranced by it. Even when he comes back from the dock with his guitar in hand, looking like a rocker, sexy and glowing, I don't say a word.

"That was beautiful, Zach." Nan kisses his cheek. "Wasn't that beautiful, Cate?" I continue to stare at my book. I haven't read one word since I sat down.

"Sure, if you like that kind of music."

"And what kind of music do you like?" Zach leans on the deck railing staring at me, the guitar positioned between his legs.

I look up from my book, trying to attempt a 'you bother me with your silly questions' look. "Definitely not hilly-billy music."

"Hmm, and my music is hilly-billyish?"

"I guess you could say that." I put my attention back into my book again.

"Don't pay attention to her, Zach. It was beautiful."

"Thanks, Ursula." Zach leaves us alone.

Why does that guy have to get to me? Every single time, he gets to me. Why don't I just sleep with him and get it over with? Obviously, that's what's bothering me. But the question is, would he sleep with me? This whole thing is ridiculous.

Most of the day, Zach and I manage to stay far away from each other till dinner time when I decide to make the meal. That's when things take a turn. For the worse or better—it's hard to say.

"Hey, Cate, one of your cop buddies got suspended for sexual harassment." Zach drops the newspaper he's reading on to the kitchen table, awaiting my acknowledgement.

A cold sweat rises to my skin and I can't turn around.

"They don't have a name. Do you know who it is? What's the story?"

No name. I'm okay. I'll plaster a fake smile to my face and casually turn around. "No," my voice cracks. "This must be new. I haven't heard anything." The butcher knife is clenched tightly in my hand; Zach wrinkles his brow as if he knows I'm lying. I turn back to my cutting and hope I don't lop off a finger.

"Isn't that typical though?"

"What do you mean?" I chop my veggies fiercely as I try not to lose my cool.

"Those guys you work with; such typical womanizing behaviour. I hope he gets what's coming to him."

I swing around, the knife still in my hand. "How can you say that? You don't know the whole story! Maybe it's a female cop. Maybe that cop was tricked into it. You don't know!" My voice wavers, my hand shakes.

"Whoa! Settle down. I was just making a comment." Zach slowly stands, his hands held up defensively.

"You know who's typical? You! You're the typical tax payer that doesn't understand a cop's job!"

"Hey, you're forgetting I was going to be that." Right. He was going to be a cop ages ago.

"That's another thing, what type of person declines a job offer as a police officer?" I slam the knife down on the cutting board, now gaining some control of myself. The conversation is veering away from the newspaper article, which is the intention.

"Not everyone wants to be a cop like you. Okay? I wasn't interested and I didn't need to be part of all the garbage that goes around the office."

"Garbage? What are you talking about?"

He doesn't have time to answer as there is a loud thumping that catches our attention. We run toward the noise and see Nan at the bottom of the stairs, groaning.

"Nan? Oh my god. Are you all right?"

"Ursula, say something."

"Damn stairs. I knew I would slide down them one day. I just didn't think it would hurt this much." Nan tries to get up, but winces and flops back down onto the floor.

"Where does it hurt?" I ask helping her to her feet.

"My arm. I think I broke my arm."

"I'll call an ambulance," Zach picks up the phone.

"No, no ambulance. I'm fine."

"Call an ambulance, Zach. She's not fine. Nan, you need to be checked over." Nan protests some more, but we refuse to give in. She's obviously in excruciating pain as she asks for the bottle of whiskey to dull it.

When the paramedics arrive, they agree that she should be taken to the hospital as her blood pressure is up. Of course, Nan gives them the fight of her life, saying I'm fine, I don't need to go, but they somehow coax her into coming with them. I thought we were going to have to strap her down and force her into the ambulance.

Finally, I climb in the back of the ambulance with Nan, and Zach follows behind in the car. The entire time, I'm blaming myself because Zach and I were arguing and all Nan wanted to do was get us to be friends. Maybe she couldn't concentrate with our bickering and that's why she slipped. A sob catches in my throat. If I wasn't so darn stubborn, maybe we'd be at the cabin right now, enjoying some wine with our meal. Another sob catches. Maybe I should have listened to her. She was trying to tell me something and I didn't listen. Why don't I ever listen? I let out a sob. Nan turns to me.

"Nan, this is all my fault. I'm so sorry."

She looks confused. The paramedic gives her a shot of morphine and continues taking her vitals, readying the oxygen mask over her mouth. She brushes it away with her hand.

"What do you mean this is your fault?"

I bite my cheek. "You were trying to get Zach and me to be civil to one another and we were at each other's throats again. That's why you fell down the stairs. God, I feel absolutely terrible about it." I bury my face in my hands and sob some more.

"Yes, well, what's done is done. You're just going to have to right the wrong."

"What?" I look up.

"You'll have to make amends with Zach, honey. If you do that, then I will feel so much better." She winces, and closes her eyes.

Make amends with Zach? I just wanted to apologize to Nan for being a pain and not heeding her advice to get along with the stupid, good-looking jerk. I don't want to make amends with him. Why can't Zach make amends with me? Why can't Nan have the same conversation with Zach?

Chapter 13
For which of my bad parts didst thou first fall in love with me? — William Shakespeare

The moment we arrive at the hospital, Nan is immediately wheeled into a room while I provide details on what happened. Following that, Zach and I wait, me shifting in a chair, wondering if I should be in the room with Nan, wondering if I should be holding her hand. Aside from the crooked smile Zach gives me from time to time, we don't speak to each other.

Over an hour passes before the doctor, an older female with graying dark hair, approaches us introducing herself as Dr. Kendall.

"You must be Cate, Ursula's granddaughter."

"Yes. What's happening..." Before I can finish, Dr. Kendall turns her attention to Zach. "I didn't catch your name."

"Zach Kennedy." Zach steps forward and shakes her hand. I watch this interaction with disdain, but then remind myself that I'm here for my grandmother.

"Your grandmother is resting comfortably now. We casted her arm, but would like to keep her for observation. Her blood pressure spiked when she took the fall, and it didn't drop until a half hour ago. Because of her age, we want to make sure it's under control."

"Can we see her?" Zach asks. I really wish he wouldn't include himself in my family's life—especially right now.

"Sure. Keep it brief though. You and your wife should go home and get some rest, too."

I'm about to say, I'm not his wife, he's my grandmother's escort, but somehow that doesn't sound right, so I leave it. Zach doesn't say anything either.

We stop in to see Nan, who barely knows we are there. She's high on pain medication and can only slur a few words before dozing off. I kiss her cheek, make sure she's warm enough, and struggle with the decision to sit by her side or go get some rest. The hospital staff ensures that she will be fine and will be in la-la land for awhile.

"Let's go." I cock my head toward the door, Zach nods and we drive home in silence, both of us knowing we are bound to get into an argument considering we're teetering on the edge as it is. When we reach the cabin, I stand out on the deck overlooking the water. The moon is full and glimmering silver through the trees. For some reason, Zach takes a spot beside me, and I wish he would just leave me alone.

"Cate," he begins. "I'm sorry about your grandmother." His eyes are soft, his words sincere.

I suddenly feel a queasiness in my stomach where butterflies flitter about. "Um...thanks, Zach."

He smiles encouragingly, almost like there's going to be hugging or something, but instead, he turns around and walks toward the cabin.

"Zach."

"Yeah?"

"Do you think she'll be okay?"

He smiles one of the most gentle smiles I have ever seen from him. "She'll be fine."

I smile, actually feeling grateful for the first time that Zach is here. He leaves me alone on the deck to sort things out, which is super nice of him, only to return later with a sandwich and hot tea

"I thought you might be hungry, I mean, since we haven't eaten yet."

I take it gratefully because my stomach has finally realized that it's empty. I take a bite into the tuna salad and almost devour it within minutes. "This is great, Zach. Thanks." There's an awkward silence. We've rarely, if ever, been civil to each other.

It's weird.

"It's getting chilly. I'll finish this inside and head to bed." I rise, hoping he won't follow me in. Honestly, this being civil business is too much work. Does this classify as making amends? I'm going to say yes.

"Goodnight." He leans back in his chair.

I finish up and get ready for bed, not really tired to sleep, but not focused enough to read. I'm thinking of Nan and how she's doing; I'm thinking about her blood pressure and her age, and her ability to heal. I'm thinking about what it would feel like to lose her and tears well in my eyes.

I need a hug and Zach is the only one in the same vicinity to offer any sort of support. I beat the pillows and toss and turn, but can't clear my head. I can't get my grandmother out of my brain, nor can I get Zach's smile out of my head.

I throw the covers off and grab the afghan from the chair, wrap it around my shoulders, and tip toe outside. The night is mild with a bit of a breeze in the air. This has turned out to be one of the nicest Octobers in the last few years that I can remember.

I stroll across the grass, the leaves crunching beneath my feet, and I imagine that I'm stepping on reds, browns, and yellows, all mixing together.

I pad out onto the dock, the hollowness of the boards echo beneath my feet, and I stand at the edge, the water lapping gently to the shore.

I glance back at the house, all is quiet. It's surreal out here. No traffic. No noise, just stillness. I look around, throwing the blanket to the side, stripping down to nothing and diving into the water, breaking the mirror image of the moon on the glass-like water. I emerge to the surface and laugh. "Holy shit, that's freezing."

"You'll get used to it," a voice says from somewhere in the dark. I scream as Zach swims out from the shadows.

"You scared the crap out of me." I spy him suspiciously. "Why are you hiding and how much did you see?"

"Only the good parts." The moon catches a glimpse of his mischievous grin as he swims closer.

"Seriously, what did you see?"

"I'm just kidding. You can't see anything out here."

I smirk. "What are you doing out here?"

"I was about to ask you the same thing," he says, holding onto the edge of the dock.

"This is my ritual. I started doing the skinny dip thing when I was about seventeen."

"Seventeen? Hmmm? Who were you with?"

"No one."

"Come on."

I sigh. "Fine, I was with..."

"Not Dan Sherman?"

"No, it was shortly before Dan and I got together. It was a guy named Gianetti DeCarlo, he was a foreign exchange student from Italy."

"And?" Zach presses.

"And, what?"

"You guys did more than skinny dip."

"That's none of your business." I swim away from him, ducking my head under water, and then surfacing.

Zach is grinning. He's closer to me now; so close I'm sure I can reach out and touch him.

"Fine, I lost my virginity to him right over there on the edge of the shore."

Zach chunkles. "Do you still keep in touch with him?"

"Are you kidding? He left for home the next day."

"Young love," he sighs.

"Why are you out here?"

"I like skinny dipping. There's something very erotic about it, don't you think?" He's about a foot away from me; he doesn't look away and I don't back down. "Lots on your mind, hey?" His tone turns serious.

"You could say that."

There is a pause and I want to talk to him about things, but can't bring myself to say the words.

Zach breaks the silence. "You look tired. You should get some sleep."

I eye him warily. "I thought you said you couldn't see anything out here."

Zach clears his throat. "You better get to bed."

The blood rushes through my body and I feel torn between leaving and staying but decide that it was safer in my room. I swim to the dock and turn back. Zach's gazing at me. "Could you...you know..." I motion my hand for him to turn around.

"Oh, sorry." Zach faces away from me and I climb out of the water putting my PJ's back on.

When I finish dressing, I hear Zach climb up the ladder and onto the dock.

"Can I borrow that blanket? I didn't bring anything with me to cover up with."

I hand him the blanket without glancing back. I wait till he's covered, then we both walk back, not saying a word.

What could we say? We're both within touching distance of each other, him naked, and the sexual tension could be cut with a proverbial knife. Saying anything might lead to something that wouldn't be a good idea. Or maybe a good idea at the time, but not the next day. Yes, my desires would be sated, but at what cost? Oh, what am I talking about? I want him and bad.

I stop in front of my room, hesitating to open the door. Zach keeps walking to his room, then says coolly, "If you need me, Cate, I'm right next door," and he disappears inside.

See, it's a bad idea anyway. I can't have sex with him. He's The Escort, my nemesis, the guy that has been a thorn in my side for the past month. Pull it together, Cate.

I toss all night, vaguely remembering having a dream about Zach. He had come into my room through the adjoining bathroom, and leaned over me, his dark hair falling across one of his eyes.

He says, "Do you want me, Cate?"

I manage a yes.

He says, "I want you, too." As he takes his shirt off, he mouths, "Cate, wake up."

"What?"

Again, he mouths, "Cate, wake up."

My eyes flash open. Zach is leaning over me looking a little too serious for my liking.

"Zach?"

"The hospital just called. Your grandmother is asking for you. She's giving them some trouble. They want you to come immediately."

"Okay." I look at the clock. It reads 8 am.

I dress quickly and we immediately leave for the hospital where Nan is refusing to eat or to have her blood taken.

"Nan, why are you giving everyone a hard time?"

"I don't want my blood taken. I just want to go home with you and Zach." She reaches out her good hand for Zach to take.

Dr. Kendall is at the end of the bed, waiting to intervene. "Her blood pressure spiked again. We want to keep her for one more night."

"Can't we take her back to the cabin? If there's a problem, we'll call an ambulance." I rub Nan's arm, giving her an encouraging smile.

"I'd like to say yes, but I don't want to take a chance. Her heart rate is at 100 beats per minute. I'm not comfortable with sending her home when it's that fast. One more night and I'm sure we can release her."

"Ha." Nan says, looking away. "You said that I'd be released today."

"Can I speak to the two of you outside?" The doctor steps outside the door as Nan yells something about 'whatever we have to say we can do it in front of her'. I'm still confused with the doctor including Zach in the decision-making process.

"Your grandmother needs to rest. You need to calm her down. If you don't, she won't get out of here tomorrow. She needs to stay here. If she can relax and give it one more night, I'm sure she'll be well enough to go home."

"I can convince her." I'm not including Zach in this. Zach isn't a part of this to begin with.

"Great. I'll leave you two alone."

Zach's about to go back into the room when I stop him. "Look, Zach, maybe you should stay out here till I have things settled. I mean, she is my grandmother."

Zach eyes up the door to Nan's room, then nods. "Okay."

I leave him in the hallway and take a seat next to Nan. "Nan."

"Cate, you have to get me out of here. I'm going crazy."

"Nan, listen. They want to observe you one more day..." she's about to protest but I cut her off. "One more day. They say if you relax, not get all worked up and do what they want you to do, they'll release you tomorrow."

"Cate, they know nothing. I know I don't need to be here."

"Nan, please. They know what they are doing."

"I can't believe you're supporting them and their quacky ideas," she huffs.

"I just want what's best for you."

"Forget it. Where's Zach? Zach. Zach," she cries out. Zach immediately runs into the room as if he's Pavlov's dog.

"Yes, Ursula?"

"Please get me out of here." Nan begins to rise, but flops back on her pillow.

"Ursula, that's not a good idea. They can take good care of you here. All you need to do is relax and enjoy yourself. Pretend that you're at the spa."

Nan laughs the girlish laugh she only uses around Zach.

"Cate and I will stay with you all day. We'll even run out and get you ice cream or hamburgers or whatever your heart desires. Okay?"

Nan's face relaxes and she smiles. "Okay."

What?! I can't believe she's listening to Zach but not her own granddaughter. "How about I go and get you some magazines, Nan. Maybe some chocolate." I'm already getting up.

"Sure. Thank you, Cate. Zach can stay here with me."

I walk out of the room, the bright hallway stinging my eyes. Now my grandmother has turned on me. It's happened. Zach has manipulated my grandmother.

"Cate, wait," Zach calls out from down the hall.

"Are you happy now that my grandmother chooses you over me?" I snarl, taking a few steps forward, my finger in his face.

"What?"

"You sure know how to brain wash her, don't you?"

"You're talking crazy. I got her to stay in the hospital, didn't I? You should be grateful."

"You know what I'd be grateful for, Zach? If you would just get out of our lives." I storm down the hall to the gift shop. Maybe it's childish, maybe I'm acting like a brat. Maybe I'm not giving Zach a chance. The fact is, my grandmother now likes Zach better than me.

All day, we sit at the hospital, watch Nan sleep, watch Nan eat, play x's and o's, card games, and watch a movie on Zach's laptop. By ten that night, she's asleep, her heart rate and blood pressure under control and she's resting comfortably. Zach and I finally leave the hospital after a long day of smelling ammonia, latex gloves, and prune juice.

I'm tired and ready to take a hot bath and climb into bed, and not have Zach harass me. I really couldn't care less what Zach does from now on.

"So, are you still pissed at me because I stole your grandmother from you?" Zach teases me, barely taking his eyes off the road; his 5 o'clock shadow is prominent in the dark of the vehicle.

"You've brainwashed her somehow. I'll be so glad to see you gone."

"You keep saying that, but I don't know if I believe you. I've grown on you, Cate."

"Yeah, like mold grows on old, stinky cheese."

"Even old, stinky cheese has its purpose."

I have to wonder what that purpose is.

We pull into the driveway of the cabin and walk to the front door, both staring at each other, no one making a move.

"Well, are you going to unlock the door or are we sleeping outside?" Zach inquires.

"I thought you had the key."

"Now, why would I have the key?"

"And, why would I have the key?" I snip back.

"It's your grandmother's place. Why wouldn't you?"

"Yeah, but you were the last to leave."

"No, I wasn't. You were." Zach walks down the deck stairs and around the perimeter of the house. "You should have taken the key since it's your place." He stands on the tips of his toes, pushing at windows as he walks.

"What are you doing?" I follow him.

"I'm trying to find an open window." He reaches up, managing to slightly slide a window, his fingertips grazing the very bottom of it.

"Okay, hop up." He laces his hands together to create a step. I stare at his hands, large, strong, secure.

"I don't trust you. What if you drop me?"

"Will you just get up there!" he grits his teeth. I place one foot on top of his hands and grab hold of the window sill, pushing the window open further, and then punch the screen in. I hoist myself up and stick my head in, my feet dangling.

"And make sure you let me in, okay?" He calls out.

"We'll see," I say.

"Hold it right there."

"Did you say something, Zach?" No answer. "Zach?"

I peer down, my body poised to slide onto the cabin floor.

"Put your hands where I can see them," the tone is firm, not unlike the one I typically use for work. "Okay, little missy, come on down from there." Little missy? Who's he calling little missy? I dangle from my finger tips, and manage to land on my feet to find the local sheriff pointing a gun at Zach and me. "Hands in the air."

"Listen, Sheriff, we were only trying to..." I start, but the sheriff isn't waiting for an explanation.

"Shut it. Both of you, up against the wall." Zach and I do as we are told and we are patted down. I've never been patted down before, except in recruit class.

"Sheriff, if you will let me explain," I try again.

"Quiet!"

"But, this can all be easily..."

"You know what you need, little missy? A mute button. Now shut it!" The sheriff yanks out his cuffs and slaps a pair on me, and puts his extra pair on Zach. "Good thing I was driving by when I noticed you two hovering around the place. Poor Mrs. Chase."

"I'm poor Mrs. Chase's granddaughter," I growl. I mean to turn around, but the sheriff slams me against the house.

"Do you ever shut up?"

"No, she doesn't," Zach mutters.

I throw him a look. "Thanks for the support," I whisper. He shrugs.

The sheriff loads us into the cruiser and fifteen minutes later we're pulling into the local police detachment. Once inside, he books us in, giving me the name of Jane Doe as I had no ID on me, not even my badge. He doesn't believe me when I tell him I'm a sergeant of Riverton Police. He pushes us into the only available jail cell, slamming the door shut.

"My grandmother is in the hospital. If you'd just let me call her."

"Forget it. Now shut up." The sheriff walks away, muttering, "If she's a sergeant, then my mother is the Chief of Police."

I'm ready to throw my shoe at this guy. I've never met someone so frustrating. I turn around to find Zach lying on the cot, his hands behind his head, eyes shut.

"Aren't you going to say anything, Zach?"

"No." Zach's eyes remain closed.

"Why not? Look where we are. We're in a jail cell and this guy is infringing on our rights. Don't you see that? I mean he's ..." I continue to talk, pacing the length of the cell.

"Cate..."

"...and if we don't say anything..."

"Cate..."

"What next? Burning at the stake? Tofu for lunch..."

"Yo', top-cop!"

I stop pacing. "What?"

Zach sits up. "As a cop, you should know that your tactic isn't going to work. The guy is a prick and he's not going to listen to us. Just let it go."

I sigh, resigned. I study the room. There's only one cot and the floor. Sensing my discouragement at the one cot jail cell, Zach pats the seat next to him and I reluctantly take it.

"So, do you think I'm still stealing your grandmother out from under you?" His tone is light considering our situation.

I give him a look. "Never mind, you wouldn't understand."

"Try me."

"Drop it, Zach. If you must talk, talk about something else. Something less controversial."

"Less controversial, hmm? Okay. What's your favourite colour?"

I roll my eyes. "That's the best you can do?"

"You said to talk about something less controversial. Unless you find there's an argument brewing in the topic of your favourite colour."

"Why do you care anyway?" I huff.

"I'm trying, okay. Cut me some slack."

He's definitely trying; I'll give him that much. "Okay, my favourite colour is yellow. What's yours?"

"Black."

"Is that even a colour?"

"Black's a colour, or why would they give it a colour name?"

He raises an inquisitive eyebrow. "What's your middle name?"

"We don't need to get into personal details, okay?" I skirt around the name issue.

"Come on, what's the big deal? It's a middle name."

I purse my lips together. I'm not telling.

"Come on. What is it?" He playfully pushes me with his elbow.

"Ocean," I mumble.

"Come again?"

"Ocean," I say louder.

"Ocean? What the hell?"

"Actually, it's my first name, Ocean Catherine Chase. But I use the name Cate." God, why am I telling him all this stuff?

"Why Ocean?"

"I was conceived near the Indian Ocean. Or so my parents say. They were out doing their crusade and had sex on some beach."

Zach's laughing, but I don't see anything funny in it. "Okay, funny guy, what's your middle name?"

He stops laughing. "I have a name that is very distinguished. A name that has been handed down from generation to generation."

"What is it?"

"Herbert."

"Herbert!" I stick a finger down my throat. "Now I don't feel so bad. Ocean is much better than Herbert."

"I think Herbert has character."

"Isn't that the name of the love bug off that Disney show?"

"It's my father's name."

"Your parents obviously didn't have much imagination."

"Okay, I'm changing the subject," Zach announces. "Favourite ice cream?"

"Easy one. Double Chocolate Fudge." I stare off into space wishing I had a bowl right now.

"Hmm, lacking in the sex department, are we?"

"What do you mean? What does ice cream have to do with sex?"

"Well, your favourite ice cream is double-chocolate-chocolate-fudgey-give-me-more-chocolate-or-else. Everyone knows that chocolate is a replacement for sex. By the longing look on your face, I'd say you've been without for some time now."

"Thank you for that analysis, Sigmund. I'll have you know that I've had lots of sex recently."

"Okay, so maybe you've had sex, but it must not have been too memorable."

I look away because those pewter eyes are burning a hole through me. "Okay, so my mind wasn't blown. And I've had some crappy moments lately. At least I don't get paid for sex."

"I don't get paid for sex," The Escort says.

"What? Yes you do."

"No, I don't. I'm not that type of escort."

"Excuse me? Now there's a type of escort. An escort is an escort, plain and simple. You can't tell me you've never had sex with your clients."

"I haven't."

I hold his eyes; he looks serious.

"Like I said, I'm not that type of escort. Yes, I get paid to accompany women to wherever they need to go, but there's never sex involved. That's part of my contract. It's stipulated specifically. Sure, women have attempted to have sex with me, but I haven't."

"Never?"

"Never." There's no flicker of lying, no wavering of his voice. Either he's a really good liar or he's telling the truth.

"Look, I know you don't believe this, but I'm not into sleeping around. I'd rather have one woman and be with her totally." He gazes into my eyes for a brief second. "So, do you still think I'm manipulating your grandmother so she'll run off with me to some foreign island so I can make mad, passionate love to her whenever I please?"

I laugh.

"Why would you think that?" he asks softly.

"You wouldn't understand." Honestly, I don't want to tell him the truth.

"You'd be amazed at what I can understand. Try me." He's serious. For whatever reason, he really wants to hear details about my life.

"You know, my parents and grandparents and I would come out here every summer. Well, not here to the jail, but you know, to the cabin. We had such a good time. I'd bring Suzanne with me. We'd swim and hike, and whatever else."

"Then, when I turned ten, after my grandfather passed away, my parents decided to embark on their 'Third World-apalooza' tour. Apparently, I was old enough to be apart from them, and they could just drop me off with my grandmother. I suppose they thought with my grandfather gone, Nan might be lonely and we could be lonely together." I convey this with more bitterness than expected.

"They'd come back to visit though," Zach said.

"Once a year, maybe. But Christmases, birthdays, school plays, graduation, they weren't available."

"But Ursula's a great grandmother. I'm sure it wasn't that horrible."

"Fact is, Zach, I have always felt abandoned by my parents. They left me. Just like everyone else does," I whisper, my face now turned the other way. I feel the tears coming on.

"What do you mean, like everyone else does? Who else has left you?"

I swivel around to eyes intense on my face, questioning, like it's absolutely impossible for someone to leave me. "Men."

"Did you ever think that maybe you push them away?"

"What? Oh, now it's my fault."

"No, that's not what I'm saying. But you do have a tendency to be a little... abrasive," he finishes.

"Really? Do you think that's because the guy I was living with screwed his recruit on our bed?"

"Okay, so he cheated on you. Not all men are like that. I mean, I'm not like that." At that point, I can't look at him because I know he's looking at me, and if I glance up into those eyes just once, I might get lost and never come back. Instead, I wish he would just go sit in the corner on the floor.

"Cate, I know you think you have to be tough and defensive. I mean, that's why you choose the men you do. Take Phil for instance..."

"You know nothing about my relationship with Phil or anyone else for that matter," I interrupt, seething.

"I know enough that you chose Phil and that young guy, Ian, because you knew they were safe and you knew that you wouldn't be able to commit to them."

"Now you're starting to sound like Susanne. Why does everyone feel like they have to figure out my life for me?" I bring my knees up and rest my elbows on them, my head in my hands.

"And, for your information, I didn't know Ian was that young. Plus, he told me he loved me."

"That may be, but I could tell by the desperate look in your eyes that you didn't want that relationship with Ian." There's a few seconds pause before Zach continues. "Hey." He places a hand on top of my hand. "I know you need to look like the rock, the one that doesn't crumble under the pressure, and maybe that's why you haven't told anyone that you haven't been at work for a while."

My eyes bulge. "How did you know I haven't been at work?"

"One day, I stopped by the police station with Ursula. Don't worry; she waited in the car while I went in. I asked if you were around and they said that you were going to be away for a while."

I want to throw up at this point.

"I didn't tell your grandmother. I told her you were on a call."
Zach's face softens even more. "I'm not sure why they asked you to
leave, and you don't have to tell me, but I think Nan deserves to
know."

Before I can think through my next set of actions, the words
tumble from my mouth before I can catch them. "I've been accused
of sexual harassment. They put me on suspension." The tears hover
near the edge of my lower lids.

"So, that was you in the paper?"

I nod. I can't look at him because I'm ready to cry and I don't
want him to see me cry. "Go ahead and laugh at me." My eyes raise
to his. That damn tear now trickling down my face. "I'm sure you
were waiting for the moment that I would break, weren't you,
Zach? Well, here's your chance to gloat."

He doesn't say anything, his expression doesn't change and his
eyes aren't cynical but possibly...compassionate? And that's when I
melt, and the tears flow.

Zach immediately wraps his arms around me, pulling me close
and I start blubbering, spilling out things that I haven't told
anyone.

"I don't know what happened. My life wasn't supposed to be
like this. I was supposed to be this great cop, and then have a
family and be in love." I sniff, my nose makes a snort. "How can I
though? I can't even keep a cat, let alone a boyfriend. I'm
commitmentphobic!" I bawl into his chest. He strokes my back, not
saying one word.

"I can't even get laid properly. Either the guy is boring in bed,
an immature 23 year old, or he comes all over my leg." I wipe my
nose on my sweater, my head resting on Zach's shoulder. "I'm not
sure if I want to be a cop anymore. It's not like it used to be. I used
to like doing police work. I have no passion for it now. The only
thing I can think about is opening up my own trendy little
bookstore." Oh, god, where did that come from? My own little
bookstore. I haven't thought about that since I was...really young.
My voice shakes and tears start to subside. I've said it all. Or most
of it. And Zach is still here, rubbing my back. Then again, where
would he go?

"You can still find a committed relationship and you can still get
laid properly. You can also open your own trendy bookstore." He
lifts my chin. "So you're a little bitter. Just become un-bitter."

Something flickers in his eyes and I realize that his mouth is
extremely close to mine. My heart pounds like crazy. But, before I
can move in, he kisses my forehead.

"Are you okay?"

I snap out of it. "Yes, um, thank you, Zach. I really mean that." I give a weak smile and shimmy out of his embrace. I wipe my face and brush back my hair, then look at the cot. "We better get some sleep."

"You take the cot," Zach says, reading my mind. He moves to the corner of the room, ready to make a bed out of the floor.

"No, that's ridiculous. You are not sleeping on the floor. Look, there's lots of room up here. We can sleep on the same cot." I squeeze up against the very back, right up close to the wall, and pat the space beside me where Zach sits. He rubs his neck nervously, which is quite cute. After a few seconds hesitation, he lies down next to me.

"Are you okay back there?"

"Sure, I'm fine. Just trying to get comfy, that's all." I shimmy around, the cold cement wall is extra chilly on my back.

"Why don't you move to the front and I move to the back? You'll have more breathing room. I'm sure I'm crushing you."

I hesitate for effect. I don't want Zach to think I'm really eager to have him spooning me. "Sure."

I scooch forward to the edge of the cot as Zach straddles over me to settle in the back. He nestles in, his body aligning with mine.

"Are you okay?" I ask, that funny feeling now drops into my stomach, like butterflies on speed.

"Yep, cozy. How about yourself?" His breath is in my hair.

"Fine. Thanks." Suddenly, his hands stroke my hair; I shiver.

"I'm just brushing some of your hair away so I don't lay on it."

"Oh, thanks," I manage to say. Silence. "Zach?"

"Mmmm?"

"Thank you for tonight. This has been one of the best nights I've had in a long time." I smile to myself. "In a strange sort of way."

"You're welcome."

How is it possible that this guy that I hate, that I want out of my grandmother's life so badly, is now sharing a cot with me? This person has moved in so easily next to me, fitting nicely against my body. "Zach?"

"Mmm?"

I want to ask him what he thought of me, what he's doing later on when we get out of jail, if he wants to kiss me... if he'd like to pass me a note in gym class...god, I'm pathetic. Instead, I stick to the standard and say, "Goodnight." It takes everything in me not to turn around and kiss him silly. But really, we're in a jail cell. Not the most romantic setting for first times, or second times. Instead, I let sleep take me.

*

"Hey, lovebirds, you've been sprung."

I open my eyes and realize the sheriff has opened the door to the cell and, in that same instance, realize that Zach's arm is around me, pulling me close to him. Zach sheepishly smiles, removing his arm and rising to stretch.

"Turns out you two were telling the truth after all." The sheriff crosses his arms over his chest, leaning on the open cell door; he has no regret on his face.

"I told you." I rub my head. The sleep on the cot hadn't been the greatest. Actually, it was the worst sleep ever. But it certainly doesn't stop me from getting the last word as Zach and I file out of the jail cell. "I could have your badge for this." Well, I don't think I could, but it sounds good anyway.

Zach clears his throat.

"What?"

"Let's get our stuff and go."

With one last glaring look at the sheriff, I grab my personal belongings that were placed on the desk for us and we walk out the doors. At that point, we realize we don't have a car. I guess we aren't done with seeing the sheriff ever again as he gives us a ride back to the cabin.

After Zach boosts me back through the window, seeing as we still didn't have a key, we get to work packing our things in silence. It's a bit weird now since we've gotten along so well in the jail cell. What next? Are we on unfamiliar territory and have no idea how to treat one another? Sure, there's a moment in the bathroom as we pack up our toiletries, and he asks me what I think of the new flavor of toothpaste noticing that I have in my bag. I say I like it and he can try some of mine if he wants. He says maybe later and that's it. Honestly, I have no idea what to say to him now. Last night was great. I revealed a lot more to him than I normally would have to any other man.

On the other hand, he's my grandmother's escort. I feel good about everything that happened last night. But now—now we're talking about toothpaste. Maybe I am the blubbering fool who can't get her shit together and needs to seek psychological help. He did say that I am abrasive.

It all comes down to the fact that I like him—really like him, and I have no idea what to do. Quite possibly, this is the first time in my life that I feel out of control.

*

Nan's colour has come back in her cheeks, and she looks like she's back on the mend. She rests in the back seat of the car as Zach drives us home.

This morning, Nan escaped her hospital room to give us a call at the cabin to come and get her. But, when we didn't answer, she got worried and called the sheriff's office inquiring about traffic accidents. Well, low and behold (those were her words), the two delinquents she was looking for were right in his jail cell.

Apparently, Nan tore a strip off of the sheriff. He apologized profusely to "Mrs. Chase", but not to us. Nan was quite surprised by the sheriff's actions considering he had just arrived to the small town after his big city training.

"He's just like you were when you started, Cate." Nan yawns from the back seat.

"I thought I was still like that?" I tease. Zach raises his eyebrows. "Yes, Zach, I can laugh at myself every now and then."

"At least you're in control of yourself. I'm sure he'd shoot himself in the foot if things got carried away, like someone jaywalking," Nan snorts. She rests her head again, content with just relaxing. This is the perfect time for me to talk to Zach, reacquaint myself with him and show him that I have more substance than that of the cry baby in the jail cell; I know I can talk to him about more important things than toothpaste. After all, we did have a moment in the cells where we were cuddling and stroking hair and kissing foreheads. That counts for something, doesn't it?

"Boy, my back is killing me. That cot really did a number on it." That was slightly forced—perhaps a little too scripted. I'm trying to lead the conversation back to the jail. Maybe he'll then be reminded that we were sleeping in the same bed.

"Hmm, not the best." And that's it—conversation over. My plan to talk about the cot and jail incident is quickly kyboshed. No reminiscing of old times when we laughed and cried; how we learned about each other's favourite colours and how I told him my real name—all of it quickly fell to the wayside. Maybe I should have started with the toothpaste conversation.

"So, I have this new toothpaste that you should try." Oh my god, did I really just say that?

"Uh, sure." Zach shifts in his seat.

What's wrong with me?

Back home, I help Nan get settled in her room, and remind her that the doctor wants her to rest so she can heal quicker. This won't stop her, not with the Halloween party coming up. There's no way she's backing down on this one.

I'm staying the night at Nan's till the nurse I hired comes to stay the next day.

I have Annie cook a nice meal for the three of us, letting Nan join us in the dining room only if she is good and gets the rest she needs—at least she's listening to me.

"Well, it's nice to see you two so cordial to each other. Looks like my plan worked," Nan sips her coffee as we sit in the living room.

Zach meets my gaze and we smile. It's kind of nice to be on an even keel, although chatting casually is not coming easy. If it's any consolation, I'm more relaxed now than ever and enjoying the decadence of the moment. I'm also happy to report that the subject of toothpaste has not been brought up once since the car ride home.

Zach has asked me to play chess, something that I haven't done since my grandfather was alive.

"You and your grandfather would play that game for hours." Nan smiles.

"I remember. He taught me all his little tricks for playing chess."

"Hmm, sounds like I might get my ass kicked." Zach doesn't look up when he says this; instead he continues to set up the chess pieces.

"Quite possibly," I murmur. We are sitting at the chess table that my grandfather and I would sit at, and I'm quite content with Zach sharing that memory with me.

A few minutes into the game, Nan rises. "Well, I'm going to head up to bed. You two can stay up as late as you like."

I immediately stand. "I'll help you up the stairs, Nan."

She waves me off. "I'm fine. You keep playing your game."

"I'm seeing you all the way to your room, so don't argue with me." I'm stern; she's not messing with me on this issue.

"Fine, if it'll make you happy. Good night, Zach."

"Good night, Ursula," Zach waves.

"And I'll know if you moved any chess pieces," I tease.

He winks my way and a fluttering happens in my chest. Are we flirting? I think this is flirting.

I help Nan into her nighty, get her some painkillers and water, and tell her to call me if she needs anything. By the time I return, Zach has changed positions—he's now sitting on the floor in front of the fireplace, the chess board lying before him, jazz is softly playing in the background. He flashes me a slanted smile.

"I thought it'd be nicer down by the fire. I poured you some wine." He points to the two glasses sitting on the fireplace hearth, then continues, "And I made sure not to mess up our game."

I take a seat across from him and sip my wine. Hmmm, this is starting to be a very nice evening.

"Okay, whose turn is it?" I ask.

"Yours." I move my chess piece and watch Zach ponder over his next move. There's more silence, which I'm getting tired of. It's time to venture into new territory...or something like that.

"So, Zach, are you always going to be an escort?" I'm not provoking an argument; I'm just curious where his future lies.

He studies me for a few seconds, testing the legitimacy of the question, and then he speaks. "Actually, I've always liked playing and creating music. Remember? You heard me play my 'hillbilly' music at the cabin." He tilts his head in a mocking way.

My cheeks grow scarlet. "I did say that, didn't I?" I clear my throat and take a sip of wine. He's still waiting for me to say something. "I guess this would be a good time to come clean. It wasn't hillbillyish. It was... beautiful. Really. I was mesmerized by it." My eyes meet his.

"I'm glad you liked it." He focuses his attention back on the chess game and makes a move. Not thinking too clearly, my next move costs me the game.

"Checkmate," he declares, knocking my king over.

"Shit, I didn't see that coming. Another game?"

He licks his lips. "Uh, you know what?"

"What?" My heart sinks. He's going to bed and that's the end of the night. I'll have to resort to borrowing sugar and hammers and soap and toothpaste just to talk to him.

"Let's go get something to eat from the kitchen." He quickly stands up. Holding his hands out for me to take, he pulls me up. He grabs our wine and walks with me to the kitchen.

"What shall we have tonight?" Zach opens the cupboards while I look in the fridge.

"Pickles," I say.

"They'll pair well with these Pop Tarts in the cupboard." Zach places the box on the counter next to the pickles. "Isn't there left over chicken?" He grabs the container of roast chicken from the fridge. "I love cold chicken."

"Do you cook?" I put some pop tarts in the toaster.

"I do like to dabble." Zach takes a bite of some chicken.

"What do your parents do?" I don't even know if Zach has parents. Maybe he's an orphan or something. I manhandle the hot Pop tarts and place one on his plate.

"My mom was a teacher, my dad was a cop."

I stare at him blankly. "Your dad was a cop? I didn't know that. He was a cop here in town?"

"Yep. Both my parents retired not too long ago, decided to become ranchers." Zach grabs the Pop Tart and bites into it.

"Is that why you wanted to be a cop?" I nibble on some chicken and a Pop Tart at the same time.

"Yep. Thought I'd follow in dad and granddad's footsteps." He shrugs. "Then I saw how stressed my dad was getting. Decided it wasn't worth it." I stare down at my Pop Tart, picking off the pink sprinkles and nibbling on those. "So what about this trendy little bookstore?"

"Huh?" I'm caught off guard.

"You mentioned while we did prison-time that you wanted to open your own bookstore. Are you going to do it?"

I wipe my hands on the napkin and think for a second. "I think I was just overly emotional last night and saying shit I didn't mean. I really don't know where that came from." I shoot my glass of wine back.

"Sometimes, in the heat of the moment, we say things that are absolutely true."

I nod. "There was one time, a long time ago, where I thought I'd open a bookstore. That and be a cop. The cop-thing won."

It's now my turn. "So, this musician thing, when did you know you wanted to be one?"

"I've always loved it. And I don't think it's a state of being, where you decide one day to be one. You just somehow merge into it."

"Do you have any songs or CDs or is it for fun?"

He doesn't say anything for a moment. "I guess you could say it feeds my soul."

There's silence again as we each finish up a Pop Tart. I clear my throat. "I've had a great time with you in the last few days, Zach."

He looks staggered, then recovers, nodding, "Me too. It's the most fun I'd expect to have a in a jail cell."

I softly laugh. "So, um, what are you doing tomorrow?" I down the rest of my food and suddenly feel full. I refuse to look at him because he'll know I'm asking him out, or maybe he'll just assume it and then he'll say no and I'll have to back pedal and explain that I'm only curious and making conversation and he shouldn't read into things—when really, I'm asking him out.

"I'm free tomorrow night. If you want to do something..." How does he do that? How does he manage to sound so casual?

"Sure, uh, what do you want to do?"

"A movie or something? I'll pick you up around 7:30."

"Great," I smile.

We stand a few feet from each other, feeling a little nervous. Zach and I are going on a date. Or, I think it's a date. We haven't clarified that part yet. Maybe it's just friends.

"I'll clean things up in here before I go to bed." I busy myself with the mess.

"I'll clean it up, you go on up to bed." Zach takes the plates from my hands and there's more silence, the silence where you have no idea what's going to happen next. And, just when I think he's going to kiss me, he turns away, placing the dishes in the sink.

"Okay. Night." I wipe my hands on my jeans, hesitate an extra moment, then walk out of the room as I hear Zach continue with dish duty.

Chapter 14
Some Cupid kills with arrows, some with traps.
— William Shakespeare

"Dave?"

"Cate?"

"Is Susanne around?"

"No, she went to yoga."

I sigh. "Shit. I needed her help."

"Maybe I can help you?"

"Doubt it. Not unless you can tell me what to wear on my date tonight."

"Oh. A date? Who is the lucky guy?" I can almost hear the 'boom chik a wa wa' in his voice.

"Oh, just a guy. You don't know him. Actually, I don't even know if it's a date. I mean, the word date didn't enter into the conversation. But we agreed to go out somewhere—but I guess I should have asked where we were going because I now have no idea what to wear." I'm nervous. I'm nervous and talking too much.

"Let's see. You want to be appealing but not come off as presumptuous. Seductive but casual."

Pause. "Am I really talking to Dave?"

"Cate, I can be very perceptive and in touch with a woman's needs. Just ask Susanne."

Susanne has never mentioned Dave's feminine side to me. I'm still convinced there was an alien abduction. "Okay, lay it on me. What kind of advice can you give me?" I'm reluctant but still willing to hear him out.

"Since we don't know where you're going, we'll have to assume that it'll be something middle of the road. Movie. Coffee. Something like that."

"He did say something about a movie."

"Perfect. Something casual, like jeans. But, just in case it's a little more upscale, wear a nice top. Something sexy, but not too sexy. What do you have?"

Hmmm. I tap my chin. "Oh, wait," I pull open the closet doors. "I have a very low-cut top and it's black with some pink in it."

"Go with that."

"Are you sure? Maybe I should wait till Susanne comes back."

"I'm telling you, Cate, the quickest way to a man's heart is by wearing low-cut clothing."

"Davvveee."

"Hey, is this the guy Susanne said is your grandmother's escort?"

I pause. Damn it, Susanne. "Umm, yes. It is."

Dave snorts. "I'm sure you'll have a good time."

"He's not that type of escort, if that's what you're insinuating." I have now officially lost it. I'm defending The Escort.

"Okay, just remember to wear low-cut. Low-cut is your best friend."

"Thanks, Dave...I think." I hang up and stare mystified at my clothes in the closet.

Low-cut is my best friend. Unbelievable. I grab the black turtle neck from the shelf, jeans from the hanger and pair them with semi-heeled black boots. I look good, still sexy, but casual enough to not insinuate this is a date in case he doesn't think it's a date.

Right at 7:30, the doorbell rings. He's punctual, I'll give him that. I do a quick check in the mirror before pulling open the door to Zach who looks amazing. He's wearing jeans, and a leather jacket. I'm relieved he isn't wearing a tux.

"Hi." He smiles. "You look nice."

"Thanks, so do you." I grab my leather jacket and slide it on.

"So, where are we going?"

"It's a surprise."

"Are you going to tell me about it in the car? A hint at least?" I lock the door and step down from the porch.

"In the car? No, not exactly."

"I'm not one for surprises. Kind of throws me off my game." Before I take another step, I realize there's a motorbike in my driveway. Zach's grinning. "This is yours, obviously."

"I thought it would be fun to ride around on the bike for bit. Are you okay with that?" Zach hands me a helmet and puts his on.

"Um, yeah. Absolutely." Zach hops on and revs up the bike, smiling the whole time. I straddle the seat, really unsure of what to do next. Do I hang on to him or to the back of the seat? Where do I put my hands?

"Hang on," Zach calls back. I wrap my arms around his waist and suddenly feel completely secure. I want to lay my head on his back, cuddle right up, and maybe close my eyes, but the constant nagging in my head tells me that this is not a date.

We ride out into the country, the sun now setting behind the trees, the road slightly deserted, the wind whistling in my ears and I realize how intimate this moment with Zach is. Just the two of us, on a bike, as close as close can be; not talking, just... being.

After what I assess to be an hour of driving—I'm not sure how long it's been as this single lane highway as the tall pine trees lining our path give nothing away—the trees suddenly break and we come upon a small diner. It looks strange out here in the middle of what seems like nowhere. It sticks out amongst the solitude of nature with its glimmering lights against the dark sky. It's quaint, for lack of a better word.

Zach points to the parking lot and I nod as he veers to the right and pulls in. He kills the engine, takes off his helmet and glances at me. "You all right?"

"Yep. I'm great. Why, do I look out of sorts?" Did my makeup smear? Did a bug fly in my teeth? What?

"Nope. You still look beautiful."

My heart beats just a little quicker.

"You want to have a bite or a coffee or something?"

I pull the helmet from my head, and try to fluff up the curls. I really hope I don't have helmet head. "Sure."

There are a few diners inside the restaurant, all of which stare at us as we walk in. Three truckers sit separately at the counter, one stool apart, not making any friends, not chatting to anyone. A young red headed woman in a pink crop top wearing white apron over her faded jeans stands behind the counter pouring them coffee. In the corner, smoke billows up in the air where two people are huddled in deep conversation.

"Take a seat anywhere. I'll be with you in a minute," The waitress calls out.

Zach points to a nearby booth and we slide in, the red vinyl is tattered and has seen better days. The waitress is quickly at our table pouring us coffee and handing us menus.

"What do you recommend?" Zach asks. "The gum at the checkout. It's the only thing the cook hasn't made." She flashes us a smile and walks off. Zach and I stifle a laugh.

"We can share a plate of nachos," Zach suggests.

"Maybe we should have something separate—you know, in case one of us gets food poisoning, the other can still drive."

Zach grins at me. "You can be quite funny when you're relaxed."

"Oh, you know, I'm one of those closet comedians," I say humbly.

"So, sweetie, what'll you have." The waitress is back and ready to take our orders. She's calling me sweetie and I'm certain I'm older than she is.

"I think I'll have a slice of your peach pie." I close the menu and wait for Zach.

"And, you, good lookin'?"

"Hmm, pie, hey? I'll have the Boston Cream." Then looks at me. "We can share."

"What a brilliant idea." The waitress grabs the menus, leaving us alone.

Aside from being in a greasy spoon and a waitress who could give a shit about her job, which I really can't blame her for, I'm having a really nice time. I still have no idea how Zach feels, but I know I like him. However, I'm not willing to let that information slip out till he says something first.

"So, what are you going to do about work?" Zach digs into his pie that the waitress slid in front him.

I stop. My job. What am I going to do about it? I am as clueless as I was when this whole thing started. "I'm not sure. And I absolutely hate the fact that I'm not sure." I pick at my pie crust and sigh a little too loudly. When I look at Zach, he's studying my face, waiting for a better reply. "You know, I don't know what I'd do with myself if I wasn't a cop. Being a cop is the only thing I've ever known." More pick, pick, picking at the pie crust.

"I guess you could say I'm at a crossroads."

"Didn't you mention something about opening a bookstore? What about that?" There was something endearing about the way he said those words.

"Bookstore. Right. That's more of a dream. Sounds like fun. Doesn't it?" I shove a piece of pie into my mouth. "I'm romanticizing it."

"Nothin' wrong with a little romance." He winks and my face turns a shade of crimson.

"You know what. Let's not talk about my career right now. I'm having a great time and don't want to ruin things."

Zach nods and clears his throat, shifting in his seat. "Um, but before we leave this conversation behind...so....is Dan Sherman still your lawyer?"

I nod my head. "Yes."

"Just a lawyer..." Zach trails off. Now he's the one picking at his pie.

I suddenly get his meaning. "Yes, just a lawyer. Dan and I dated ages ago and seeing him again made me curious about him and...well, us. I guess I wanted to see if there was a chance of rekindling something."

"And, is there?" He twirls the fork between his fingers waiting for my answer.

"No. Definitely not." I make this last point very clear. Zach nods and smiles and continues to eat his pie.

We share a nibble or two of each other's pie, drink our very strong coffee and talk about Zach's work. He has many interesting stories to tell about his escort service, which, amazingly, doesn't bug me too much. He's had women try to marry him and octogenarians try to sleep with him. I can see what the enticing part of being an escort. He goes to interesting places, meets interesting people and has new experiences while being paid for it.

"That's why I do it. It's just fun."

I play with the remnants of my pie with my fork. "So, you wouldn't give it up for anyone, then?" Now I'm dancing around words.

"It depends who that person is." I stop what I'm doing and shift in my seat before glancing up. Zach smiles sheepishly. "Ready to go?" I nod and we head to the till.

"So where are you two goin'?" The waitress punches in the bill.

"No idea," I shake my head. "He's in control of the date...I mean, evening," I correct myself quickly. "He's in control of the evening." I repeat. I said 'date'. I didn't mean to say it, now Zach's going to get all funny on me, thinking I thought this was a date when he was thinking this was just an outing. Then he'll think I want something more...and I do, but he doesn't need to know that.

"You could say it's a date full of mystery," Zach tells her, paying for the pie and coffees.

"You two enjoy yourselves. And here, this is for later. On the house." She slides a package of mints toward us and winks.

"Thanks." Zach pockets the mints and we leave, the whole time my brain is thinking 'date'!

"Where to now?" I put the helmet on, now comfortable with wrapping my arms around Zach.

"I have an idea."

"What is it?" I yell over the roar of the engine.

"Hang on." And I do.

*

We ride down a dark stretch of road amongst a dense forest; the asphalt stretches out before us on an incline and the only light is the moon, still full and plump and bright. It's so still out here, so serene and I'm so relaxed. Is it possible to fall asleep on a bike cruising down the open road? I place my head on Zach's back for a few brief minutes till we pull into a private, well-treed road. At the end of the road is a house, lights brightly shining, absolutely welcoming us to its front door. Pulling in closer, I notice the ranch house has a huge deck out front that winds around to the back. A dog, a medium sized Heinz 57 type, runs out to welcome us, barking and sprinting alongside, only stopping when the engine is killed.

"Hello, Fletcher," Zach pats the dog's head. Fletcher pants, licks his chops and runs up the porch where two people are walking onto the deck.

"Zach?" I question. He grins widely, or maybe wildly, and hops off the bike as soon as I do. I pull the helmet from my head and try desperately to make my hair look half decent; it's a lost cause.

"Zach, what a surprise." The woman hugs him, then he hugs the man. "What are you doing out this way?"

"We were just taking a drive." Zach nods at me and the couple smile. "Thought we'd stop in."

"Wonderful," the woman says.

Is anyone going to fill me in on what's happening?

"Mom, Dad, this is Cate Chase. Cate these are my parents, Vivian and Herbert Kennedy."

Parents? What? Parents! I step forward to shake their hands; instead Vivian wraps her arms around me, holding me tight.

"Oh, Cate, nice to finally meet you. Zach has told us all about his client and her granddaughter." Herbert does the same thing, only kissing my cheek. The whole time I'm feeling the love, my brain is racing on why Zach is introducing me to his parents and why they said they were finally glad to meet me. What has The Escort been saying?

"Do you two want tea? Or something stronger? We have wine, beer." Vivian lists off drinks before she even has us in the house.

"Tea's fine," I say, feeling Zach's hand on my back.

Vivian and Herbert strike me as two very genuine people—friendly and accommodating to anyone. Vivian has the total mom-look down pat, with the short dyed chestnut brown hair and the loose fitting jeans and top. Her large round glasses fit easily on her round face, while her gold chunky earrings look out of place in the ranch type setting. Herbert is completely gray, with a moustache that he must have grown when he entered the police force. He has his bi-focals propped on the end of his nose, which he promptly removes when we get inside.

The living room is cozy and inviting, a rustic house with comfy chairs, wood mantel fireplace and log cabin feel. There are family pictures and school pictures hanging on the wall. Zach looks pretty much the same as he did then, except for the platinum blonde hair that he said his ex-girlfriend dyed one night just to see what it would look like. He was about sixteen then.

The moment Vivian and Herbert head to the kitchen for drinks, I turn to Zach. "Your parents?"

"Yep, those are my parents."

"No, what I mean is, you're introducing me to your parents?" Before Zach can answer, Vivian and Herbert return with a tray of tea and cookies. They scatter around for a few seconds, pouring out tea and asking about cream and sugars before sitting down.

"What were you two up to?" Herbert asks.

"Just going for a ride. Stopped at the diner. Had some pie. Teaching Cate the fine points of being spontaneous."

Now, why did he say that? "Your son thinks I should relax a bit more."

"Cate's a cop." Zach places a hand on the back of my neck and tickles; I'd purr except for the fact that I've just been introduced to Zach's parents, which, by the way, I'm still stunned about.

"Oh, that's right. Zach had mentioned that before. I'm sure Zach told you he wanted to be a police officer once, but decided he could make more money in the companion consulting business," Herbert nods at his son.

"Companion consulting? Is that the politically correct term for it?" I throw Zach a mocking look.

"Cate had some issues when I became her grandmother's companion. But she's accepting it now."

Is he being patronizing? He sounds patronizing.

"I assure you, Cate, Zach's intentions are always honourable."

"Mmm hmm." Did Zach set this whole scenario up thinking I'd be in agreement to what he does? What a load of crap. Maybe he's just trying to win me over and manipulate me into bed with him. I'm not about to be manipulated—I'll still sleep with him, but I'm not willing to be manipulated. "So, Herbert, I understand you were a police officer." I sip my tea, shifting away from Zach, whose knee is slightly touching mine, now totally aware he's manipulating me.

"Yes, let's see...for about 25 years. Had to give it up when I began having heart problems. The stress was getting to me."

"What area were you in?"

"I managed to make my way through all the districts, eventually ending up in the Homicide unit for a bit. When I left, I had been deputy chief for a few years."

Deputy Chief. Zach didn't mention any of this. We discuss more police related topics till Zach's mom says, "Herb, she didn't come here to talk about police work the entire night. The kids are on a date. Let them be."

I blush and down my tea. Mom's a sweetheart, too bad her son is a manipulator.

"Why don't we go sit on the deck for bit? Look at the stars. You'll never see stars like this in the city." Zach grasps my elbow, but I casually pull away as I stand.

He leads me out the back way to the patio where everything is dark, except for some Christmas lights hanging around the railing that Vivian turned on as we made our way out the door. Other than that, it's very secluded and very quiet.

Zach sits down while I lean back on the railing facing him. "Were you patronizing me in there?"

He looks surprised. "Patronizing? No. Why would you think that?"

"It just sounded like you were." It's silent for a few moments.

"Did you plan this out, Zach? Bringing me to your parent's place. Showing off that your parents think what you do is acceptable. Calling yourself a companion consultant. Really? What's that all about?"

Zach stands next to me. "Honestly, it wasn't planned. I realized at the diner that we were close by and thought it would be nice to come out here." Zach moves closer, he doesn't touch me but I can feel the heat from him.

I edge away. No, this isn't convincing enough for me. I feel something's up. Maybe I'm being overly sensitive, or maybe the whole cop sensors are kicking in, but I'm extremely confused and I don't like being confused. "Maybe we should go," I suggest, walking toward the door.

"You're feeling insecure again, aren't you?" Zach says from the railing.

"What are you talking about?" I thunder toward him, now only a foot away.

"Like I said, you only dated Phil and Ian because they were safe. You'll only get involved if it means you're in control. Right now, you feel completely out of control."

I narrow my eyes at him. "You're ridiculous, you know that."

Zach grabs my arms and squarely faces me. His voice is soft and low, but alluring. "I like you. I've liked you for a long time now. And...I'm going to shut up and kiss you and I'm really hoping you won't slap me."

My head is starting to pound and I want to melt and crawl away into a small hole at the same time. Zach brushes my hair aside and leans in for a brief, soft kiss, my lips obey, and I'm floating somewhere around the moon and stars.

He pulls away for a second. "Again?"

I nod because I really can't say anything at this point. Zach presses his lips against mine for a second time, lingering there a few seconds longer, pulling me into him a little. There's something so different, so real and so...loving about the kiss, I feel completely lost.

When he pulls away, I am unable to speak when he asks me if I'm ready to go.

He takes my hand, leading me inside to say goodbye to his parents, which is all a complete blur.

I believe his parents hugged me, told me to come again, but I couldn't say for sure because I was lost somewhere in the memory of that kiss.

The entire drive home, I'm thinking of the kisses, of how much I want to invite him into my house, how I've never ever felt tingling in my toes like that before.

At midnight, we roll into my driveway and both dismount, taking our helmets off, standing around, feeling awkward.

"I had a nice time, Cate, and I hope you don't think that what happened tonight was all orchestrated. It really wasn't." I nod. I trace the top of the helmet with my finger. "The last thing I want is a bunch of misunderstandings between us."

I nod some more and move in closer to him. "So, do you want to come in?"

He takes a half-step back, scratching his head. "I'd love to, but I don't think I will."

"Huh?" No one's ever said that before.

"Let's call it a night, okay?" He takes my hand.

"A night?" Why the hell doesn't he want to come in? "Sure, I-I guess. So...um... good night then." As I step away from the bike, confused by what has happened, I realize I'm still holding onto the helmet. I spin around to hand it to him and Zach leans in and kisses me again, moving in closer till his body is pressed against mine, our lips connecting easily. It's another brief kiss, but it's not enough.

"Come in," I whisper.

"I have to go." He plants one last kiss on me before getting on his bike. "I'll call you tomorrow."

I wave, still all fuzzy warm from the kisses, but still wondering why he didn't come in. I walk to my front door replaying the night, replaying the kisses, replaying meeting his parents, replaying what he said on his parent's deck; I suddenly realize I'm having a panic attack.

Chapter 15
Over-analyzing is like drinking the poisoned Kool-Aid.

My sleep is restless as I over-think my date with Zach, my feelings for him and how everything is so confusing and bunched up into one huge emotional ball. Yes, I like him. I've established that already. But he took me to his parents. They knew all about me before we got there. I didn't even know Zach had parents until just a few days ago. I mean, I always thought he was the Devil's Spawn since coming into my grandmother's life. Sure, that changed, but I seriously thought he was just one of those people.

Let's go back to the whole kissing thing again. He kissed me, and I really, really like him. More than I've liked anyone before. And he likes me too. And he didn't come in last night. There's only one reason for all of this—he's manipulating me. Why else would he take me to his parents on date numero uno?

Zach calls me later the next afternoon—of course I screen the call. He leaves a message telling me he had a nice time and to give him a call, maybe we could do something later. I don't return his phone call. Instead, I make plans with Susanne for later that evening. I need therapy.

*

The Black Duck has now become my favourite place to go. The dirty glasses have become less dirty looking and Earl the bartender seems to polish them up a little bit when he sees Susanne walk through the door. Susanne and I have warmed up to all the regulars there and I'm surprised she still comes with me— definitely a true friend.

Cindy, the ex-con, has now become my new best friend as past difficulties are forgotten and we forge a new, closer and supportive relationship. Alright, the last part isn't really true, but Cindy does show up with every intention of not hiding her face anymore. She knows I'm around, and I know she's there.

Even the lumberjacks buy us a drink now and then, but they refuse to come near our table. No, I still scare them.

"Dave said you went on a date last night with The Escort." She raises her eyebrows. "I knew it. I knew you'd get together."

"Susanne, we aren't together. We're not even in the vicinity of one another. He's just...a guy. And really, after last night, I don't know if I like him that much." I sip my beer, see that the bartender has cleaned the glass just for me, and give him a cheers from across the room.

Susanne eyes me suspiciously. "You're falling in love with him."

My eyes widen. "No, I'm not. The guy absolutely annoyed me last night."

"Even if he annoys you, you're still falling for him!"

I exchange fierce looks with her. "Susanne, that's impossible. The guy is an escort. He reeks of machismo and ..and... hangs out with prostitutes. I'm a cop. This obviously is not a compatible match. I don't know what I was thinking going out with him last night."

"So, what happened? How did this all start? You obviously have something to talk about or you wouldn't have met me here at our new dive." It's true, when I have something I need to get off my chest, The Black Duck seems to be the place to go. Well, the last couple of times it's been the place to go.

I shrug. "Nan forced us to come with her to the cabin."

"And?" She leans forward, waiting for the punch line.

"And, we went skinny dipping." I put my hands over my eyes, hoping to make it all go away.

"You what?"

"Well, it wasn't planned. I went out there for a moonlit walk and decided to go for a dip, and discovered he was in there already."

"Did you sleep with him?" she says easily.

"No, of course not. But he might have seen me naked. And he was swimming really close to me and I, oh god...." I pause realizing how much has transpired in the last few days.

"Okay, so that's it?"

"No. We made a trip to the local police cells."

She leans in, eyes wide.

"It was a mix up, but we ended up sleeping on the same cot. Well, in my defense there was only one cot. But I cried in front of him. I was a blubbering mess. I was talking about how I was suspended, how my exes cheated on me and how my parents have abandoned me." I downed my beer and motioned for Earl to send me another.

"And?"

"And he was really sweet, and held me and let me cry." I scratch my head nervously." The beer arrives and I take a long sip.

"And? Come on. Stop stalling!"

"When we got back to Nan's place, we had this really nice night of chess and Pop Tarts, and I thought we were bonding and I thought he was going to kiss me, but he didn't."

"Cate! Does this story ever end? What happened last night? Tell me what happened last night." She says as she watches me take another swig of my beer.

"Last night, we took a ride on his bike. Drove through the countryside, had pie at a seedy diner and laughed. It was probably the best date I've been on." I close my eyes for a few seconds.

"So, what's the big deal?"

"The big deal is he took me to meet his parents. And it was corny and I'm sure it was planned. And it was bogus, and he's a manipulator, and then he kissed me and told me he likes me." I notice that I am almost done this beer and wave to Earl for another. Earl nods as if we've forged a wordless relationship based on wants and needs.

"Did you sleep with him?"

"Susanne! No! He wouldn't come in. He didn't say why, he just said no." I shift in my seat uneasily.

"Okay, so what's the big deal?"

"It just is."

"To me, it sounds like you're in love."

"What? The guy is a fake. He's trying to prove to me that his business relationship with Nan is on the up and up. He's trying to manipulate me…I'm not in love."

"I'd say you are. So what? He took you to his parent's place without you knowing first. Maybe he did plan that part, but shouldn't you feel flattered? He's obviously into you. Why are you making a big deal of this?"

I shrug and wonder when the waitress is bringing my next beer.

Susanne takes a sip of her drink. "I know exactly what your problem is, Cate."

I give her a dirty look. "What?"

"You're commitmentphobic."

"I'm not commitmentphobic. The guy is an escort. He's a manipulator, a-a womanizer. He and I have no future together. It's ridiculous." I thank the waitress for the beer, and take a large sip. I feel a little woozy as I try to remember how many I've had. Three? Four? Did I arrive here before Susanne and start without her? Shit, I can't remember. All I know is things seem a little jiggly.

"I better take you home." Susanne stands to help me up.

"Do I love him, Susanne?" I peer bleary eyed into her brown eyes.

"I'd say you're teetering on the edge. Come on."

I stop for a few seconds, looking around the bar. "You know what? I'll take a taxi. You live on the other side of the city. Look, there's a taxi right here."

Susanne knows something is amiss. She doesn't have to say anything, but I know she suspects that I'm about to do something crazy. And she has a right to.

I'm not heading home.

*

The cab drops me off at 1130; I pay the driver and go around back to the guesthouse. In my split second decision making at the bar, I had decided to tell Zach all of it—my thoughts, feelings—everything. Part of me, the slightly sober part, is wondering what the hell I'm doing here. You're telling him how you feel, you idiot. But what am I going to tell him? I'm torn between telling him I'm in love with him and telling him he's a phony-baloney-manipulator-boxer-short-wearing escort.

I walk around the side of the house, stepping carefully through the dark; tree branches hit me in the face, large rocks stub my toes, till I finally stumble onto the patio area. The guesthouse has a light on outside and one light glowing inside—he's possibly up.

I stagger to the door, and knock, adjusting myself, patting down my hair, trying to look sober and business-like. A few seconds later, the door opens and Zach has no shirt on and a pair of jeans. He looks amazing. Oh, god. I can't do this. I almost turn and run, but I know that's ridiculous.

His face brightens. "Cate! I didn't expect you this late." He takes a look closer. "Are you okay?"

"Fine. I have something to tell you; I won't take long." I try to confidently walk in the door but instead stumble over the threshold where Zach catches me.

"I'll get you some water or something."

"No, no. I'm fine. I won't be long." I hiccup again, coming into the living room of the guest house and lean up against the couch—it stops the room from swaying.

Zach waits for me to say something, but all I can do is hiccup.

"I'll get you some water." He leaves me for a minute, returning with a large glass and hands it to me. I drink it back, a little too fast, and burp.

"Last night!" I blurt out. He stares at me confused. "You're phony-baloney, mister. Don't know what you're tryin' to do to me but I ain't falling for it." Looks like I opted for the phony-baloney speech. I didn't see that one coming. "Maybe you think maniplatin' me is a shadistic way off yours of seekin' pleasser." Hey, my words are slurring together!

"Cate? What are you talking about? I'm not manipulating you. I just want to get to know you. I like you. Why do you think I introduced you to my parents?"

"Two words." I hold up what I think is two fingers.

"Grandmother." Yes, that's only one word and I think I have three fingers in front of my face.

"What does your grandmother have to do with any of this?"

"You want to get on my goosside."

He sighs. "Not everyone has a hidden agenda like you think they do."

"Right." I snort. I start feeling not so hot. Especially after guzzling that water.

"God! You drive me crazy!" He throws his arms up in the air, then runs his hands through his hair. "You're drunk and obviously don't know what you're saying."

"I'm not drunk, buddy, you are!" No idea why I said that. I am drunk and now my stomach is churning. "An' anotha thing, you didn't come in my house las' night. Who does that?"

"You're mad that I didn't sleep with you? Is that it?"

"It's weird." I place a hand on the wall to steady myself.

"You want to know why I didn't come in last night? Because I respect you. I want you to trust me. And believe me when I say it took every ounce of restraint I have not to follow you!"

I blink. I hope I remember this in the morning. The look on his face is so sincere. I could stare at him forever. "Oh, god." I hold my stomach.

"What?"

"I'm going to..." Puke. Right all over the floor. "I feel shitty."

"No kidding. You smell like a brewery. Lie on the couch, I'll clean this up," he mutters while I take a seat, grab the blanket and curl up. God, I smell like puke. Please don't puke again. Maybe if I squint my eyes hard enough, the feeling will subside. Then again, squinting my eyes may not be such a good thing. I can hear Zach somewhere off in the distance getting cleaning supplies; pails are rattling and water is running and the all too familiar smell of cleaning products hits my nose. In that moment, he places a garbage pail by me and I throw up in it.

By this time, my head is pounding and my throat is dry. I sip a little water and settle myself.

Zach is busying himself with the cleaning, and I feel terrible for not helping, but I can't even stand at this point, so, instead, I fall asleep.

The next morning, I wake up to the bright sunlight shining on my face. The clock on the DVD player flashes 12:00 to the beat of my hangover and I wish it would stop. Over on the coffee table are some crackers and more water and the rest of the house is quiet. I feel like crap.

For a moment, I have a memory lapse. I have no idea why I'm in the guesthouse on the couch, with a shag carpet pasted to my tongue. But it doesn't take too long to remember that I told Zach he was a phony, or rather phony-baloney. And, oh, shit, I puked all over the floor. And, fuck! He cleaned it up! Incredibly embarrassed, I leave, vowing never to return again.

Chapter 16
Hesitation breeds discontentment

Zach calls later that day to see if I'm okay. I don't answer the phone. Not only am I in love with the guy and don't want to admit it, I puked all over the floor and he wiped it up. And he's still calling me! After he called a few more times during the week, and after I don't answer or return his calls, he stops calling. Good! Well, sort of.

Fact is, Nan's ultimate Halloween party is coming up on the weekend and Zach hasn't asked me. Not that I want him to. Okay, I do want him to, but I don't. You know? I'm mortified by my actions, unsure of my feelings, and after I let my brain calculate it all out, I decide I've never been good at math, or relationship math. Two days before the party, Zach still hasn't called. At this point, I decide I better get a date. Actually, the clincher was when Nan told me Zach had his date all set up. Then she asked why haven't I arranged a date yet? I told her I was busy—busy calling people phony-baloney and avoiding phone calls.

Now it's time to dig through all my past dates and see if anyone will come with me on such short notice. Yes, I could go alone, but Zach is bringing someone. I can't let him upstage me like that.

I list off all my options. Phil—no. Ian—no. Mark—no. That Todd guy from Susanne's wedding last year? Definitely not! Dan—maybe. He's my only real option. I take a breath and dial Dan's number.

*

I slip into my Cat Woman suit all the while surveying myself in the mirror. My reddish-brown hair spills down my back, the tight spandex suit hugs my body; the high heeled boots, cat ears and mask all add sex appeal. Cat Woman always had a seductive, edgy look about her. Yes, I'm trying to seduce someone tonight, although he doesn't know it. No, it isn't Dan, and just as I think his name, Dan's not Zach's, the doorbell rings.

Dan didn't tell me what he was going to be wearing tonight; he said it would be a surprise and that I would love it. I can only imagine. Maybe a pirate or Frankenstein or Luke Skywalker, or something completely evil. But, when I open the door, I'm rendered speechless. Dan's outfit is reminiscent of Liza Manelli in Cabaret. He has on red lingerie, fishnet garters, high heels, a black wig and an incredibly made-up face.

"Dr. Frank-N-Furter is here, darling."

Dr. Frank-N-Furter from Rocky Horror Picture Show. That's what he's dressed up as? My night is officially ruined.

I blurt out, "What the hell?"

"What do you think?"

I want to make Zach jealous, not laugh at me. I wanted Dan to be a superhero or super villain. "Uh, it's great."

"Madam," Dan gives me his arm and I take it reluctantly. Now that Dan is dressed as a Dr. Frank-N-Furter, things are a little less compelling.

It's amazing what a swanky-do Nan has put together; and every year she outdoes herself. The roadway is lined with large jack o' lanterns, their lights flickering in the breeze, the front yard is adorned with orange and black garland, flickering orange lights, witches on broomsticks and ghosts hanging from trees. Once inside, an upright coffin greets us at the door where a mummy has found its final resting place; however, it still manages to flash its eyes whenever anyone walks in. At first, I thought it was Syd the butler, but then Syd apparates from out of nowhere dressed as Lurch from the Addam's Family.

"Syd, you look awesome as Lurch!" He holds out a tray of drinks for all the arriving guests. The tray is filled with some sort of drinking potion that spews fog from the dry ice sitting below it.

"Who's Syd?" Syd doesn't crack a smile; he continues his stare as if in total role- playing mode.

"Right, sorry, Lurch."

All throughout the darkened foyer and main hall are more lights, more flickering pumpkins, gravestones and ghosts as if we're partying in a makeshift graveyard. Nan said something about a cemetery theme this year. Last year, it was a haunted house theme and the year before that it was all about the mad-scientist laboratory.

Other guests in a variety of costumes are milling about, reading the epitaphs of the dead, like, I.M. Dead, Ima Goner, and M.T. Tomb.

"Your grandmother really knows how to throw a party." Dan does a little dance as he enters the house.

Throughout the hall are more pumpkins, more garland, witches, vampires and ghosts. Tables are set up around the room, making way for a dance floor. At the front is a band playing a sixties montage of surfer tunes. They're also dressed in their own costumes of what appears to be Devo.

Nan, dressed in an angel costume, is in a far off corner speaking to an older gentleman; she is a vision of extreme angelic-ness, clearly happy, especially as she continues to touch the stranger's arm when he says something. "Nan. You did a great job. Much better than last year."

"Isn't it great? Oh, hi, Dan." She forces a smile.

"Hi, Mrs. Chase. It's been a while since I last saw you."

"Yes. Well, you look...interesting tonight," Nan says. I stifle a laugh. "You have a good time while you're here."

"Cate." A hand taps me on the shoulder, and I realize it's Susanne dressed in a Wonder Woman costume.

"You look awesome." I hug her.

"You, too." Then she notices Dan. She gives me the 'what-the-hell' look. "You do too, Dan."

"Time Warp, baby. You and me. I'm going to request it right now." Dan runs off in his high heels.

"That's rather disturbing, isn't it?" Susanne stares after Dan.

"Yeah. And for some reason I can't look away." Dan leans against the stage; he has one heeled foot in the air as he talks to the lead singer.

"Please make me look away."

"Isn't that Zach over there?" Susanne asks.

"Where?" I glance around the room, then realize Susanne is joking.

"Have you seen him yet?"

"Nope. No idea what he's dressed as." I continue to scan the room, barely acknowledging Susanne in front of me.

"There's a cowboy over there, maybe that's him." Standing by a very buxom woman with extremely long hair that I could only assume is Lady Godiva, is a cowboy in brown chaps, blue flannel shirt, red handkerchief around his neck and a Stetson. "Nope, that guy's too skinny."

"It's hard to tell with all these people wearing masks."

"Well, it is a masquerade party," I say. "Oh, wait. Look at that guy over there. The Frankenstein." It's a strange costume with a mishmash of different items, the ripped pants, turtleneck and blazer, the green face. "Or is he supposed to be The Hulk?"

"I don't think that's him anyway."

"Oh, god, Susanne, what am I doing? I'm here with Dan but I'm looking for someone else."

"I was about to ask you the same question. Why are you here with Dan?"

"Because Zach didn't ask me. Because he was going with someone else and I didn't call him and I puked on his floor and he cleaned it up..."

"You should be on Jerry Springer."

"Oooooooo. Oooooooooo. Hello, ghouls!" A ghost, with an ordinary white sheet and a few holes cut out, waves his arms before us.

"Hi, Honey," Susanne leans in to kiss the ghost where the mouth is supposed to be.

"Hi Dave, nice costume." I raise an eyebrow at Susanne.

"Dave decided to create his own costume."

"You should be supervising him when he plays with scissors."

Dave flaps his arms. "I think it's the best thing I've ever made. No one goes as a ghost anymore. I'm starting a trend."

"I suppose it could be worse..." And before I can say more, Dan appears with drinks.

"I hope everyone is okay with champagne as a starter. Come on, everyone take one and we'll make a toast." I take my champagne and raise it up next to Dave and Susanne's.

"Okay, Frank-N-Furter, what shall we toast to?" Dave says. It's obvious that Dave is already drunk, but no one can really say for sure what's happening beneath that sheet.

"Halloween, old friends, new friends, and rekindling an old flame," Dan throws an arm across my shoulders, kissing my cheek with his Frank-N-Furter lips.

I glare at Susanne, hoping she can hear my thoughts, "If he thinks we're rekindling anything, he seriously has another thing coming."

"Um, cheers." We all clink glasses and take a sip, except Dave and Dan who are having a drinking contest as they both down their drinks in record time.

"Another?" Dave's slurring already.

"How about a shooter?" Dan's already off to the bar again.

"We'll get them. You guys stay here and discuss your costumes." I pull Susanne by her magic lasso and drag her to the bar.

"Susanne, I can't do this all night. Dan is already driving me crazy. The only thing I can do is ply him with drinks and hope he'll pass out under a table somewhere."

"Four tequila shooters," Susanne orders. I give her a questioning stare. "Plying them both with drinks may not be such a bad idea, and tequila is a good place to start."

"You're the greatest." I kiss her cheek.

"I know. Oh, wait, your cat ears are all wonky." Susanne reaches over and yanks them, almost pulling the hair from my head.

"Oww!"

"Sorry!" She winces "You better go fix them yourself."

"Okay, just wait here till I get back. I want to do a shot with you." I walk off to the bathroom down the hall, hoping that maybe I'll run into Zach at some point. I have no clue where he is, who he is, or if he's even arrived yet. Maybe he didn't even come tonight. I suppose that's a possibility.

I reach for the doorknob to the bathroom without thinking of knocking first. Apparently, I should have done this as I wasn't expecting what I saw behind the door—poufy, dark-haired pantless woman straddling an equally pantless Zorro on the toilet seat.

"Hey! Close the door!" she yells. And I do, a little unsure of what I just saw. No, I know what I just saw; I'm just having a hard time grasping it. I'm torn between kicking their asses out of my grandmother's party or just letting them have at it. I decide I'm in a 'who gives a shit mood' and let them go to it. It's Halloween, after all.

I walk back to Susanne who has four tequila shooters on a tray. "You won't believe what I just saw!"

"What?"

"Two people screwing in the bathroom."

"Remind me not to use that bathroom. I've already plied Dave and Dan with four tequila shots and I'm going in for another round." Susanne indicates the tray in her hands. "And I ordered two shots for us." She hands me a creamy looking shooter and clinks mine with her equally creamy looking shooter. We shoot them back and slam the glasses down. "What are you going to have?"

"Hmm, I think I'll stick to beer." The bartender cracks one open and hands it to me.

"So, Cat Woman, we meet again." I catch my breath because I know who it is. I turn to meet familiar eyes behind a Batman mask.

I compose myself and nod. "Batman." Susanne stands beside me, holding her tray. "You remember Wonder Woman."

"Wonder Woman. Nice to see you again."

"You too, Batman." Then Susanne gives me a quick look. "I've got work to do." She lifts her tray and walks away.

"So, I see Dr. Frank-N-Furter has escorted you tonight." There's a flicker in Zach's eyes of …I don't know what. It can't be jealousy. Or can it? Let's just say it is, just to make me feel really good about myself.

"Uh, ya. We're having a great time." I glance down at my boots, scuffing them on the floor. "And you? Where's your date?"

"Um, around here somewhere." Zach half-heartedly searches the room. "Not sure."

There's silence and I really don't know why I'm standing here. Does he even want to talk to me? What do I say? I mean, we really haven't spoken since I threw up on his floor.

"Would you like a drink?" He asks.

"Um, no thanks. I have a beer." I hold up my bottle.

"Are you going to be okay with beer? Maybe water is more your speed." He grins. He looks damn sexy in that Batman costume.

I blush. "I'm sorry about that night when I threw up on your floor. Thanks for cleaning it up, by the way."

"I guess I should apologize for pushing you too quickly."

"Pushing? What do you mean?"

"You know, the night we went out, and I said some stuff and took you to my parents, and kissed you..." He trails off. I then realize what he's apologizing for. Was he pushing me too fast? God, am I that transparent? Before I can say anything further, the band finishes playing a Buddy Holly song and time warps to the '80s with 'True' by Spandau Ballet.

"Do you want to dance?" Zach holds out his hand. My stomach churns.

"Sure." I take it and he leads me to the middle of the dance floor, in the midst of many other dancers dressed up in an array of costumes. Some big, some flashy, some awkward looking and some just really bizarre. There's a headless guy who's carrying his head while his neck spurts out blood; he keeps bumping into people, which is quite entertaining.

Zach slides his hand around my waist then takes my other hand in his waltz-like style and pulls me close.

I place my other hand on his shoulder and look into his eyes. I really don't know what's happening. Actually, I do know what's happening, I just don't want to admit it. His heart is beating close to mine, our bodies meshing together...well, I suppose this is how people slow dance and these things do tend to happen.

"Did you dance to this song in high school?"

"Who didn't?" I laugh.

"We should dance this the proper way then."

"What do you mean?"

"Like this." He places both my hands around his neck and then wraps his arms around my waist, pulling me closer.

"Oh, right. This type of dancing." I smile. I can hear his own laugh right next to my ear, his breath tickling my neck.

Flashbacks of telling him he was a phony-baloney come flooding back and I realize I need to apologize.

"Zach?"

"Yes?"

"I want to apologize for calling you a fake the other night."

"Oh, you mean the phony-baloney bit. Right."

"And for calling you a manipulator."

"Uh-huh, and...?"

"And, you aren't those things. I was just being...me, I guess. I mean, I really enjoyed our night out at the diner and your parents place and....all those things you said." I don't look up.

"And?"

"And? What more is there? I already apologized for puking on your floor."

"I have a feeling there's more," he pries.

There is more. I love you. I want to be with you. I take a breath. "Well, I also feel..."

"There you are, Zach. I've been looking everywhere for you so we could dance. This is my favourite song." It's the puffy haired woman who was screwing Zorro in the bathroom.

"This is your date?" My respect for Zach is waning.

"Darci, this is Cate. Cate, Darci."

Darci gives me one of those once-overs that size you up, analyzing the intruder who has stolen her boyfriend. "Who are you supposed to be?"

"I'm Cat Woman. Who the hell are you supposed to be?"

"I'm Pat Benatar."

"I don't think Pat Benatar was a hooker."

Darci has beady little eyes that become beadier as she squints at me; her hair is so puffy, I could have sworn she stuck her finger in a light socket.

"Wait, don't I know you from somewhere? Oh, yes, the bathroom." I glare at her, knowing her little secret. Her eyes flicker with surprise.

"Okay," Zach steps in. "How about we go get a drink, Darci?"

She takes her eyes off of me giving Zach a seductive smile, all the while running her finger down his arm. "Mmmm," she moans sexually. "Sounds good."

Oh, how I want to gouge her eyes out, start a real cat fight right here on the dance floor, and pull Pat's puffy hair. Scary thing is, I think that hair is for real and not an embellishment for her costume.

Zach walks away, his smile apologetic.

"What happened?" Susanne had been watching the whole thing from the sidelines.

"Well, that's the ho who was doing Zorro in the bathroom. Now she stole Batman away." Darci continues to latch onto Zach's arm as they stand at the bar.

"Does he know she's a ho?"

"I don't think he cares."

"Did you tell him how you feel?"

"He's obviously not interested. Besides, what would I want with him anyway? He's a manipulator and dates hoes!" I look around.

"Where's my date?"

"He's getting sloshed with my husband." She smirks.

"At least if he's passed out, he won't try to sleep with me."

"See, there's a positive to everything."

The song fades into the distance and the band goes on a break, turning on their round of downloaded music. I hadn't moved from my spot yet, unsure of what to do next. I don't want to go over to Dan, and I don't want to watch Zach and his date. Nan is talking to an older gentleman who has her laughing, and I'm glad that she found someone her own age.

Over in one corner is Zach being fondled by his date, and in another corner stand Dan and Dave laughing about something. I shiver and make a decision. "I've got to get out of here."

"Where are you going?"

"I need air. Maybe I'll go home. I don't know. I can't stay in here."

"Don't leave because of Zach. Go over and tell him what's going on."

I hesitate for a split second. Tell him how I feel. I've already tried that. I shake my head. "Nah. I'm getting out of here. If you don't see me back here in about an hour, I've left the building." I'm going to make my exit, not say goodbye to anyone, and let them all think I'm still around. But before that can happen, someone yanks at my arm.

"Cate, we haven't danced yet." It's Dan, his eye make-up now smudged, his lipstick needs a touch up and he looks hot under that wig.

"Dan, um, I don't really want to."

"Come on, honey," Dan yanks me close, grabbing my ass. "I can't wait to get you home and take your clothes off..." And I shiver. This is not happening. This is not how my night is going to end. Before Dan can utter one more thing, I push him away.

He doesn't give up and grabs my arm, and that's when my reflexes cut in. I swing around, twisting his arm behind his back in one quick movement and have him prostrate on the floor in seconds.

All around me, people are staring. On the floor, Dan is wincing in pain. I realize what I've done, and release his arm, running out of the room and out onto the patio. How embarrassing. I threw a friend to the floor. What is wrong with me?

Around me are a few people smoking, Mr. Potato head, Danny and Sandy from Grease. They clearly aren't concerned with me or with what's going on. I'll calm down, maybe go back in, apologize and hopefully Dan won't sue.

"Cate."

I don't turn around; I know full well who it is. "Don't you have your 'girlfriend' to be with?"

"She's not my girlfriend. She's just a date. And besides, why do you care? You're here with Dan Sherman." Zach says Dan's name with disdain.

"I care, because...."

"Because?"

I change the subject. "Did you know I found her screwing Zorro earlier tonight?"

"I'm not surprised." Zach rolls his eyes.

"If you knew she was like that, then why did you bring her?"

"Because I needed a date and she was available." He steps forward.

"If you needed a date, why didn't you ask me?" I blurt out.

"Because I didn't think you were interested. I mean, I told you my feelings, I kissed you, took you to meet my parents. You then berated me for being a manipulator, puked on my floor and didn't speak to me again. I had no idea what you wanted, so I thought I would leave you alone." Zach takes another step forward. "You didn't say why you cared that I'm here with Darci."

I avert my eyes.

"Cate." Zach touches my arm, sending a bolt of electricity running through me.

I stare at him and shake my head. "This is absolutely ridiculous. I can't talk to you like this."

"What? Yes, yes, you can. You can talk to me."

"No, I mean, I can't talk to you with your mask on. Can you please take that stupid thing off?" Zach pulls his Batman mask from his face as do I. Zach's eyebrows arch as he waits for my answer. "I have a thing for you," I whisper.

"What?"

"I have a thing for you," I say louder.

He grins. "Is that your way of telling me you like me?" He's teasing me.

"Look, I'm not good at this. Oh, forget it." I wave him off.

"You're so incredibly stubborn. You know what your problem is?"

"What?"

"You haven't been kissed properly." Zach grabs my hand pulling me toward him; he plants his lips on mine and they meld into this hungry kiss that has been left smoldering for far too long. I don't pull away, don't run for cover, but instead, I hop up, wrapping my legs around his hips, his arms tightly holding on to me. With whoops and cheers from Mr. Potatohead, Danny and Sandy, Zach carries me off to the guest house, slamming the door behind him.

Clothes and capes are yanked at and unceremoniously discarded on the living room floor. We have some issues with spandex and boots being a little tricky, but once that's out of the way, we fall onto the living room sofa and finally release some pent up passion that has been hanging on since the day we met. And, that night, we christen almost every room in the house.

Chapter 17
Excuse me, but I think I love you.

The next morning is a bit of a haze. As I lay in bed with my eyes closed, my mind pieces together what happened the night before. I could very well just be having another fantasy and have suddenly become lost in my own world where I don't know what's real anymore. But, as I open my eyes to Zach's smiling face, it occurs to me that everything that happened last night really did happen.

I cover my mouth, my hand muffling a good morning.

"What are you doing?"

"Morning breath," I muffle.

He pulls my hand away, kisses my mouth, face, my neck, between my breasts. I laugh, not at him, but just at a thought I'm having. "What?"

"I was just thinking—apparently, I haven't had a lot of things done to me properly." I raise a brow. It's true.

"Glad I could fix you up, ma'am," Zach does his best southern accent, tipping his imaginary cowboy hat. His hand falls to my belly and tickles, slowly tracing circles around my belly button.

"So do you think our dates were okay that we ditched them?"

"I think they'll be fine. After you put the boots to Dr. Frank-N-Furter, Pat Benatar stepped in to help him up. She might have been giving him mouth to mouth." I grimace at the thought.

Zach pecks my lips with a couple of kisses, then whispers, "How about you sleep and I'll make some breakfast."

"Mmmm. Sounds wonderful." I watch him get up, sneaking a peek as he slides his arms into his black robe. I close my eyes and snuggle into the pillows, thinking about this totally unlikely pairing if there ever was one. For some reason, he makes me want to stay in bed with him and never leave.

Now that we've had incredible sex, what happens from here? Are we a couple? Do we pretend nothing is going on in front of Nan and have a secret love affair? And what about being an escort?

Is he going to give that all up for me?

I sit up. What if he wants to continue being an escort? Can I live with that? I don't think I can. I mean, he'd be taking other women out on dates and I'd be sitting at home knitting. So, I don't knit, but that should be me on his arm, not those other girls. What if this is just one of those one night stand things or a friend-with-benefits thing? What if I have to resort to borrowing his other tools just so I can make excuses to see him? Look at me talking about commitment; who would have thought I could even say the word?

I pull on a shirt from Zach's closet and walk into the kitchen. The smell of sausage and coffee is in the air. Zach is sitting at the table, his feet crossed at the ankles, and he's reading the paper. He looks up, surprised by my presence while spying my attire. "I like your outfit."

"I have to know, and you have to be completely honest with me. No beating around the bush." My hair is all in knots from last night, and this morning, and, well, you get the picture. I'm sure my black eyeliner that I painted on last night to look like a cat has now become a big blobby mess under my eyes. "What are we? Are we just a good time for each other or are we dating exclusively? If we are exclusive, are you done the escorting business? And do we tell Nan? Or, is this just a one night stand? Because let me tell you, I can't keep coming over here asking for sugar every time I want to see you."

A smile plays at the corners of his mouth.

"What? What are you smiling about?"

"You're so cute when you get excited." He stands, pulling me to him.

"Well, what is it?"

"Yes to all of the above. Well, minus the one night stand."

"Yes to all of the above? Can you remind me what I said, again?"

"Yes, we are a good time for each other and yes, we are dating exclusively. Yes, we should tell Nan, and yes, my escort days are done. And I really hope you come over more often for some sugar." He kisses me, pulling me tightly into his arms. I undo his robe, pushing him back in the chair, straddling his legs. As the sausages sizzled in the oven, we went about christening the last room in the house.

*

Cate, it's Susanne. Give me a call when you get in. I want to hear all about your night.

You'd think I'd been gone for a week with all the messages I have on my voicemail. Five from Suzanne with an urgency to call, one from Dan apologizing for getting so drunk last night that he went home with Pat Benatar, (and I should call him so he could explain himself and maybe we could go for coffee when his headache subsides). The planets have aligned. Dan went home with Pat Benatar. I wonder how that went.

There was one very important call from Zach telling me to hurry back. I left Zach in bed at the guest house completely satiated. I'll return to satiate him even more after I freshen up and get normal clothes on. All I had with me was a cat suit, so I wore home the shirt I grabbed from his closet and a pair of sweats. The outfit isn't very stylish with my Cat Woman boots, although Zach really likes them, the boots that is, and wants me to wear them when I return.

Before I can pick up the phone to call Susanne, she beats me to it. "Where have you been?"

"I was just about to call you."

"I've been calling all morning. Did you just get home?"

"Well, yeah."

"Tell me what happened," she presses. "Don't leave out any details either. My night was crappy, my husband passed out in the car and I had to leave him there to sleep in the driveway. I had to check on him every hour so he wouldn't aspirate on vomit or something. Finally, at five this morning, he was able to walk in the house by himself. I'm living vicariously through you."

"Oh, nothing much happened," I tease. I really want to blurt everything out, but I want to make her work for it first.

"What? Come on, something must have happened. Last I saw, Zach was chasing after you, and Pat Benatar was soothing a very inebriated Frank-N-Furter. And neither of you came back. So, spill the goods, sister."

"Okay, here's the condensed version..."

"I don't want the condensed version, I want the two hour movie," Susanne whines.

"You want me to tell you how he touched me and where?"

"Well, I don't need all the details. But give me something more than we talked."

"Okay, he likes me, I like him. We kissed; he carried me off to the guest house..."

"He carried you off? Oh, how romantic," Susanne gushes.

"Well, I did wrap my legs around him, so he had no choice but to carry me off. It was more awkward and clumsy. We then tore off each other's clothes and...well, it was a busy night." There was silence on the other end. "Hello?"

"And?"

"And...it was amazing."

"What about the escort thing?"

"He says that's done."

Susanne squeals in my ear. "I'm so happy for you. Really. I knew you'd get together. I don't know why you just didn't do it in the first place."

"Okay, okay. I admit I'm a little commitmentphobic..."

"Ha!" Susanne blurts. "A little....!"

"Okay, a bit more than a little. But, I've moved on and realize that I like Zach...a lot. Maybe even love..." I trail off because I realize what I'm saying.

"Cate, if you love him, then say so."

"Susanne, we barely know one another. I mean, we spent the first month at each other's throats and now I'm in love with him? It doesn't work that way."

"Who says it has to work a certain way? I think you liked him from the start but were afraid to trust yourself. Just go with it."

Susanne is right, as usual. I guess that's why she has the PhD in psychology. I resolve to Suzanne that I will 'go with it', then hang up to go see Zach again. I even pack an overnight bag including a toothbrush and fresh undies. Maybe this is all a bit presumptuous, but we are dating now.

I remind myself that my career still hangs in the balance, and that maybe I shouldn't be having so much fun. On the other hand, all I have been doing is stressing. I decide that tonight I will tell my grandmother about the suspension. It's time.

*

I reach the guest house just before dinner, rapping softly on the door before entering. "Hello?"

"Hey." Zach appears out of the kitchen wearing a pair of jeans and green t-shirt. He leans in and kisses me. "You smell nice." He presses his nose into my hair.

"So do you. You want to skip dinner and just go straight to dessert?" I push him back toward his bedroom.

"Hmm, I'd love to, but Ursula has invited us to dinner. I don't think she'd want us to be late because we can't keep our hands off of each other."

"We'd be quick."

"Really? Like you said this morning when I wanted to finish making breakfast. I don't think we ate breakfast till two."

"It was a late brunch," I reply as I hastily pull his shirt up.

Zach grabs my hands and kisses them both before his eyes fall to the knapsack at the front door. "What's this?"

"Oh, just some provisions."

"Provisions? What kind of provisions? Like 'I'm going to be stuck in the woods for three days' provisions?"

"You don't need to look."

He unzips the bag and peeks in. "Toothbrush, toothpaste, cleanser...oh, so the 'I'm going to be stuck at my boyfriend's place for three days' provisions." He yanks out the pink lingerie that I had thrown in there at the last minute. "Maybe your grandmother can wait." He pulls me in.

"We better go." I'm tormenting him.

We walk out into the backyard where the pumpkins and lights from last night have already disappeared just as all the decorations inside the house have. "How do you think Nan will take it that we're together?"

"Well, she likes me and I can only assume she likes you..." Zach grins. "I think she'll be happy."

Zach grabs my hand and leads me into the house and to the living room where Syd told us she was waiting.

"Nan, we have something to tell you," I call out. I'm ready to blurt out everything, but am floored at what I discover.

"Mom? Dad?"

"Cate!"

My parents! My parents that I haven't seen in a very long time are standing only a few feet away. And, in the perfect Hallmark moment, I run in, embracing them both at the same time. Tears well up and I can't believe that I'm holding them after a year and a half. I can't believe it's them. I take in their scents—they're so very familiar that it catches me off guard and I let out a sob. My back is rubbed by arms tightening and pulling me closer. I sob some more. Finally, when I have control, I step back and take them in.

As I wipe the tears from my face, I realize that Dad looks almost the same—dark short hair, dark eyes, except now he has a beard, more grey, and a receding hair line. Mom's red hair is still radiant and long, and only a few wrinkles dot her fair complexion. They have a healthy glow, which is enhanced by their bohemian wear—both with hemp button down tops, dad with a pair of khakis and mom in her long brown broomstick skirt.

"I'm so happy to see you."

"I know it's been a long time, sweetie. You look wonderful." Mom brushes my hair back—mine is a slightly darker shade than hers—I almost nestle into her when she strokes my hair. It reminds me of so many nights when she would tuck me in.

"This is a surprise," I finally manage.

"I knew about it," Nan pipes in. "I didn't want to tell you."

"This is wonderful." I bring them in again for another embrace. Their eyes suddenly fall on Zach who has been sitting on the arm of the sofa. "Oh, Zach. Meet my parents, Forest and Flora Chase."

Zach reaches his hand out. "This is Zach," I pause for a moment. "My... boyfriend."

"What? Boyfriend? How did you meet?" Dad asks.

"Oh, well..." I look to Nan for guidance. Explaining that my new boyfriend is Nan's escort isn't something I want to get into at the moment.

"I hired Zach to help me with some things around the house. He lives in the guest house right now."

Relief spreads across my face. After everything that has happened, I just want to put it behind me and be happy that Zach and I are together now. Zach tells my parents about his music, not saying one word about the escort service he had going since, well, since this morning. I also realize how hard I'm falling for him or, rather, have been for some time now. Sometimes, all you need to do is embrace it.

With Mom and Dad here, I feel as if things are bound to work out.

"I'm so happy you guys are here. Finally!" I sit between Mom and Dad and cozy in like I did when I was young, suddenly feeling all those lost moments and memories rushing back. "So, what's on the agenda now that you're back? You probably want to look for a house or condo or something. I have a real estate agent I can refer you to. And maybe mom and I can look for some towels and dishes and all that stuff."

Mom's face twists up in alarm, and Dad is doing the confused thing. Something isn't right. "You are staying now, right? I mean, after all these years, you are staying in one place, getting sedentary, right?" Panic sets in as the inevitable happens...again.

"Oh, Cate, honey. We had no intention of stopping what we're doing." Dad clasps my hand.

"Sweetie, we need to get back. We still have work to do."

"So, how many days are you back for?" My voice quivers and I know that a big crying session is about to ensue. I don't want it to, but my parents have been gone so long, it'd be a dream for them to stay home with me.

Dad hesitates. "Oh, um, a week."

"What?" I stand abruptly. "A week? That's not a visit! You've been gone for years now. You can't stick around for a month, maybe two, maybe forever? Instead you have to go off and do....god, I don't even know what it is that's so important there. I'm not important? Aren't my birthdays important?" I yell, now feeling the tears lingering on the edges.

"Cate, we didn't mean to make you feel..." Mom rises to embrace me, but I race around the sofa away from her.

"Well, you did. You made me feel less of a daughter. You made me feel like I didn't matter. No wonder I'm so untrusting of others. No wonder I'm so... so... commitmentphobic," I rage. Here it comes. Everything that I had bottled up comes out in one fluid sentence. "No wonder I've been suspended from my job and charged with sexual harassment!" It's done, out in the open. I'm not quite sure how that relates to my parents being away, but it's done. And it's a relief.

"Cate, we-we didn't know..." Dad starts.

"How could you know? You're never around! Listen, don't come near me, don't talk to me, and don't follow me. Go back to where ever it is that you came from. I don't want you here!" I scream, tears now falling crazily down my cheeks. I run from the room, out the front door and get into my car. I rev the engine, ready to squeal down the driveway and never come back. Where would I go? Who knows. Does it matter? Maybe.

"Cate?" A yell and a knock on the car window stops me from racing away with Zach's arm. "Cate, wait."

I unroll the window, wiping my tears. "Don't stop me, Zach."

"I'm not, I'm not. It's just...let me drive. I don't want you driving like this. I'll take you wherever you want to go. You can vent, cry, whatever. I won't say anything unless you want me to."

He's making sense—probably the only sensible one in a fifty mile radius at this point. I agree and slide to the passenger side so he can drive my car.

"Where to?" He puts the car in drive and heads out onto the open road a little too slow for my taste.

"It doesn't matter. Just drive." I wipe my tears with a tissue and blow my nose, then start talking about everything. My childhood, how my parents were always there until they decided to be crusaders. How Nan was great but my Mom and Dad would have been better to have around, just because they were my Mom and Dad. I tell him how they disappointed me and how having them back in my life would make me feel complete. I cry, I yell, Zach listens and drives. I don't really pay attention to where we're driving to, but after what seems like two hours, Zach pulls into my driveway.

He turns toward my questioning stare. "Why are we at my house? I thought we were driving till we hit Mexico."

Zach's hands are in my hair and he gently rubs the back of my head. "I thought maybe I'd make you something to eat, some tea. You can have a hot bath, we can talk some more. If you still feel like driving around, then we'll get back in the car and drive."

I exhale for the first time since hearing the news about my parents leaving again. I nod and we go inside where Zach proceeds to find something to eat while I run a lavender bath and slide in the tub, trying to get my head straight, trying to make sense of it all. Trying desperately to figure out how I'll get over my parent's absence once more. I get out, feeling a bit more relaxed, a bit dazed from the up and down emotions, and the hot water.

As I slide on some yoga pants and a top, the phone rings and I can hear Zach talking. Who's he talking to? I walk downstairs to listen.

"No, she's doing fine. Don't worry, I have her safe here with me." Pause. "She's a little upset, Forest, but I'm sure with a little sleep, she'll be fine."

I march into the room. "Is that my father?" I yell. Zach turns away from me, plugging his ear. "You tell him that he and my mother can go to hell. I don't need their pity. I don't want them as parents. You hear that!" Zach hangs up the phone; his look says I didn't need to yell.

"Why did you tell them I was okay? I'm not going to be fine with some sleep! I'll never be fine! Do you realize that, Zach? I'll always be untrusting of you, of everyone. I'll never, ever be able to commit to a relationship because my parents could never ever commit to me!" I break down, crying again. I was doing fine till that phone call.

Zach blankets me in his arms, stroking my hair. He doesn't say anything, he just lets me cry for a few minutes till I calm down and turn my attention to him.

"Take me upstairs," I whisper, seductively kissing him, all the while reaching under his shirt.

"Cate, I'm not going to sleep with you as some sort of revenge against your parents. I'll sleep with you because you want me."

"Ha! See, that shows just how much you know about me. I don't want revenge sex." He actually has me pegged.

"I'll be here as long as you need me, but no revenge sex."

"Why do you have to be so good? Why can't you be a dickhead and sleep with me like any other guy would?"

"Because, I like you."

I sigh, and realize there's a sandwich on the table. "So, you found something else to eat besides oatmeal." I run a hand down his back.

"The cupboard was pretty bare, so I made you a tuna sandwich." He sits me down in the chair and we share a meal together, and I briefly forget about my parents, realizing that Zach is one of the good ones. Especially when he takes me upstairs, tucks me in bed and crawls in beside me, cuddling me in his arms the whole night.

"Are you sure about the revenge sex?" I ask in the dark of the room. "Because it can be really good sometimes."

"No one can ever accuse you of not being persistent," he mumbles in my hair. "Goodnight, Cate." He kisses my shoulder; I shiver and fall asleep.

Chapter 18
I love you for developmental reasons.

Zach is already awake when I get up the next morning. Actually, after searching the house, I realize he's gone. He left! I can't believe it, just as I was looking for some morning revenge sex, he isn't even around to oblige.

"Okay, 'Mister I'll be around as long as you need me'," I mutter. So much for the support. I knew he wasn't perfect. No one can be that perfect, and now he has a black mark on his record. As I proceed to throw on some jeans, I hear the front door open and footsteps coming up the stairs. I toss the jeans aside and sit on the bed in my underwear.

"Cate?" Zach calls just as he enters the bedroom.

I cross my legs and lean back on my elbows. He raises an eyebrow and closes the door. "I'm over my revenge sex issues; I'm ready for real sex." He doesn't rush to the bed. Okay, so this plan isn't working. Maybe he needs a bigger hint. I get up and plant a kiss on him then proceed to undo his belt. "Where'd you go anyway?"

Zach clasps his hands on mine. "I went and got your stuff that you left at my place." He points to the bag he placed by the door. The one with my 'provisions'.

"That was very sweet of you. Now let me thank you for that." I tug him over to the bed till he falls down on top of me.

"Cate, I'd love to do this right now, but I have a surprise for you."

"Can't the surprise wait?" I yank him down again.

"Um, no. Get dressed and meet me downstairs." He adjusts himself, leaving me in my undies. Surprise? What kind of surprise?

I quickly get dressed and run down the stairs. This better be good. "Okay, Zach. Where's the surprise?" I walk into the living room. There, sitting on my couch, are my parents. Zach stands innocently by the fireplace. Apparently, they have already served themselves something to drink. That was nice of them to make themselves comfortable. "What are they doing here?"

"Just hear them out, okay?" Zach grabs my hand and sits me down on the chair across from them. I glare while they stare gently at me. "Well, now that everything is under control, I'll leave you three alone." Zach slips on his coat ready to bolt. I automatically stand up.

"Wait a minute, bucko. You're leaving? Where are you leaving to?" I follow Zach to the door. He can't throw me into the lion's den.

"I'm going out so you can talk to your parents. I'll be back later." He kisses me hard on the mouth. "It'll be fine." He kisses me again then leaves—taking my car! Now I really can't escape.

I look back toward the living room where my parents sit. Maybe I can run out the front door and down to the mall. It's only a half hour walk. Only problem is, they would still be here when I came back. I suppose hearing them out for five minutes won't be so bad. "You have five minutes." I sit in the chair and cross my arms. I can't even look at them at this point.

"Cate, honey, we want to apologize. We had no idea that our absence affected you this way. We always saw you as a resilient child," Dad begins.

"One that always bounced back from situations," Mom throws in. "We thought you would be fine staying with your grandmother because the two of you had always gotten along."

I shake my head. I'm stunned I have to explain myself and my developmental needs. "You don't understand. It wasn't just living with Nan, it was that you weren't around to see any of my achievements. Graduating high school and from the police academy. Making sergeant. Birthdays, Christmas, Santa Claus, losing a tooth, my first boyfriend. You weren't there to see that. Sure, Nan's a good substitute, but that's all she is, a substitute. I want the real deal. I've always wanted the real deal!" Tears are welling-up again. My eyes are still puffy from last night's crying fit. More puffiness will ensue later tonight. "I've always had crappy relationships, always finding the ones that wouldn't be a threat to commit. Not trusting anyone." I break off. This is the first time I'm actually honest with myself. It's a bit unnerving but calming at the same time.

"If we could take it back, we would. We would change everything that we did. But we can't. All we can say is we're sorry for depriving you of the chance to have real parents. We want to start now to make it up to you," Mom explains.

"How can you say that? You're going away again. When are you going to be around long enough to make it up to me?" I'm now standing, pacing, ready to bolt when the pain becomes too much.

They both stare at each other, lost for words. "This is our last trip."

"You said that last time. It's always the last trip."

Dad nods. He knows. "I'm sorry, Cate. We made this commitment...we need to do this. When we're done, we will be back for good."

I laugh. "So, I have to wait two years till you can make a commitment to your daughter."

Dad shakes his head. "Not two. One. Only one year. We made a commitment to go back, and we don't want to go back on the commitment. But, we are coming back for good next year. We have blindly gone about our business without taking your feelings into consideration, and that was terrible parenting on our part. We can't bring back the past, but if you give us a chance, we will begin a whole new future."

Dad stands and walks toward me, arms open. "Please, can't we enjoy this time we have together? When we get back, we'll...we'll start over."

"We love you, Cate!" Mom and Dad flank me. "We will make this better."

Dad's speech has moved me and the tears flow. I nod, unable to speak because my heart is in my throat. "One year. Okay. I can live with one year. Just one!" They kiss me.

"Just one!" Dad says. "Now, what about this sexual harassment charge?" I cringe. "What's that all about?"

I begin to tell them what happened, how it isn't possible, how I really need them to believe me, and they do, offering me full support, whatever I need.

"And, how's Nan? She didn't know any of this," I say guiltily. "I should have told her ages ago."

"She's fine, honey. She loves you. She's not sure why you didn't tell her, but Zach explained that you were worried about how she would take it," Dad points out.

"Zach seems like a very special guy," Mom says. "It takes some kind of man to pick up his girlfriend's parents and request that they speak to their daughter to make things better."

I blink. Zach did that? "You two didn't request to come over here?"

"We were planning on calling first, but then Zach came by and insisted we come over and talk it out."

Zach did that....for me? I can't believe he did that. I swallow the lump in my throat because I think I've done enough crying for one day.

*

It's a couple of hours later when Zach returns with groceries. My parents and I visit the whole time, catching up. What has turned out to be a crappy reunion, is now a beautiful day.

"What's with the groceries?" I ask, pouring another cup of tea. Mom and Dad are relaxing in the sunroom.

"For the barbeque," he says, pulling out ribs, potatoes and everything else to go with it.

"What barbeque?"

"The one that we're having here tonight."

"I don't remember planning a barbeque."

"Well, I kind of took it upon myself to call up Susanne and Dave and your grandmother, and my parents."

"I don't think I've ever had a barbeque at my house before," I say, stunned. "Do I even own a barbeque?"

"You do. It's hidden behind some bushes in the backyard."

"Oh, right." I smile. "I guess I'm having a barbeque."

"It's about time you broke the house in." Zach kisses me then busies himself in the kitchen.

"Where did you come from?" I'm still stunned by him and the way he takes care of things.

He places tin foil and potatoes in front of me. "You can start with this."

I get busy wrapping the potatoes, talking to Zach, happily discovering how much he makes me laugh.

When everyone arrives, I realize how I've been depriving myself of those amazing things that life can give you: family, friends, love. Why have I not had people over before?

And why didn't I trust those who love me to be able to handle the chaos in my life? Why haven't I reached out before for support? Even approaching Nan and apologizing for not telling her, I wondered why I didn't say anything. She would never see me as less of a person. She's always been there for me, what made me think she wouldn't be?

As I look around the table at the others laughing, eating and drinking, I realize my incredible luck.

Then there's Zach. This man I've known for short time, who I never thought would have won me over, has worked his way into my heart.

He winks at me, placing a hand on my upper thigh, tickling the inner thigh; I'm sure my eyes are rolling back into my head. By the time everyone leaves a few hours later, I'm ready to jump Zach as soon as the door closes. He senses this urgency, but doesn't take it. Instead, he pushes me against the wall and kisses me, his hands resting on my hips, not moving anywhere else. His knee is strategically placed between my legs. I begin unbuttoning his shirt, but he stops me, taking my hands and holding them above my head against the wall, my whole body humming.

We linger in the front foyer for a few minutes, me wanting to get upstairs immediately, while Zach takes his time, kissing, brushing lips, licking earlobes. Finally, he leads me upstairs, and slowly takes my clothes off, meticulously kissing me, running his hands up and down my body, driving me crazy with his touch, and then, he tenderly makes love to me.

Chapter 19
Crazy, Beautiful, and the In Between

Parents—they're always solidified in your life whether you want them there or not. Somehow, some way, they still intertwine their lives with yours, either making your life miserable and crazy, or sweet and beautiful. I think I have both sides of the coin. I came to that conclusion during the last few days spent with my parents.

Zach was able to take it further for me, pointing out that, no matter where my parents are, I've always had the support I've needed. Even when they were away, I have always had my grandmother. Nan has never wavered. She took on the role of caregiver to her granddaughter without hesitation. Mom isn't the woman at home baking cookies and Dad isn't the guy in the garage building a five tiered bookcase. This is my reality. It's never going to be perfect.

And then there's Zach. He's been great. Hanging around, helping out. You'd think I'd be sick of this, wanting him to go home and not come back for at least a month; but I love having him around.

The only thing is we can't hang out like this forever. I need my career back and the man needs a job.

So, after questioning him on what he's going to do now that his escort days are behind him, he only laughs and tells me I have nothing to worry about.

Which brings me this moment of us lying in bed in the dark of my room, legs entwined, our bodies radiating post-coital heat, and I ask him what he plans on doing now that the companion consulting business is done, and can't believe I just called it that.

"I have my music," he tells me.

"Your music? What does that mean?"

He's silent.

"No, seriously. What are you going to do?"

"You're cute when you're worried." He kisses my forehead.

I push him away. "I don't think having a plan is crazy."

"Music is a legitimate career, Cate. I know you think that, 'oh, he's one of those musicians that sits in his basement playing oldies but goodies, dreaming that he'll make it big', but I'm not."

"I just think it sounds wishy-washy, that's all." Suddenly there's dead-air and I wonder if he's pissed at me. "I was just voicing my opinion," I explain, moving away from him. If he's going to be overly sensitive, then there's no point in me trying to communicate with him.

"There's something I need to tell you," Zach finally says.

"Great, you're married." This was meant to be funny, but Zach doesn't laugh. "You're married?" I panic.

"No."

"Then what?" I turn to him and squeeze his arm. "You're dying!"

"I'm not dying. Look, not many people know what I'm about to tell you and I really hope you'll keep it to yourself."

"Sure." Still panicking.

"I've written and sold many songs."

The panic subsides. "Ooookay. You really know how to spread some juicy gossip."

"I used to be in a band at one time."

I turn to him. "I'm still not seeing how this is really hot gossip. Lots of people have been in bands, playing gigs at bars."

"I used to play bass for Agent Zero."

Absolute silence. "You did not."

"I did."

"Agent Zero. The '90s band that sang Sweet Venus?" I question.

"Yes. Actually, I wrote that song."

I sit up. "Come on."

"I'm serious." More silence. I quickly jump out of bed and grab my robe, running down the stairs to the storage closet near the living room. I begin digging through my tapes that I still have left over before CDs became popular. I know I had that tape somewhere in here. I continue to dig, sensing Zach behind me, waiting. I finally find it and stare at the tape. The cover gives nothing away as the band isn't even on the front; instead it's just a picture of a big 'o'. I open it up and pull out the insert, letting it unfold four times. Inside the folds are the pictures of all four band members. One of them being a picture of a guy with longer hair and a fresh face that could pass for Zach's younger brother, but it's not, as the words, 'Zach Kennedy, Bass Guitar' are written beneath it.

I slowly glance up at Zach. He smiles sheepishly, the blanket from the bed wrapped around him.

"Why did you leave?"

"Didn't want to be in the limelight anymore." He sits down beside me on the floor, the moonlight streaming in through the windows.

"And escorting was your second choice for a vocation? What, you couldn't get enough of the women hanging off of you?" I stand up and retreat to the couch, the tape cassette still in my hand.

Zach sits beside me. "It's not about the women. It's never been about the women."

"Then what is it about, because I'm having a hard time understanding." I continue to stare at the picture of Zach, also scanning the credits for each of the songs. Most of them are Zach's. Then my brain goes back to the cabin and him sitting on the dock playing his guitar and singing. How embarrassing! I told him his music was hill-billyish. God, I'm so pathetic.

"It was about finding out who I am, outside of the fame, the expectations. I wasn't fulfilled, Cate." He stops for a moment watching me study the tape. "You know why I do the escort service?"

I stare at him. He's using the wrong tense.

"Sorry, did the escort service?" I continue to stare, unsure if I want to know the answer. "Because I enjoy seeing other people feel good. It's the same when I write a song and someone plays it—it helps people feel good. But being on stage, I felt people only saw the superficial part of me. I had to get out. And that's what I did. You may or may not remember, but I dropped everything and split from the band one day, and the press went crazy. I honestly didn't think they would care. I left the country in the middle of the night. Lived in Europe for a few years, over to Australia for a few more till I knew it was safe to come back. I just needed time to let the press die down. It worked, because now it's the perfect set up. I write songs, other people sing them. No one knows who I am. No one remembers."

"But if you're making money writing songs, then why the escort business?"

"To meet people. To have fun. When I came back, I thought I would go into the police force, but you know the story behind that. That's when the escort business came to me."

I slowly let a breath out. Zach is a rock star. Wow. "I know you didn't like me to begin with because you saw me as a criminal. A guy who has sex for money, but now you know that's not the case. And...." He pauses for a second.

"And?"

"And, I wouldn't have met you if I hadn't been one." He smiles. "I think two people would be extremely unhappy right now."

Now I'm smiling. He pulls me in closer, my head rests on his chest. "I'm happy you're in my life, Cate. I don't want to screw this up." My heart flutters. I turn to him, my lips swiftly move to his, engaging in this soft, sweet kiss—sweeter than ever before. We part, and Zach gazes at me. "I love you, Cate." I must look horrified because he quickly says, "And it's okay if you aren't ready to say it yet." That's a relief, because I'm not ready to say it yet.

Zach then pulls me down on top of him and I'm taken back to the place he always manages to take me. The whole time, all I can think about is that I love Zach Kennedy.

The next morning we both get up, me the 'suspended cop' and him the 'ex-rock star/out of work escort', and drive down to the office where I intend on meeting with Mark face to face, who, by the way, hasn't returned my calls after I have left several over the last few weeks.

I say hello to Joan, who has been my ally this whole time. She's managed to find out that there is a possible conspiracy happening and everyone in the office, except her, is in on it.

Zach waits outside the door, reassuring me that I can do this, that he's not going anywhere. It gives me energy for when Mark greets me at his office door. He gives Zach a once over. At that moment, Zach pulls me in for a passionate kiss and releases me, saying, "I love you." I only nod, still unable to say those words.

The moment I'm in Mark's office, he closes the door. "So, what's up, Cate?"

"What's up? I've been calling and I haven't heard a thing from you. What's going on? This whole harassment thing has gone on far too long. I want this resolved. I want to get on with my life."

"Cate, you know this is out of my hands. I'm just doing you favors by delaying the release of your name. It's up to Internal Affairs now. They will get in touch with you when they have a date set for the hearing."

"Internal Affairs! Ha! They haven't even called me. Doesn't that seem a little odd?" I eye him up. Something's not right. He's barely made eye contact with me the whole time I've been in his office. "What's really going on?"

Now his eyes are on me; they change from trapped to curious in a few seconds flat. "I don't know what you mean."

"You know something, or there's something you aren't telling me."

"I don't know what you are talking about."

"I've seen that look before—usually when you're lying. Same look when you slept with that little recruit." Notice how any woman involved with the cheater is a 'little' so and so. That little hussy.

"You're paranoid. Relax. I'm working things out, okay?" He comes over to hug me but I back away; this throws him off his game. "So, is that your boyfriend out there?"

Boyfriend. I giggle inside. I like that word for Zach. "Yep. And he's wonderful." Mark lets out an exasperated breath. "And don't start changing the subject on me; you always did that. I'm here to talk about the case and why it's taking so damn long."

"We're working on it, okay?"

"I'm calling Internal Affairs."

"I don't know why you haven't yet. I expected much more from you, Cate, being the cop that you are."

Man, I could really do with slapping him upside the head right now. But I'm the bigger person here. I escape the clutches of Mark, and meet Zach's smiling face.

The next course of action is to contact my lawyer, Dan Sherman. The person I haven't spoken to in a while, the person that I used semi-sex as payment for his services; the man that dressed up as Dr. Frank-N_Furter, and the guy that I took down at a Halloween party. I've only spoken to him once on the phone since that night, in which he apologized profusely for going home with Darci, and that he would dump Darci if I wanted to get back together with him. I didn't want to break his heart and tell him we weren't together in the first place. I debated if I should lead him on by telling him that he broke my heart by dating Darci or maybe tell the truth about Zach. I tell him the latter.

Dan is quite surprised to see Zach with me when we arrive at his office later that day. He quickly pieces it all together and says, "Oh" when it makes sense. "So, I guess you having dinner with me is out?"

"Yes."

"Well, Zach, you have a wonderful woman there. Don't let her use some excuse to run away. She tends to do that." Dan walks around his desk and sits.

"Dan! I don't run away." Zach and I also take a seat. Zach grasps my hand.

"What's happening with the inquisition, Dan," Zach says before Dan can say anything further about the night we spent together.

"I don't know much more than you do. I've been running into road blocks, not receiving any of the information I've requested. IA isn't cooperating and I may have to get a warrant for info."

I can't believe that work isn't willing to give information. Something definitely isn't right.

When I return home, I call Internal Affairs immediately. They tell me the guy working on my case is out of town and should be back next week some time. I can leave a voicemail and I do. The guy's name is Quinn Gervais and I'm not familiar with him. Not like I'm really cozy with most of the people in IA, well, except for lately; I don't think this guy has been around long.

I hang up and walk out to the sun room where Zach is playing his guitar and writing a song. It's now mid-November and it's becoming colder. Outside my window are large flakes of the soft white kind floating down to the earth; everything looks freshly coated in icing sugar. Zach looks up and stops playing. God, he's handsome sitting there. I feel like cozying up inside his arms and staying there forever. He sees my need and wraps me up.

"Dead end?" he asks, his lips on my shoulder.

"Yeah."

"Don't worry. We'll get it sorted out." I like how Zach has now made my problem his problem. We'll. I'm not alone in this. For once, I don't feel absolutely alone in this.

"What can I do to make you feel better? Tea? Coffee? Chocolate?"

I look out the window. What would make me feel better? I grin.

"Sweaty sex."

"By the fire."

"On a bear skin rug," I add.

"You don't own a bear skin rug."

"We'll improvise."

Chapter 20
The Bargain Basement

I'm playing phone tag with the Internal Affairs dude, Quinn Gervais, which has become increasingly annoying. I leave him messages with my list of questions and he phones back, leaving me messages that are short and lacking info. "I'm looking into your file as we speak. I'll call you when I have all the documents."

Documents? It's been, what, a couple of months and he doesn't have all the documents? Each time I call him back, I, again, get voicemail and I'm officially annoyed. Something doesn't seem right, and I believe now it's time to stop being all passive, which isn't my style, and jump on this thing. I call the receptionist of Internal Affairs and ask for Gervais' schedule. She said that he'd be in on Monday from 8 am to 4 pm. I don't make an appointment because I have a feeling that, the moment he sees me scheduled in, he'll need me to reschedule. The man is being evasive and I need to find out why. Two months has been too long without answers.

Zach agrees to go with me as support; I know I can get this resolved easily with him in my corner.

*

"So, where's Zach tonight?" Susanne asks. She finishes applying her makeup with a few swirls of her blush brush.

I lean forward in the mirror and put on lip gloss. It's Saturday night and Susanne and I are having some girl time. We are heading to the martini bar at Riverton Inn where her husband Dave agreed to drop us off and pick us up when we were ready to come home.

"He has a friend in town that just split from his wife and he's meeting him to offer support." I press my lips together and smile at her.

"You're really smitten," she says. I blush, which is something I rarely do, but seem to be doing a lot lately.

"Nah." I am, though. "I have to admit that this relationship is much different than the others." I put the lid back on the lip gloss. "I'm borrowing this." I stuff it in my purse, Susanne doesn't bat an eye. She's used to it.

"Of course it is. You actually like him!"

I grimace. Yes, it's true. And, as of the other night, I love him, but I'm not going to say that too loud.

"We'd better go. Dave's texted he's outside." Susanne adjusts her skirt and top and we head out on the town.

"I'm glad you've found someone who suits you." Susanne gives me a sideways glance as get out of the car in front of the bar.

"He told me he loved me the other night," I say coolly. I can't believe I'm being so casual about this. Really, my whole insides are flipping.

Susanne stops me. "He did! That's great. What did you say?"

I bite my lip. "Nothing."

"What? Why?"

"I wasn't ready to. He actually said 'I understand if you aren't ready to say it back.' So, I didn't."

"Do you?"

I sigh. "Love is so complicated, don't you think?" I start walking again.

"Cate..." Susanne catches up to me.

"I have reason to believe that I do love him."

"Come on, Cate. This is your best friend you're talking to, not a court of law. Do you love him?"

I take a deep breath and stop walking. "Yes, I love him. There, I said it."

"I'm not the one you need to tell it to." She winks.

"I know. That's the next thing on my to-do list."

"I'm going to ask you about it tomorrow, so you better get around to it."

"Okay, I will," I toss her a look. "I promise." I smile cheesily as we walk through the last of the slushy snow in our high heels.

Finally, for once, things are beginning to balance out.

We take the steps up to the hotel where a porter in a long black coat opens the door for us. I toss around the idea that maybe an Irish coffee might be the first drink of the night instead of a Martini, just to keep me warm.

However, before I can make a decision, I turn around and run into Zach... and his date.

My smile fades and cold creeps in to my bones. The sensation of vomiting is hovering somewhere in my throat.

You know when your life seems so perfect for at least a minute, and then it shatters in an instant? This would be that moment.

My mind does quick calculations; I take note of the black overcoat, the hint of a black tie underneath, and realize he's wearing a tux. The woman next to him is in black fur over a green ball gown, and she's older than him. Doesn't she know that fur is so 1980s?

But, all this doesn't matter, because my heart is in my throat as Zach's expression confirms that he's been caught.

"You're friend who just split from his wife?" I question through gritted teeth.

"Cate…"

"You lying bastard!" I slap him hard across the face. I turn on my heel and run out the doors, my hand stinging, my head pounding, my feet becoming increasingly wet in my strappy shoes.

"Cate, wait! I can explain." Zach's footsteps are not far behind me and I try my best to run faster in these damn heels.

I stop, looking both ways for a cab, hoping one pulls up right now to take me away from this place forever.

"Cate, it's not what it looks like." He slides up to me, his shiny black shoes slipping all over the place; I wish he would fall right on his ass because I've heard all these lines a million times before. Mark used that line as he stood naked before me.

"So, what is it exactly? You're an escort again! You said you were done with it. Oh, god, I'm so stupid. Out with a friend! Ha!" I continue to hold out my arm, waiting for a stupid taxi to stop. Why aren't they stopping?!

"Cate, there is a good explanation for this if you just give me a chance." He grabs my hand and I pull it away.

A cab finally arrives and I open the door. "Don't bother." One last look at Zach tells him not to follow me as I get in. As we pull away, I don't intend on glancing back, or at least, I don't want to glance back without giving it a few seconds. When I do, Zach is running his hand through his hair and I realize I will never touch that hair again.

*

By the time I get home, Zach has called my answering machine sixteen times and my cell phone, which I turned off in the cab the first time he called, twenty.

Cate, please call me, it's not what you think.
Cate, it's Zach. I can explain everything.
Cate, I told Susanne what was going on, please call.
Cate, it's Susanne. I spoke to Zach and I think you should at least hear him out. I hope you're okay. Call me to let me know you are okay.
Cate, listen, she's a friend. Honest to god. Please call me.

A friend. That's rich. As much as I want to believe him, he still lied about meeting his buddy. I grab a beer from the fridge and take a long swig. Bastard. I take another swig. Asshole. And another. Jerk. And another, till I can't find anymore words to insult him with in his absence. By that time, the beer is gone, and I grab another and lie on the couch in semi-darkness. My strappy shoes are wet and lying misshapen by the coffee table.

My feet throb from the cold and I yank off my nylons, warming my feet with a blanket. He lied. And I can't believe I fell for it again. Did I really think he would quit the escort business for me? Did I really think that I could have an honest relationship?

The tears slowly come and I force myself to stop crying. But that only lasts a few minutes and the water-works begin.

I must have dozed off because when I awake, I'm still in my clothes and there's pounding at the door. I look through the curtains. Zach. Of course, it's Zach. Who else would it be?

"Cate, I know you're in there. Please let me in. I can explain everything."

"Go away," I yell.

"Cate, come on!"

"Go away, Zach!"

"I'm not leaving till you open the door and talk to me." A pause. I'm not opening the door. "Cate!" More banging. I don't say anything. Maybe he'll go away if I keep quiet.

"Cate, honey, she's a friend. She's married. I was doing her husband a favor. He was a guest speaker at some ceremony tonight and he wanted someone to take care of his wife. He's a good friend. I couldn't refuse. I didn't even get paid for it!" Oh, brother. Now we're really grasping, aren't we?

"You lied, Zach," I say through the door.

I think I hear a sigh on the other side. "I know. I should have told you the truth. I didn't think it was going to be a big deal..."

"You didn't think you'd get caught," I reiterate.

"Cate, I'm sorry. I handled this all wrong. Please, let's...let's just talk about it."

"Talk about what? Talk about how you faked your way into my heart and then screwed me in the end. Talk about how I trusted you and then you did something I absolutely cannot stand. You're the one that's been talking about winning my trust, and then you go back on your own word. Obviously, there's nothing to talk about!"

"Cate, please, just open the door..." he says softly. I peek through the curtains. He has his head and palms resting on the door. He looks so tortured. Good. Then I hear, "I love you."

He loves me.

Why does he have to play that card? I was doing so well before he said those words. I still don't know what I'm going to do as I open the door. I'm torn between making up and slamming the door in his face. Zach looks absolutely relieved. "Thank you," he breathes. He takes a step toward me, but I put up a hand.

"You lied, Zach."

"I know, I know. I'm so sorry. If I could, I would change everything. Please, tell me how can I make this right?"

I then realize that there is only one thing he can do to make it right. And, in turn, it is the hardest thing I will ever have to do. "You can't, Zach. I can't give a liar a second chance."

"Cate..." he whispers. "This isn't how it's supposed to be. God, I love you so much." He reaches to cup my face in his hands, but I can't look at him.

I put my hand to his chest and push him outside. "I can't, Zach." And I close the door.

*

Two weeks. Two whole weeks have gone by since Zach lied to me. He's phoned a zillion times. Sometimes I'll pick up; most times I'll let it go to voicemail. It's the same old thing, anyway—'I'm sorry, please, let's talk. I didn't mean to hurt you. You mean everything to me. I love you.' Of course, I cry my head off, lie in bed a little too long, and eat too much junk food, but I manage. To make matters worse, I can't even get up to go to Internal Affairs. I can't face them. Basically, everything is crumbling all around me and I don't know how to stop it.

There have been many times when Zach has come by, tries to get me to talk. I don't want to see him; it's hard seeing him. He looks good, even though he hasn't slept much and has dark circles under his eyes. Also, there's a chance of me melting if I see him, letting those warm arms wrap around me protectively.

After the third attempt to try and get into my house, I tell him to leave or I'll call the police, and, if he comes back again, I'll have him charged with trespassing. He doesn't come by again.

Susanne wants me to call him, to talk it out. What she fails to understand is that he still lied. Nan knows all about the incident and of course sides with him. "We all have our little lies and secrets, Cate. You didn't tell me about your job suspension." Oh, sure, she has to throw that into the mix.

"That's different, Nan. Zach is my boyfriend...or was my boyfriend. He shouldn't be lying to me about escorting. If he explained it to me, I'd have understood." Really, I would have. But Nan snorts anyway, obviously disagreeing with me.

"How does he look, Nan?" I ask. I'm just curious. If he looks rough, well, good.

"If you're so interested in how he's doing, then come over and see for yourself," she says sternly.

I'm not giving in. It's impossible for me to take back a liar. Okay, not impossible. But right now, I don't feel like talking things over. I don't feel like trying again. He's hurt me too much.

Chapter 21
Dangling the Carrot

Where would we be without retail therapy? I know where I would be: still sitting on the couch in my housecoat and slippers feeling sorry for myself. After I finally got my butt off the couch, I head straight to the mall. I feel much better just breathing in the recycled air, the greasy fries, and eating some chocolate. I buy numerous outfits, shoes, even towels for the bathroom because the bathroom needs a little love too. This all gives me the boost that I'm looking for, even if it's only for a short time. I even plan to tie up loose ends, call Mark, and the guy in IA, the one that's being elusive and has not told me one single thing. But, I don't care. Is it bad that I don't care? What's happening to me?

Really, I'm finding this time off to be a blessing in disguise as I try to deal with the whole Zach-deception thing. Maybe I'll even call Zach when I get home, just to say hi, see what's going on.

We'll see.

I guess I shouldn't say I've been doing nothing but be a couch-potato. I did manage to head out to the Black Swan with Joan the other night and we had our man-bashing session. She had a marriage that ended in divorce about five years ago and told me her ex wasn't that upstanding.

We have a few too many beers with Earl the bartender giving us some sage advice: "Don't take any of his crap."

Well said, Earl. Well said. Cindy, the ex-con, even gets in on the conversation, relaying her experiences with men...none of which have anything to do with prostitution. She said it, not me. Maybe she saw my questioning stare.

As I throw the bags from my shopping excursion onto the floor, my call display indicates that Susanne, Nan, and Zach called. Zach called. I'm relieved but leery. I won't call him just yet. I'll put my purchases away, grab something to eat, clean the house a bit. I'll take some time to mull it over before calling. I do want to talk to him. I've missed him so much, but that hurt feeling still lingers there. How do I get rid of that?

I putter around a bit in the kitchen, thinking about what to say, how to say it. Should I invite him over? Obviously, he should come here since he's the one that needs to do the begging. I'll let him come over for an hour and then tell him to leave. Tempt him with the dangling carrot, then take it away. Repeat.

Two hours later, I finally listen to his message. What I say to him will depend on what he says on the message. I fast forward past Nan's and Susanne's messages, heading straight to Zach's.

"Cate, I'm truly sorry for everything that happened. I wish I could change it. I wish I hadn't been such a....jerk. I'm hoping you'll speak to me again, one day. Anyway, I just want to say goodbye. I'm leaving town for a while. I got in with a band and we're touring around Europe for six months. I just wish I could say goodbye in person," he pauses as if he hopes I'll pick up the phone. "I love you," he finally says, then click.

He's leaving? Europe? Six months? I thought...I thought...I don't know what I thought. No, I know exactly what I thought. I thought I would let him slowly work his way back into my life, and I'd slowly start trusting him again and eventually things would get back to normal. Instead, he's going away for six months and probably will never return. He'll probably forget about me the moment he steps on the plane, and run into some other woman's arms in first class. They'll laugh as they drink the complimentary champagne and he'll tell her how he made a big mistake but has learned and would like to make a fresh start...with her! And he's joined a band? I thought he didn't want to be in the 'lime light' anymore?

I pick up the phone, hesitating for a half second, then dial the number. No answer at the guest house. I dial his cell phone. The number you have reached is out of the service area. Please try again.

When was he leaving? He didn't say.

I dial another number. No answer. Where the hell is everyone? I hop in my car and drive over to Nan's, which is still at least a half hour drive, dialing her number on my cell phone every five or ten minutes. Dialing Zach's number, with still the same message.

I pull in front of Nan's place just as she's entering the door with Syd.

"Nan! Where's Zach? I need to speak to him."

"Cate, honey, he left this morning."

"This morning? Why didn't anyone tell me?" Tears stream down my face; I really need to get a hold of this whole crying thing. "Why didn't you call me?"

"You told me you didn't want to hear any more about Zach."

"You should know by now that I never know what I'm talking about on a day to day basis." I wipe my nose on my jacket sleeve. It occurs to me at this very moment that I don't know what I'm doing and never have. Years ago, everything seemed so clear. Everything fell into place. But, now, I really don't know.

"I fucked up, Nan."

She doesn't say anything about my swearing; instead she sits me down on the bench outside the front door. Syd has left us alone. "I want him in my life, but I can't trust him. God, I screwed up. I should have listened to him. Talked to him about it. Now he'll never know that I love him," I bawl.

"Honey, life gives you choices. You have to decide which choices you want to make."

"That doesn't make me feel better."

"Sorry, but you're going to have to figure this one out on your own."

"Nope, still not making me feel better. Honestly, Nan, what are you trying to do to me? Zach is gone and I feel like crap. I can't even run off to the airport to stop his plane, because, apparently, he left this morning." I slap my hands over my eyes and cry. "Will someone just make me feel better?" She rubs my back, puts her arms around me and waits till I'm ready to move. It becomes too cold to tolerate sitting outside, so Nan invites me in, but there are too many memories there, and besides, I'll probably just go to the guest house and smell his pillow or something. This isn't good for getting over him. He's gone and I missed my chance. That's the truth.

*

The things I've learned during my process of trying to get over Zach:

- Chocolate is a must-have comfort food.
- If there's no 'regular' chocolate in the house, those little chocolate baking squares are just as good.
- If there's no baking chocolate in the house, canned icing is a good alternative.
- If none of the above are available, pancake syrup is an easy stand-in.
- If that doesn't work, hitting the 7-11 is in order.

And I'm not above shuffling my way down there in my PJs and slippers for some chocolate comfort. Okay, so slippers aren't a great idea in winter, but my high heeled boots over my pink and grey plaid pajama bottoms are a nice fashion statement.

There are a few people staring at my fashion faux pas, my bed-head hair that is severely twisted into a rat's nest, my puffy eyes from on-and-off crying, and remnants of chocolate still hiding in the corners of my mouth. Come on? As if they haven't seen the likes of me before down near the river; the only difference is that I haven't started talking to myself...yet.

I place five chocolate bars on the counter and a bag of chips to take the edge off of all the sweetness. The clerk at the counter sports a green faux-hawk, which he's matched up with a silver headband. His fingernails are painted purple and it's all so surreal as he wears a 7-11 uniform. He eyes me up as he scans my items, on the verge of saying something.

"These for you, darlin'?"

"Yep."

"Got it pretty bad, huh?"

I nod and burst into tears.

"Oh, honey," he grabs a tissue and hands it to me. Meanwhile, ten people have lined up behind me. "You listen to me now. There is no one as fabulous as you. You stand tall, darlin' because there ain't no man out there that is worth those tears." He then pushes my snacks toward me. "These are on the house." I wipe away the stray tears and leave the store with my stash, wondering what exactly happened in there.

I walk the block or two back to my home and stumble to the couch where I've been lying around for the past week. What have I been doing the whole time? Let's see, I've absently flicked the channels while stuffing Kit-Kats into my mouth; screening my calls, avoiding Susanne and Nan and anyone else—by the way, none of those calls have been from Zach. It's obvious he did forget about me the moment he stepped on the plane.

Oh, wait, Karate Kid's on. I love this show; too bad it's almost over. I settle in with my chocolate bars on my stomach, ready to unwrap the first one. I decided to try a different kind, one with peanut butter. I don't usually go for the peanut butter/chocolate combo, but today it just seemed right.

Just as I stuff the first bar into my mouth, and as Mr. Miagi fixes Ralph Macchio's injured knee because that blonde jerk pretty much broke it, the phone rings. Caller ID tells me it's Susanne—again. I decide to answer. Her last message warned me she would come over if I didn't pick up the next time she called. If I want to avoid visitors, I should at least tell her I'm good and quite happy with my stash of chocolate. What else do I need?

"Hi."

"What are you doing?" She's gruff. Doesn't she know I'm in mourning? She could be nicer.

"Oh, just watching Karate Kid."

"Are you ever going to get dressed and start living again?"

"Hmm, not sure. Oh, wait, it's the very end. Ralph is doing that thing, that stork thing."

"It's called the crane," she corrects me.

"Here it comes..." I hold my breath till Ralph kicks his opponent with one swift move. "Yes! Ralphie baby!" My voice quivers; I'm sitting up, glued to the TV.

"Are you crying?"

"No."

"Yes, you are! You're crying over The Karate Kid."

"So? It's a great moment in history."

"Cate, you can't sit around watching '80s movies all day. You need to get up."

"For what? I don't have a job to go to. No boyfriend to be with." I pause. Oh, god, my state of affairs is worse than I thought. At least I thought I had a job to go to, but I haven't done one thing about it. It's like I dropped off the face of the earth.

"I'm coming over!"

"Don't bother."

"I'm coming over. You better have that weenie butt off the couch and showered."

Before I can protest and tell her the weenie butt has inflated to that of a large chocolate macaroon, she hangs up. I don't follow her orders, but continue to lie on the couch and open up the bag of chips. I wonder what else is on today.

Half hour later, while I'm watching Footloose, Susanne is at my door. She looks like a little piece of heaven, all glowing, and smelling like oranges. Ooo, orange chocolate. That would taste good.

"Get up," she orders.

"Get up? Why? Zach's gone!" I blubber. It has to be the chocolate talking.

"Yes, Zach is gone, but that doesn't mean you have to sit here and wait till the hurting stops. You're a fighter, Cate!"

I eye her suspiciously. "Either you tell that same line to your clients or you saw it in a movie."

"For Pete's sake! Stop wallowing in self-pity and get off the couch. You kicked him out of your life; he's gone. You either track him down or you move on. Just stop playing the victim."

I'm appalled. Her words really cut me deeply. I'm not the victim. How did I become the victim? Why me?

"Thanks, Susanne! I really didn't need that!" I bawl into my hands.

"Yes. You. Did." She pulls me to my feet, surveying my pile of chocolate bar wrappers. Then she surveys me in my rumpled PJs and matted hair. Come to think of it, I don't know if I've showered in a few days. "You're a mess. Get thee to a shower!" She pushes me towards the bathroom. She brings me my new fluffy purple towels from the closet, turns on the water and leaves me to my devices.

I reluctantly shower, and won't admit I feel a bit better. I'm still stinging by her words and don't feel like being her friend at this point. Why can't she just cuddle me and make me feel better, or take the pain away? Fortunately for Susanne, I know that she's only trying to snap me out of it.

I come out, my hair wrapped into a towel, my robe on. I bite back wanting to tell her off and kick her out of my place for good. Instead, I make a bold move on my part, and decide to let her take charge. "What next?" Susanne's rummaging through my closet pulling out clothes.

"Here, put these on. Have to use the bathroom." Susanne literally runs off, which I find bizarre. My eyes fall to the jeans and shirt sitting on the bed. I look through the closet again seeing as I don't like the shirt she's picked for me and come across a shirt that doesn't belong to me. I hold my breath. It's Zach's. Zach's shirt. The one I had worn home the first time we got together. It's still here in my closet. I pull it out and smell it. It smells like him...and me. I lie down on the bed and place it over my face, taking deep breaths.

"Are you smelling that shirt?" Susanne demands.

I take another deep breath. "Yes, it's Zach's." I don't even save face by removing it; instead I continue lying there. "Susanne, I miss him so much." My words are muffled. I can feel another crying fit coming on but restrain myself because Susanne has run off to the bathroom again. What is with her? Small bladder? Or—I get up and stride to the bathroom door, hearing the water run. When she opens the door, she's a tinge of green.

"Are you pregnant?" I ask. I'm still carrying Zach's shirt, except now it's draped around my neck like a scarf.

Susanne bites her lip and nods.

"Susanne! Why didn't you say something? How long? Tell me all about it!" I hug her and walk her back to my room where I continue to hold Zach's shirt to my nose.

"It's just confirmed. I didn't want to say anything because you're going through your own stuff and felt it would depress you even more."

"You're ridiculous. So, when? When is this baby due?"

"July." She pauses a moment catching her breath, then nods that she's fine. "I think it happened that night you and Zach had that barbeque. We've been trying for some time now—and nothing. And then the night of the barbeque, we went home and I think it just took."

Right. The barbeque. That was a perfect night. I sniff the shirt again and feel my heart plummet once more to my stomach.

"I'm sorry, Cate, I didn't mean to rub that in your face."

"No, no. You tell me all your happy news. It makes me feel better." I get dressed and put on Zach's shirt and my jeans. I feel better wearing it.

"I thought maybe you could use some retail therapy. You can buy yourself something nice, I can find something for the baby, I mean, if you are up for it."

"You're like a sister to me, Susanne. Of course I want to help you shop for the baby." I then address her non-existent belly.

"Isn't that right, baby? We're going shopping for you." I grab my purse and jacket. "And thank you for getting me off the couch. I've now seen all the episodes of Dawson's Creek and don't know if I can force myself to watch Top Gun for the third time in two days."

*

This turns out to be a perfect day. Aside from having to stop twice for Susanne to throw up, things go well. We buy some blankets and unisex sleepers for the baby, and a pair of pants and a pair of shoes for me. We also end up getting a pedicure. Sadly, this is the first decent lunch I've had since last week, aside from chocolate.

"I know this is hard for you, Cate, but I think it's time to get your career problems in order. Maybe call Mark or Dan. Take a more proactive stance. Ever since Zach left, you've kicked everything to the curb. I hate to see this happen to you, I mean, since you love your job and all."

I nod. I love my job. Right. I loved my job is more like it. "I know. You're right. Tomorrow. I will do it tomorrow." Susanne has to have caught my unconvincing tone; I mean, even I don't believe myself.

But, by the time I get home, work has beaten me to it. "Cate Chase, this is Chief Norman. I would like to arrange a meeting with you tomorrow to talk about this harassment charge. Please call me to confirm." What? The Chief is calling me? This has become serious. Feeling only slightly panicked, I quickly phone his office and get his secretary. She's made arrangements for me to come in the next morning, not giving me any indication why I'm coming in or what will be discussed. What should I wear? My uniform? No, I can't wear that. I'm suspended. I guess it'll be civies. I can't wear Zach's shirt though, I suppose it has to be something a bit nicer. My new pants and shoes and some sort of top? That'll work.

That night I sleep in Zach's shirt knowing that I'll have to one day throw it in the wash. I try my best not to spill jam on it just so I can wear it to bed the next night. In the morning, I part ways with it, telling it I will return to it the moment I get home.

*

I pull in front of headquarters fifteen minutes before our meeting. It's been a while since I've been here, and deep down inside, I know I haven't missed it.

I sit in the waiting room listening to another officer's radio bleep in the background about a traffic accident with injuries and I find myself tuning it out, finding myself not interested in how many units are headed there, how they're blocking off traffic, and if there are any fatalities. This is the stuff that used to get me going. I'm not that interested now.

Finally, the door opens and the chief walks out. He's wearing his uniform pants, white shirt and tie. His dark hair is receding and has dashes of white on the sides. I haven't met him in person before; I never had a need to until now.

"Cate, thanks for coming by. Come on in." I walk into the office and take a seat. I'm nervous. Is this the day I get canned? The chief is now involved and that means something major is going to happen. It must be worse than I originally thought and I brace myself for the inevitable.

The chief sits behind his desk and lays out some papers before him. He places his long fingered hands on top of the pages, as if protecting them. "I'm sorry I didn't get back to you sooner. As you know, Internal Affairs always handles these cases and I merely get an update on what's going on. Turns out, I should have been inquiring about this situation all along."

He wanted to inquire about this investigation? When did the chief investigate Internal Affairs' complaints?

"After I met with Zach and Herbert Kennedy, and after Zach told me what was going on and how it was being dealt with, I had to step in."

I'm sure my eyes are bulging out of my head right now. "I'm sorry, did you say Zach Kennedy?"

"Yes, didn't he tell you?"

"Tell me what?"

"That he called me."

"I'm sorry, could we back up a bit? How do you know Zach Kennedy?"

"Zach's dad and I worked the street together many years ago. Then Zach's father and I were both Deputy Chief together. I'm a good friend of the family. I've known Zach ever since he was very young."

I can't speak at this point. Why didn't Zach say anything? Why didn't he tell me he saw the chief? Why didn't his Dad tell me he was best buds with Chief Norman?

"Zach and Herb came to talk to me, let's see, over two weeks ago. Told me the situation and asked me if there was anything I could do."

Zach called the chief for me?

"And I looked into it. I checked out your history—very impressive Sergeant Chase." He smiles. "Then I checked things out at the station. Spoke to some people. A woman named Joan is very fond of you."

Joan! Joan spoke on my behalf. I have chills.

"I also spoke to some other officers. What I discovered was that it all came down to one thing—this is a false claim. It shouldn't have been issued in the first place."

I want to throw up. "So, are you telling me that the charges have been dropped?"

"Yes, that's exactly what I'm saying. The plaintiff has been relegated to front desk duty." His eyes twinkle when he says this. I want to hug him right about now. "And his accomplice has been let go." He sees my questioning stare. "Quinn Gervais was in on it too; that's why nothing was getting done." I nod. Okay, it's making sense now. "You can return back to your same position with your team tomorrow."

Tomorrow? That soon. After all this, why is my heart screaming 'no?' I must be releasing some emotional stress right now. My brain probably hasn't acknowledged that I'm getting my job back. I stand, shaking the chief's hand. "Thank you. Thank you, so much."

"You should thank Zach. He's the one that got the ball rolling."

I sigh. "I can't. He's...he's left the country." I'm not going to cry. I'm not going to cry.

"So I've heard." I shake his hand one more time and turn to leave the room. "If it helps, he spoke very warmly of you."

I hold my breath.

"I could see it in his eyes. I've known him for a long time; I'm pretty good at judging what's going on." He smiles knowingly.

I feel like hugging him and telling him my problems. Instead, I tell myself once again that I'm not going to cry. No matter how paternal the chief is being, I cannot cry in front of him. "Right. Well, if I get a chance to talk to Zach, I will thank him. Thank you, Chief Norman, for everything." I leave the office knowing this hollow feeling has everything to do with going back to my job.

*

I show up for my eight a.m. shift, ready to face my co-workers. I have my first meeting with my team and notice how attentive and willing they are. I note the new recruits on my team that I plan to shape and mold; I also notice one of my team members is missing—Sabinski. Yep. He was a trouble maker. I guess he's on desk duty now.

I walk to my office and get rid of the stuff that doesn't belong there: gym bag with sweaty clothes still inside, dirty plates, pictures of someone else's kids. I set up shop, putting my pictures up, arranging my dungeon the way I like it, and spraying air freshener to get rid of the smell. I organize my pens, sign on to my computer and look at all the emails that I missed. I delete most of them without reading them.

Joan comes to visit, asking me how I'm doing, almost setting me up with another son. This one is eighteen years old and is going to be a dentist—one day. She tells me her son Ian has found a girl and they've been dating ever since we split. That seems like eons ago. She asks me about Zach; I don't want to talk about it, so she leaves, squeezing my arm and telling me she's here for me. That's sweet.

Mark is next in line, welcoming me back, hitting on me; obviously, he knows Zach and I broke up. Joan must have said something. Not that I really care. I tell him I'm off the market, well, his market anyway, and that if he ever comes in here again to hit on me, I'll make his life a living hell, just as my life was made a living hell. He looks scared and immediately leaves.

Next up is Erickson. I'm on a roll today. "So, you got any big plans your first day back at work? Maybe let some criminals go because you feel sorry for them."

I keep my attention on my computer as Erickson doesn't deserve anything more. "You know...I missed you, Erickson."

I sense he's thrown off of his game for a split second. "Really?"

"No. Now get the hell out of my office." And he does. Chalk one up for keeping it simple. I don't really feel like heading out today, but now that Erickson has pissed me off, I change my mind. I manage to give a few tickets to people, arrest someone on a warrant for a lame failing to pay a transit ticket charge and assist another unit with a domestic complaint, but I refuse to get into it. I only attend the call to make sure my team members are doing all right, then leave. And all the while, something is missing. Something doesn't feel the same anymore. My heart isn't into it. I wish I had known this when I was on suspension, then at least I could have made some progress in figuring out what to do to get out of this job. There was too much going on back then. Too much drama.

My computer bleeps and I hit a button to see a call coming in for a vehicle stolen not too far from here. The dispatcher comes over the air and announces it to all units, describing the car as a 2006 blue Honda Civic, license plate 3245LF. Fuck, a stolen vehicle! Memories of my last few stolen auto pursuits still linger in my head. They didn't go well. Then, again, my team was against me.

A few of my team's units voice over the radio that they're going on the call, but I don't say anything. I'm nervous. What the fuck am I doing? I'm their sergeant. I should be on this call. Why am I not speaking up? Deep down inside, I'm afraid of screwing up. I don't trust myself and I don't trust my units. Just like my relationship with Zach. I didn't trust him from the beginning, and sure, he did lie, but really, he earned my trust up until that point. He never did anything else to make me question his credibility. Then he went and spoke to the chief for me. He wouldn't want me to hide from my job, the job that I was always so good at.

I click my radio and announce I'm on the call as well and drive to the area with nausea setting in and my brain stabbing away at all of the doubts.

Focus. Focus. Okay, blue Honda Civic.

Just as I approach the next street, a blue Honda Civic careens out of the back alley, cutting me off and speeding away. I take a few seconds to realize that this is the stolen vehicle, but my instincts manage to kick into high gear.

I grab my radio. "4750 to dispatch, I'm behind a blue Honda civic heading southbound on 32 St crossing 52 Av. Confirming license plate: 3-2-4-3-lima-foxtrot. Two occupants, speed at 75 kms/hr."

"Chase, is this a pursuit? Road conditions are shitty," Inspector Mark yells over the radio.

"No, this isn't a pursuit." It really isn't. I haven't flicked on my overheads or my sirens, so technically, it isn't a pursuit. "Roads are clear and traffic is minimal," I say sternly. This is a lie as there's a bit more traffic out here than expected at this time of day, and the roads are a tad icy. However, if I tell him that, he will call it off, and I'm not letting this one go. I put my foot down on the pedal and turn down 66 Ave right behind the offenders. With the heavy traffic, I finally decide to put on lights and sirens.

"Dispatch, I'm primary," I announce, meaning I'm the one calling the shots as I'm right behind the vehicle; this is now a pursuit. "Now westbound 66 Ave approaching 31 St. Speeds at 75 km/h. Not slowing."

Another cruiser pulls in behind me, lights flashing. "4758 is secondary."

"4733 is on 29 St approaching 66 Ave."

"4733, they are headed your way. Lay the spike belt," I order.

"10-4."

"Chase, call it off! Speeds are too high for residential!" Mark booms. I ignore his request and keep going.

"Roads are clear. Speed at 100 km/hr," I bark into the radio. This is my pursuit. I call the shots.

"4719 is 28 St and 66 Ave."

"4719 and 4758, if he continues over the spike belt, we'll box him in. There's a chance they might off shoot the next two turn offs."

"10-4."

Now all that has to happen is for these guys to continue to 29 St. They might try to elude me by turning off. Or, they might continue straight on as they have the speed for it. My guess is they will go straight till they hit the major thoroughfare, which is only a few blocks away. Please don't turn. Please don't turn! My breath now suspended somewhere in my chest. I can see the lights of my secondary unit right behind me; the sound of sirens fills the entire car and I can feel that this is going to work.

I hold my breath as we approach 31 St, then 30 St, and when they don't turn, I know they are mine. Coming up to 29 St, I see 4733 has the spike belt positioned, the street is blocked off. It's almost too perfect. Can it be this perfect? Have the planets aligned for me today?

They have to know that this is it, it's over for them. They didn't expect the spike belt, it's obvious, or they would have driven on someone's lawn. They fly over the prongs, two tires puncture and they roll down the road, the rubber flipping and flopping around and around. Within a minute, the vehicle slows. 4719 takes the front of the vehicle, I take the side, and 4758 takes the rear, boxing them in. I hop out of my cruiser, and safely position myself with my gun drawn. Wilkins, who laid the spike belt, positions next to me. My other officers have their eye on the car.

"Hands to the ceiling of the car," I yell. The two offenders quickly do as I say. Looks like some kids going out on a joyride. They've probably wet their pants by now.

"Driver, step out of the car with your hands in plain sight." He does and I get him to move around to the front of the car. In a matter of minutes, I have him and his partner lying prostrate on the ground, cuffed and crying.

Everyone who didn't think I could do it can eat it. Sabinski, Mark, that guy in IA, even though I never met him, and anyone else who didn't think I had it in me.

But really, who cares what they think? I just want to phone Zach and tell him all about it and that I need him. I want to tell him that I want to leave police work for good and I need him with me when I do. But that's not going to happen.

Chapter 22
What we achieve inwardly will change outer reality. – Plutarch

"Good work on the stolen auto." Mark is at my office door. He steps in like I invited him or something. "But, I'm pretty sure I told you to call it off," he says, arms folded across his chest.

"Thanks, I'll take the kudos, but I'm not going to justify my actions." I turn back to my paperwork. I've actually become organized since returning back to work. My desk is clear, my work is filed immediately, and I have zero Internal Affairs complaints. I guess it's only been a day.

He sighs. "You don't seem too happy about it."

I sit back in my chair and lick my lips. They taste sweet from the mochachino I just had. "I guess I'm happy. I'm happy that no one was injured. I'm happy the outcome was positive. I don't know, Mark. What else do you want me to say?"

"This is what you've been waiting for, isn't it? Make some sort of major imprint on your police career."

"I don't think a successful stolen auto pursuit will go down in the books as anything major. And besides, I've done many other 'major' things during my career that I can certainly be proud about." Where was this coming from? Was this the new me or was it the old me resurfacing? Perhaps a mixture of the two?

"Well, next time this happens, ensure that the roads are clear and traffic is minimal. When you are out there, be straight up with me." He turns to leave.

"Just like you were being straight up with me?"

Mark stops in his tracks. "Huh?"

"During this whole sexual harassment thing. You weren't being straight with me. You knew about it, didn't you, Mark? You knew it was a false allegation." I slowly stand, my hands on my duty belt.

"What are you saying? I protected you."

"You protected your own interests. I don't know what happened, or what kind of deal was struck with you, or who else was involved, but you went along with this whole charade. It didn't occur to me till just recently, but it makes sense now."

Mark is speechless. He's too busy thinking of some perfect comeback. "So, you're going to tell the chief on me, is that it? Now that you two are best buds because of your boyfriend."

I take a dramatic pause before saying, "I'll take care of it." I walk out my office door. I actually don't have 100% proof that Mark had been involved, and was only taking a stab in the dark. However, it really does align with who he is and our history, doesn't it? He's a liar and a cheat, and always will be.

*

Starbucks Coffee House, seven o'clock on a Tuesday night. This is our new place to meet now that Susanne is with child. She sips tea, I sip coffee and we talk about work and Zach.

"Mark was in on it? The bastard!" She growls.

"I know. I can't believe I dated that guy."

"I can't believe you lived with him."

"I can't believe I slept with him," I shiver.

"So, what are you going to do now?"

"I could say something, but I'd need more proof. Or, I could hold onto it like blackmail."

"By the way, what's it like being back at work?"

"Hmm, good. Making lots of progress getting back into it, you know....and...and...you know," I pause.

"No, I don't know."

I sigh. "I hate it."

"What?"

"God, I hate my job."

"I thought you loved it. It's all you've ever talked about."

"I did like it. It's just not in me anymore. I want to own a bookstore."

Susanne almost chokes on her tea. "What? A bookstore. Where did this come from?"

I rub my neck. Zach was the only one I told about this. I can't believe I never told Susanne. Maybe because I thought it was lame. "I've always wanted to own a bookstore, but thought it was silly, so I never told anyone, except Zach on the night we were thrown in jail."

"Oh, Cate. Why don't you then? Just find out what you can about opening one up. Lord knows we need a decent bookstore in Riverton. That quasi bookstore/comic shop downtown just isn't cutting it."

"Too bad Zach wasn't here to help," I say absently.

"Why don't you call him?"

"I have no idea where he is."

"I'm sure someone knows. Nan. His parents."

I nod.

"You don't seem to gung-ho about it."

I shrug. "I don't know. Well, I guess I do. I was rotten to him, and wouldn't allow him back on my property and now he's gone and I haven't heard from him since. I treated him like a criminal and he got my job back. I've lost him for good, Susanne." I wipe a tear away from my cheek.

"You don't know that for sure. Talk to him."

"What would I say?" I snivel. "Oh, forget it! It was a dumb idea anyway. I'll just go back to my job. It's really not that bad. Really. I mean, look what I accomplished since being back. I threw some teens in jail...their parents must be proud." I sniffle some more.

"Take some time off, Cate."

"Time off? I just had a bunch of time off. I can't just take more time off because I hate my job."

"Why not? You've gone all these years without taking a real holiday. You have tons of holiday time. They owe you a relaxing break, and now that you have your job back, you can start concentrating on what you really want to do."

"I don't need to take time off to know exactly what I want to do. I already know."

"Then do it. What are you waiting for?"

I'm silent for a moment. This is all a bit crazy. "Can I really do it?" I hear myself say out loud.

"Yes. I know you loved being a cop, but since being away from that job, you've turned into this.... human being."

"And, what, I wasn't a human being before?"

"No."

"Susanne!"

"Sorry! But you're less tense now, less angry, more tolerant. I'm sure that some of this has to do with Zach. Honestly, being away from that place has changed you. You're more relaxed. I like this Cate. The old Cate is gone. Please don't bring her back."

She's right. Things have changed. This job isn't me anymore. I've outgrown it. "I'll think about it." I say. I'm not committing just yet. There's still work to be done, plans to be made.

"And find Zach. Someone knows a number or something."

"You're starting to sound really motherly, you know."

"I know. Pregnancy has imparted some sort of wisdom on me."

"I could call his parents," I say meekly.

"Then do it."

"But what if they hate me."

Susanne looks me square in the eye. "Zach and his dad helped you get your job back. I doubt that they hate you. Now get on that phone and call them."

*

Turns out they do love me. As soon as they heard my voice, they insisted I come over before I could say another word. When I arrive at the ranch house just after seven the next evening, they're waiting out front for me just like they did the first time I met them.

"Herbert, Vivian, hi." I hug them, knowing that they won't accept anything less.

"We're so glad you called, Cate. We were worried about you. I mean, after that misunderstanding between you and Zach." Vivian pats my arm, but won't say anything further regarding the 'misunderstanding'. "Come in. Let's talk."

They lead me into the ranch house and we sit at the wooden kitchen table, drinking coffee and eating homemade cinnamon buns that Zach's mom made.

"So, how have you been?" Vivian starts.

"Great. I'm back at work now, as you know. And, Herbert, thank you so much for handling that for me. I really appreciate it."

"I can't take all of the credit. Zach was really the one who spearheaded the meeting. I just went in to give him some back-up." He winks at me.

"So, um, how is Zach?" Come on. Why am I being so dancey around the Zach issue? Obviously, they know I'm here to talk about Zach.

"Zach is doing well. We spoke to him, when was it, Herb?" Vivian eyes her hubby.

"Two nights ago. He was in Paris. Heading over to London. Should be there now, hey?" Herb gives Vivian a look. I guess everyone is dancing around the issue tonight.

"I'd say. Hmmm, now let's see. Where did we put that number?" Vivian searches by the phone. "Oh, here it is." She magically produces a small piece of paper with the word 'Zach' on it and an overseas number.

"Oh, I don't need to call him." Right. I need to smarten up when I say stupid things.

"Just take it, you know, in case. And if he phones here, we'll tell him you came by and he should give you a call."

"No, no. Please don't get him to call me. Just...um...just tell him I say hi."

"He did ask if we had heard from you. But, of course, this was before you called us."

"Is he...meeting new.... people?" It sounds awkward. Thankfully, Vivian, bless her heart, gets my meaning.

"Oh, you know, a few buddies here and there, but they're really too busy to form any friendships. He misses everyone." Vivian nods.

"Of course." I take another sip of my coffee, willing the phone to ring while I'm here. Hoping Zach will call so I can nonchalantly get on the phone and chat with him. But it doesn't. After another cinnamon bun, and Herb and Vivian chatting some more about Zach and what he said, I get up to leave. "I better go. Thank you so much for everything."

"Any time. Please, come out for dinner sometime." I nod, they hug and I'm gone. I have a date with a shirt.

*

I put Zach's shirt on and stare at the phone. It's about six in the morning in London. He'd have to be in his room, right? I dial the number and am immediately connected to the front desk.

"Zach Kennedy's room, please."

"Zach Kennedy?" A male with a strong British accent echoes me.

"Hmmm, no, no Zach Kennedy on our reservation list. Is it under another name?"

Crap. Another name? I have no idea. "He's actually with a band and they're staying at your hotel. Does that ring any bells?"

"Band? That doesn't sound familiar."

I sigh heavily. "Okay, thanks anyway." Of course I wouldn't be able to talk to Zach. That would be too easy. What about email? I could always email the guy. I'm sure he still checks it from time to time. I flick on the laptop and sit down to type some sort of message. How should I start it?

Dear Zach, how's it going? That's great you got on with a band. Send my love to the Queen!

Nope, not enough emotion. After a few crappy attempts, I end up keeping it short and sweet.

To: ZachKennedy213@mymail.net
From: CateChase24@mymail.net
Subject: Catching up

Hi Zach, I hope things are going well on your trip. You got in with a band. That's great! I met up with your parents today. They gave me your number. I tried calling but you must not have checked in yet. I want to say thank you for getting my job back. It means a lot to me. I had my first successful stolen auto pursuit as a sergeant. I wish you were here so I could tell you about it.

Well, good luck to you. Write if you have time.

Cate

Not the world's greatest email, but there's a lot said in a short span. I hit send and realize how much it sucks. I surf the net for about an hour, checking my email every ten minutes, hoping that he might write back. But he doesn't.

It's time to think of something else. My bookstore. Could I really do it? What would it take? It seems like an option, it feels like the right thing to do. Maybe I should just use up all my holidays and start up the bookstore. Let's see, with all the holidays I have saved up, I could easily take four months off. Yes, four months! I have loads of unused holidays and banked time. It's time to use them.

Just the thought of going back to my dungeon tomorrow doesn't really excite me. I pull my quilt up to my neck and look out my window. It's starting to snow. I gaze out at all the Christmas lights on the houses and in the trees. In my state of despair, I've totally forgotten about Christmas. In the living rooms on my street are decorated trees, people getting excited for the holidays and I realize I've worked too many major holidays, and this year, I will spend my time with Nan. It's decided. Tomorrow, I will demand time off, and Mark will have to give it to me.

Chapter 23
Hanging on for Dear Life

I arrive at work the next morning focused and set on what I'm about to do. I complete my meeting with my team, then march directly into Mark's office without knocking. He's surprised to see me....and maybe a little nervous.

"I need time off."

"Didn't you just have time off?"

I lift an eyebrow. "You call being suspended 'time off'?"

"Does this have something to do with that ex-boyfriend of yours?"

I squint. This guy doesn't seem to get it. "This has nothing to do with him and if it did, it wouldn't be any of your business anyway."

"How long do you want off?" Mark opens the schedule on his computer, searching through the days. I can see the days are filled with other people's time off. It almost deters me from my mission—almost. But then I remind myself of all the hell I've been through.

Stay focused. "I want four months starting tomorrow."

Mark almost chokes. "Four months? Are you nuts? I can't give you four months. The best I can do is two weeks starting January 2."

"I want four months. I have sacrificed everything to get where I am today and I want what's due. You can find someone to fill my shoes for four months and don't tell me otherwise. You did it pretty quickly when I was suspended."

"Cate, your suspension was a special situation. We didn't have the manpower then and we don't have the manpower now. How about three weeks starting December 26?"

"Am I speaking a different language than you? I said four months. I deserve my holidays and this is how I want to take them. Or did you forget about your little indiscretion?" His eyes are wide. I stare him down. "I want four months."

"Cate, this is not possible. My hands are tied."

"Blah, blah, blah. I've heard this all before. It is possible. You know why? I have tons of info on you. Not only regarding this whole bogus sexual harassment complaint, but also your conduct around female police officers." He visibly gulps.

"Two months." He throws back.

"You're not listening," I sing. "How does 'conduct unbecoming an officer' sound?" That got him right where it hurt.

"This is blackmail, you know."

"I know. I don't care."

"I could have you fired."

"I could have you fired," I say back.

He huffs. "Fine. Four months."

"Starting tomorrow," I coach.

"Starting tomorrow. But if I know you, you'll be bored by next week."

"That's the point, Mark. You don't know me, and you never will." I walk out with a renewed sense of control. It's back. I'm back. I'd like to know where I was all this time.

Like clockwork, Joan is in my office twenty minutes later. "I just heard. You really told him off, didn't you?"

"Yeah, I guess you could say that." I smile.

"So, what are you going to do with yourself these next four months?"

"I have some plans," I say surreptitiously.

"Make sure you keep us up to date on how you're doing."

"I will. I just can't believe I'm going to do this."

*

That night, I set up my tree—the tree that I had been neglecting for a couple of years because I was too busy to decorate it. I even bought some groceries, made some shortbread cookies and sat down with a hot chocolate for some Christmas movies. Being that this is Christmas, a time of giving and receiving, I call Zach again at the London hotel, now knowing the name the room is under, according to Vivian and Herb. Unfortunately, they already checked out. When I called Zach's mom to let her know they were no longer at the London hotel, she said they were heading over to Ireland for a night, and would call when they were staying in one place for a few days. I checked my email. He hadn't emailed back.

I'll give it a few more days.

*

It's the week before Christmas and I invite Susanne over for dinner and a gift exchange. She's still glowing, still slightly ill, but otherwise, feeling good. Over the next few days, I hook up with my real estate agent to look at commercial properties, asking Nan to tag along for guidance and feedback. We haven't found anything yet, but I'm positive something will come up—the perfect place, my perfect place.

The days before Christmas are difficult. I attempt to keep myself busy with getting the ball rolling with my business and finding financial backing, all the while trying hard not to think about Zach and how he hasn't called or how I can't reach him. Maybe it's really over. He's moved on and has more important things to do.

Two days before Christmas, I get my first gift—a bank loan approval. I'm nervous, but feel it's the right thing, and continue learning the inner workings of the bookstore business. By the time Christmas arrives, I've got orders set up for books to show up at my place for the end of February. I still have no place to put them, and I'm antsy that I might have thousands of books sitting in my living room with no bookshelves to put them on.

I spend Christmas with Nan, making her dinner at my place so Syd and Annie wouldn't have to work. She spends the night here and the next morning, we drive out to Zach's parent's place for breakfast, me hoping that Zach will call while I'm there—but he doesn't. I hope that maybe there will be a voicemail when I get home, but that hope is futile. Just before New Year's Eve, as I grab the mail from my mailbox, I find a card inside with a Barcelona postmark. I rip it open, not showing the envelope any mercy. On the cover is a Christmas tree decked with lights and presents. Inside is a Spanish greeting that I can only assume means Merry Christmas or something of that nature.

Opposite from that is Zach's handwriting.

Cate,

I am truly sorry for everything that has happened. I know that these words do not make up for my behavior and how I have hurt you. But, I am hoping that one day you will be able to forgive me. I love you.

-Zach

He loves me. Still. I don't know if I should jump up and down or break down and cry. How can I get excited when I can't even call him? I have no idea where he is, and his cell phone is almost useless. I place his card by my bed, wondering what to do next. The only thing that comes to mind is to continue to concentrate on my goal of finding a location for this bookstore.

And, just before New Year's, the perfect place lands right in my lap. It's in an older area along the river, a small bookstore with a loft that had closed down ages ago. It's perfect, it's quaint, and it's mine. I sign the papers and by the time January arrives, I'm fairly organized. Nan, Susanne and Dave help me paint, redecorate and do whatever upgrades are needed to get the bookstore running. Even Zach's parents lend a hand. Herb is quite good with construction and any type of electrical work and helps bring the place up to code.

But, even with all of this activity, I still miss Zach. Still no word from him except for the card, I've decided to stop wearing his shirt to bed. I wash it and store it back in the closet, saying hi to it every now and then. I'm not ready to completely relinquish it just yet. I still like looking at it. I'd like to believe that he'd be back, one day. But I can't continue to hope. A card isn't enough. I need contact. I need to talk this out. But, it isn't happening, and I need to move on.

Then one day, Dan Sherman calls. He's been thinking about me and would like to pick up where we left off (wherever that was) and he invites me out to dinner. Dinner? I never thought I would go for dinner with Dan Sherman again. But, things change and I really need to get on with things. I decide that this might be the push I need.

"So, what happened to Darci?" I ask.

"Oh, we didn't work out. She was sleeping around."

"Noooo?" I say. I'm sarcastic. The way I saw her bounce around from guy to guy the night of the Halloween party, it's not surprising.

"Yeah, I never would have thought it either. But there she was, screwing some guy in our bathroom. After that happened, I really got to thinking about the women in my life; you are the only one that popped in my head as being the consistent one. A stable fixture. I was a fool for letting Zach get his hands on you."

Zach's hands on me. That's all I register. Zach's hands on me. It's been ages since Zach's hands were on me. I miss those hands on me. But, it's now the end of January and nothing since the card. Yes, I guess it's time to move on.

"So, do you want to go back to my place?" Dan says. For some reason I start to nod. Maybe I actually think I'll get over Zach if I start dating again. Unfortunately, I'm only lying to myself as there's still a part of me that's hanging on for dear life.

Chapter 24
Once More with Feeling

The moment we step in the door of Dan's condo, he's making the moves on me. He's not wasting time. Actually, he says something about how we've been wasting too much time since meeting in his office that fateful day. Yes, he used the word fateful. I'm not calling this fate.

As he kisses my neck and earlobes, and, as I desperately try to put my heart into it, I discover that fate sent me to him to realize what we had is in the past... and should stay there, undisturbed, forever. I want to prove to myself that I can move on, that Zach is out of my life, but deep inside, something is crumbling. This isn't right. It's never been right. I stop it right there.

"I'm sorry, Dan." I hold his hands and give him a gentle smile. "I can't do this. You know I've had a really good time with you. And it's really nice to talk about old times, but I think the time we spent together should remain in the past."

"It's Zach, isn't it?"

I'm going to say no, but decide it's no use lying to him. "Yes. It's Zach." Dan doesn't say anything; we just stare at each other for a few seconds. Is he going to beg me to stay? Convince me of how we're so good together? He doesn't say anything, so I break the ice. "Take care of yourself, Dan." I kiss him on the cheek and leave.

*

The end of March. That's when I'm opening my bookstore, the bookstore named 'Water's Edge Books', because it's actually by a body of water. Who knew running a business would be more complicated than it appears. There are employees and accountants to hire. There are permits and regulations and codes. Plus, all these new employees need to be taught coding, inputting, and shelving of books. Thank goodness Dave saves the day and sets up my computer system. Susanne, now showing a little bit of belly, tends to the details of the café.

Dan, now recovered from the shock of leaving him that night, has resurrected himself and is helping me with any legal questions I might have. And, by the end of the day, I view my store and realize that it's all mine, with a little help from my friends. I send out invitations for the pre-opening celebration, my way of thanking everyone for helping out. I have champagne, hors d'oeuvres, music and am surprised at myself and at my ability to do all this. But it feels right. All those years of being a police officer seemed right for that time. It felt right when I was young and before my sergeant days. It's what I needed. I've out grown that part of my life now. This is where I'm supposed to be.

Dave pops the cork, pouring out libations to everyone present as I give my speech. "I want to thank you all for coming and for helping and supporting me in this new venture. I never thought it would ever become a reality. But here we are." I choke back a tear. "Now, please, have fun before I start crying." I sip my champagne, tuning out the clapping because I'm really on the edge of bawling. I sit down beside Nan and Susanne.

"You've done well and I think this bookstore is going to be a success." Susanne squeezes my hand.

"I guess we will see tomorrow how we do."

"I'm really proud of you, sweetie. You did what you wanted to do." Nan grasps the other hand.

"You've come a long way from where you were before...." Susanne trails off. I know she's going to say before Zach came into my life.

"You know he called me yesterday morning," Nan says.

"Who?" I'm teasing.

"Zach. He asked how you were. I told him you were opening your store this week and that we were having a celebration tonight. He said he wished he could be here."

"Right. I'm sure he said that. And did you ask him why he hasn't called me? Did you tell him that a Christmas card isn't enough? I can't wait around for him, Nan." I roll my eyes. "It doesn't matter. I've gone on with my life."

"I'm disappointed that you guys didn't work out. I mean, after all the trouble I went through," Nan says as she inspects her fingernails.

"What do you mean? What trouble did you go through?" I frown.

"Oh, you know, hiring Zach for you," she simply proclaims. I blink a few times. "You hired Zach for you. Remember?"

Nan shakes her head. "No, dear, I hired Zach for you."

"You hired me an escort?" my voice cracks.

"Yes. It was my big ploy to get you a man. We had that talk that night when you suggested I find a man for companionship. Then you made that joke about finding a man at the senior's centre. Anyway, I just took it upon myself to find you the companionship, but someone your own age."

"But he was an escort, Nan. How in the world did you think we'd get along?"

"Well, I didn't, really. I just called up Zach and spoke to him on the phone. I liked his voice and asked him to come over. I liked how he looked and got a good vibe from him, you know?" She nods like it's all completely natural to hire an escort for your granddaughter. "I really thought this one was going to work out. I'm sorry, dear." She pats my leg. My own grandmother had set me up with an escort. On top of it, she'd found the one and only guy that I could relate to on every level and the one and only guy that she approved of. How does she do it? I don't think I will ever know.

I mingle a while longer and around ten o'clock, people start to leave, thanking me for a lovely evening, wishing me good luck on the store and that they'll pop by to see how it's going.

Herbert and Vivian also come by for a brief while, hugging me and being overly ecstatic for me. Joan came with her new boyfriend. She's quite happy with him and he's only 15 years younger.

"I guess I should be going too. I'm feeling tired all of a sudden." Susanne awkwardly rises as if she has a huge belly.

I say goodbye to her, to Dave and then to all my other guests, till finally Nan leaves with Syd, and I'm alone in my own store. I still can't believe it. The only thing I know is, regardless if it does good or bad, this is my venture and I tried. I stroll upstairs to the loft, gazing at the gleaming coffee making equipment and all the syrups, the display case where cookies will be on the first day of business.

The bell to the front door rings, and I'm ready to yell out that we are closed, and come back another day to buy lots of books. But, when I peer down, I realize who it is.

"I need a book on how not to be an idiot," Zach says.

Zach! Zach standing in my store...like he never left. He has that same 5 o'clock shadow that I love. That hasn't changed. He's wearing a black wool coat with a black scarf, and his hair is a little longer than the last time I saw him. But, he's still my Zach.

I run down the stairs, unsure what I'm going to do when I get down there, stopping only a few feet away from him. I'm ready to run into his arms, and ready to run away at the same time. I need answers, first and foremost.

"What happened to you? Why'd you leave? No word for months, except for a Christmas card. Now, you decide to show up here like nothing's changed. Why are you here, Zach?"

"Cate...."

"You didn't call. Why didn't you call?" What I really want to say is: 'Why didn't you chase me? Why didn't you call to win me back?' Because I wanted him to win me back. I wanted him to show me how much he cared. But, the bottom line is, I knew he wouldn't play those games. I had told him to stay away—and, though my hurting heart meant it at the time, I knew that I didn't mean it forever.

"Cate, let me explain." He took my hands; so much sincerity in his eyes and his voice.

"I loved you," I blurt out. Zach's surprised. This is the first time I've said the word 'love' to him.

"You loved me?" he questions. "Loved, as in the past tense?"

I grit my teeth. I can feel a part of the old Cate re-surfacing, closing up. "I can't go through this again. You left without saying good bye."

He shakes his head. "Cate. Listen." He inhales deeply. "I can't take back what I did. It was a dumb move on my part. I do not blame you for kicking me out of your life. And, I know I could have called more.... do something to show I cared. But...." he paused. "But, I was so stuck in my regret at what I did to you that I knew that there would be no words to make up for it. I knew you needed time, and so did I." He squeezed my hands. "I knew I wanted to be part of your life, but, betraying you the way I did...obviously, there was something in me that I had to figure out. I was running away from you." He sighs. "But, if you let me in, I promise that you will never question my love for you again."

I wanted to agree to everything he said, but there were things I needed to understand. "What about the band? Why'd you come home? Why'd you leave?"

"After I screwed things up with you, I had to leave. Being at your grandmother's just made me think about you even more. I couldn't stand the fact that we lived in the same city and didn't even speak to one another. So, I gave the band thing another try. Turned out to be a bad idea. The other guys and I weren't well suited for each other. When I found out you were opening a bookstore, I knew I had to quit and come to you." Zach edges forward. "I'm here now, Cate. I love you."

Those words, all of his words, mean everything, and the tears come fast. "I will do whatever you ask. Just, please, can we start all over again?"

Whoa! Start all over again. I fight back more tears. I have to think this through. Start all over again! I release his hands and step back. Looking at him, I know I can't start all over again. But, man, do I love him.

He looks worried when I stop pacing and take his hands. "No. I'm sorry. I can't do it. I can't start all over again."

Chapter 25
At the end of the day

"Susanne, you have to name this cutie something super cute. If you don't, I will have to disown you," I hold the little pink bundle in my arms. She's absolutely adorable with mounds of dark hair on her head. Susanne looks rather beautiful after pushing out a seven pound baby a few short hours ago. "Please don't give her a name that she's going to hate because her quirky parents thought it would be fun. I know what I'm talking about."

"Her name is Juliette Catherine."

I smile. "A beautiful name for a beautiful girl."

Zach puts his arm around me. "I don't know what you're talking about, I like the name Ocean; kind of stormy." He kisses me, and goo-goos the baby sleeping in my arms. "Why don't you tell them our good news?" He says.

"You guys are getting married!" Susanne cries out.

I laugh. "Are you kidding? No, it's better than that."

"You're pregnant!" Dave throws in.

Zach and I grin at each other. "No, but close. We're getting a puppy."

"We figured this was the next step. You know, with Cate's bookstore and me writing more music, and then moving in together, we thought we could use a puppy," Zach explains.

Susanne and Dave are dumbfounded. "So, no wedding? No baby?"

"We like the way things are right now. Sleeping in, well, when we can, breakfast in bed, sex wherever, whenever…" I taper off and realize Zach and I are staring into each other's eyes, grinning stupidly.

"Ugh, you two are too mushy. You just wait. When that puppy comes, you won't have any time for sex. Will they, honey?" Susanne hasn't even started the late night feedings and she's already anticipating her lack of free time.

"No. Nope. You're right," Dave isn't very convincing.

"I think Dave just realized that your sex life is history," I say.

"Dave does look shell-shocked," Zach whispers.

"It's only for the first few months, honey," Susanne reassures him.

"Well, should we get going?" Zach stands.

"Where are you two off to?" Dave takes the baby from my arms.

"Oh, we're going to Nan's cabin for a couple of days." I stand, giving the baby one last kiss. "We decided we deserved a mini vacation together. Just the two of us."

"Well, have a skinny dip for me," Susanne says. I hug her, kissing her cheek.

"You can count on it." I wink.

*

It's been four months since my bookstore opened, four months since Zach came back into my life and four months since I told him that I love him. When he showed up that night at the bookstore, I told him I wasn't willing to start all over again.

Starting all over again would mean going through all the phases of disliking him, to lusting him, to liking him, to loving him and then being sad. It was a roller coaster ride, one that I didn't care to ride again. I wanted to start right then as we were.

The old Cate—gone, The Escort—gone.

And, for the first time, I love you meant something more to me than ever before. I knew I loved Zach before this all had happened, but never said it. It was new territory for me since I had never said those words to any of the other men I had dated. Or I had said it and never really meant it.

Zach came home with me that night after the bookstore event and never left, only taking a week before all of his things were moved in. We were going to take it slow—I guess this was as slow as we could stand it.

In those few months, the bookstore has exceeded my expectations. Zach can still write and share his music without having to do the world tours. It's just the way he likes it.

We've both been so busy, we realized we were in need of a quick holiday, and the cabin was the perfect place to be—skinny dipping as the sun sets out onto the water; finding comfort in his hands on the small of my back, his lips touching mine, and whispering I love you to him like it was the most natural thing on earth.

Thank you for reading my book. If you enjoyed it, please consider leaving a review at your favourite retailer.

Thank you!
Tamara Hanson

About Tamara Hanson
Tamara Hanson is a non-fiction and fiction author, freelance writer, relationship blogger, awkward romantic, and all around nice person. She enjoys long walks on the beach, spending time with her children, and creating new stories that inspire and enlighten.

Visit her website at www.tamarahanson.ca

57297305R00123

Made in the USA
Charleston, SC
09 June 2016